# No

# True

# Believers

# No True Believers

## RABIAH YORK LUMBARD

CROWN
New York

Text copyright © 2020 by Rabiah York Lumbard and Soho Press
Jacket art copyright © 2020 by Peter Strain

All rights reserved. Published in the United States by Crown Books for Young Readers, an imprint of Random House Children's Books, a division of Penguin Random House LLC, New York.

Crown and the colophon are registered trademarks of Penguin Random House LLC.

Visit us on the Web! GetUnderlined.com

Educators and librarians, for a variety of teaching tools, visit us at
RHTeachersLibrarians.com

*Library of Congress Cataloging-in-Publication Data*
Names: Lumbard, Rabiah York, author.
Title: No true believers / Rabiah York Lumbard.
Description: First edition. | New York : Crown, [2020] | Summary: High school senior Salma Bakkioui, who has a connective tissue disorder, faces prejudice and hidden danger, especially after being framed for a Muslim terrorist act she did not commit.
Identifiers: LCCN 2019009357 | ISBN 978-0-525-64425-5 (hc) |
ISBN 978-0-525-64426-2 (epub)
Subjects: | CYAC: Prejudices—Fiction. | Terrorism—Fiction. | High schools—Fiction. | Schools—Fiction. | Family life—Virginia—Arlington—Fiction. | Muslims—Fiction. | Ehlers-Danlos syndrome—Fiction. | People with disabilities—Fiction. | Arlington (Va.)—Fiction.
Classification: LCC PZ7.1.L846 No 2020 | DDC [Fic]—dc23

Printed in the United States of America
10 9 8 7 6 5 4 3 2 1
First Edition

*To my three fierce,*
*creative, and kindhearted daughters,*
*Layla, Rayhan & Tasneem*

———

Don't let anyone or anything in this crazy *dunia*
stop you from being you.

Mommy loves you more than words can say,
so go out there and conquer the world

(but first you must conquer your *nafs*).

# PROLOGUE

## THE LETTER

*Dear Mr. Epstein,*

*I'm writing you because you know me. U.S. mail is the only safe way I could think of to get in touch. Weren't you the one who told me that the federal government was mostly just a postal service at first? A funny fact from a music teacher. I'll miss those funny facts.*

*I have to ask two favors.*

*First, you know that I am not capable of doing whatever it is they say I've already done, and whatever is about to come next. So please tell the federal government or anyone else who comes knocking on your door that I am not the bomber of May 3. They are.*

*Second, you have to promise me that you'll watch over Salma B. Her life is in danger. If you trust me as much as I trust you, then you already know that she is even less capable of this insanity than I am. Although*

right now I honestly don't know what I'm capable of.
I'm sure that's what they wanted.

And I don't care about incriminating myself with
that thought, because it's too late.

I keep thinking of the word you always use to get
me to practice scales, to play the way I wanted to play,
so that one day the instrument would almost feel like
an extension of my body. "Discipline." That's what
they have, on a level that I still can't understand.
Their instruments are human beings, and their music
is death. I know how crazy that sounds, but if you
remember it in some way, it might be enough to keep
you safe. And if you think I've lost it, maybe that will
keep you safe, too. Either way: please tear up this letter
and the envelope when you're finished and burn the
scraps.

I guess that's three favors.

Take care,
A

# THREE WEEKS EARLIER

# 1

WE NEVER SEE the world exactly as it is. We see it through whatever lens we choose. I never understood the difference until that sunny Thursday afternoon, the last day of April, when I stood face to face with Mariam in her driveway. In that moment the world became clear in all its stark ugliness. I was losing my best friend. Mariam Muhammad: my soul sister, lifelong neighbor, and general co-conspirator in all things.

My eyes fell to the driveway. It was ridiculous; even the pavement made me want to cry. We'd played hopscotch here. And there was no use spinning it as "Oh, she'll come back to Arlington all the time." We knew better, both of us. Seeing each other from now on would involve passports and expensive airfares, clearances and checkpoints. Also, eight time zones. The truth was that she wasn't moving. She was fleeing. She and her whole family were now refugees—off to Dubai, the new Promised Land—an escape from Mason Terrace, a cul-de-sac so ridiculously safe and suburban that local real estate sites featured it to prove the entire neighborhood's safety and suburban-ness.

Comical, if it weren't so depressingly false.

When I looked up, Mariam was smiling, of course. Mariam

the brave. Mariam the good. Cheery in the face of stress and sorrow. I lurched forward to hug her, the bright side of the Salma-Mariam moon. We *were* a unit in that way: visible yet detached, maybe a bit mysterious (we hoped)? Yes, we'd stay in touch. Through Twitter or WhatsApp or whatever. "Even old-fashioned letters!" she'd said. Mariam wouldn't let me slide, even though videoconferencing was illegal in the UAE. Which didn't help diminish the sudden and intense loneliness. Our moon would be all darkness now.

*How am I going to survive the rest of senior year at Franklin without you?*

"It's going to be okay, Salma," Mariam whispered in my ear.

I stepped away, wiping my eyes. "Can't you just stay through till the weekend, till the grand fundraiser? I was thinking of raiding the mosque's funds. Pay off your parents' mortgage or at least get y'all a ticket for later in the month. I've never celebrated an Eid without you."

"Yeah, pretty sure stealing from the *masjid* won't go over too well with the Lord of the worlds," she joked, trying to snap me out of my funk. "Besides, if you wanted me to stay that badly, you should have hacked into Air Emirates. Gotten us cheaper tickets."

*If you only knew,* I thought miserably.

"Hey, look at it this way. Now you get to spend more time with Amir." Mariam gave my hand a final squeeze. "And that brother is way too cute for you to be so sad."

She was right about that, at least.

———

6

Amir and I began several months ago at one of Vanessa Richman's legendary "Hey, my parents are out of town" parties. We were packed in the basement with thirty other kids from Franklin, mostly Vanessa's friends, though I'd brought a couple of mine: the usual twosome, Lisa and Kerry. Or as they jokingly referred to themselves, "Dora and Boots."

Lisa de la Pena happened to be my physical therapist's daughter, but she had recently become my go-to party pal. Kerry Morrison, a willowy redhead with a Southern cowgirl style, was basically Lisa's Mariam: like Mariam and me, they were a unit, BFFs since toddlerhood. The self-made *Dora the Explorer* nickname came in middle school. Apparently Kerry had come up with it after some idiots had bullied Lisa for being Latinx and accused her of being an "illegal." (According to Lisa, Kerry was also unafraid to use her cowboy boots for "butt-whoopings" of bullying idiots, though I'd never seen her be anything but likeably goofy.)

Mariam's parents had a sixth sense about parties and road trips and generally all things "haram"—so as far as Mariam was concerned, Vanessa's place was never an option. But Lisa and Kerry were always game.

Point being: It's always better to arrive with a posse. And Lisa and Kerry were in fine form that night. Maybe that's why I was already feeling more comfortable than usual. Plus, after months of hounding, I'd finally convinced Vanessa to screen *Fight Club* for the obligatory 72-inch surround-sound feature presentation. I'd claimed I had a shameless crush on Edward Norton. Which wasn't *false*. (He always looks so lost and vulnerable.) But the secret truth was that I'd wanted to share with Vanessa—a less judgmental friend than Mariam, I admit—this treasure I'd only recently discovered on the more secure chatrooms. *Fight Club* was the cult classic every hardcore anonymous online activist revered.

As it turned out, Vanessa had been hiding a hidden agenda of her own.

"I know a boy who loves that movie as much as you," she'd told me the moment I arrived.

In typical Vanessa fashion, she refused to say who. But I forgot all about this mysterious boy once the movie started. Ten minutes in, the keg suddenly arrived. At first I thought it was a shared aversion to cheap beer; Amir ended up being the only other warm body to remain in the basement. We'd always been a part of the same social scene, the circles of friends that orbited around Vanessa. But I would have never pegged him as a fellow *Fight Club* fan. He didn't exactly give off that vibe. He gave off the opposite, in fact—a hippie-hipster musician, with an old-school guitar pick and feather dangling from a slim black cord around his neck. Then again, I, of all people, should have known how deceiving looks could be . . . and his looks are fine.

I couldn't help but sneak glances. He kept tucking loose strands of that thick, dark hair behind his ears. And he was definitely a *Fight Club* fan. He was whispering the lines.

Eventually I stopped paying attention to the movie.

I didn't care how obvious I was being, staring at him. I couldn't get over it. I couldn't believe this boy I'd known but not known was a kindred spirit. But how kindred? Message-wise, the film was timeless. Take the general social commentary and apply it to Snapchat: As outward tastes are being engineered, so, too, our inward bigotries. *Bam!* Mind blown.

I wanted to test Amir. Test his knowledge. I scooched down the couch, just a tad, to better hear him.

He murmured another line. Perfectly.

I made a point to whisper the next line with him.

He did the same. All of a sudden we were in a quote-for-quote competition. He inched toward me, too. Soon it felt like we weren't even at Vanessa's at all, like there wasn't a party upstairs. I started to laugh.

"What's so funny?" he asked me.

"That you know every line of this movie."

He turned with a smile and leaned even closer, as if he were letting me in on a secret. "It's not the movie. It's Edward Norton. I love that guy."

In that moment I was so Amir-struck that I almost forgot that we were speaking. I nodded mutely and stared back into his dark eyes . . . vulnerable maybe, but not lost. Then we turned back to the screen and sat snuggled against each other like that right up until the crucial scene where the two main characters, Tyler Durden (Norton) and Marla Singer (Helena Bonham Carter) hold hands and watch their world collapse. *"You met me at a very strange time in my life,"* says Tyler Durden.

I turned to Amir. Without warning, he leaned in and kissed me. His long hair tickled my cheek. I pulled away, then leaned back in, returning his kiss, intoxicated. I had no idea how long we'd been making out when Vanessa appeared at the top of the stairs and drunkenly cackled, "Oh my *God*! I *knew* it!"

We jumped apart, faces flushed, moment ruined.

Vanessa then proceeded to turn off the lights, which for

some reason shut down the massive TV system, too. Amir and I exchanged a few awkward giggles. We fumbled our way out of the darkness, holding hands. I let go only when we reached the kitchen, so I could stop by the sink to splash cold water over my red-hot face. I couldn't stop smiling. Lisa and Kerry snickered and blew kisses at me from the doorway, and I *still* couldn't stop. Then my back pocket buzzed. I assumed it was my parents checking up on me. But when I pulled out my phone, I saw Amir's face.

My silly smile grew even wider. Vanessa had given him my digits in advance. That figured.

The next time we hung out alone, we made a point not to tell her beforehand.

Alone in the driveway now, I reached for my back pocket again. But I couldn't bring myself to pick up the phone. What could I say that he didn't already know? *"Hey, I just lost my best friend to a one-way ticket from Dulles to Dubai because her dad can't make a living anymore because people hate 'Mooslims' and that's the shitshow we're living now."*

No doubt he would answer with something annoyingly positive.

Amir had friends in the UAE. Online friends, like mine. Fellow musicians. (The tragic difference: I kept my online friends hidden from him, even after we became an official thing.) Amir plays the oud, one of the oldest instruments known to man. Literally: like beginning-of-time old. It's a Middle Eastern guitar, a cousin to the lute. He would never admit how talented he is, but he first met these friends because of videos he posted—just him playing alone in his room.

Naturally the cool people he met led him to believe that the UAE was a cool place: international, open-minded, stress-free. He kept insisting that Mariam was off to greener pastures. I knew he was trying to make me feel better. But I didn't need gentle reminders of how lucky I was, that *we* were, that my parents were tenured professors at George Mason and his were comfortably retired . . . that we had stability. I didn't give a shit about any of it. I wanted my friend. I refused to put on a happy face because I didn't have to flee, myself.

*How would you act, Amir? If you lost your soul brother, if you had a soul brother?*

I took a deep breath and wiped my damp cheeks with my free hand. Definitely best not to call him. Why take it out on him? I shoved my phone in my pocket. No . . . better to wallow alone in a coma of self-reinforcing misery, and mine craved only one type of company: fresh buttermilk scones.

Twenty-three hours later (I'd been counting), I sat in our cushioned bay window, staring out at Mason Terrace. I hadn't slept much. I hadn't really moved much, aside from periodic scone binges. Luckily, my sisters and parents were thoughtful enough to leave me alone. All on our street was leafy green and springtime sunny, as it had been yesterday. Yet lifeless. Deserted. *Abandoned.* I was about to pull out my phone for the millionth time (to do nothing) when I heard a car approaching.

I sat up straight. There was a glint of shiny black metal at the cul-de-sac entrance. My heart jumped.

For a blissful delusional moment, I thought Mariam's family had come back. A Ramadan miracle? Yeah, right. Stupid me. Funny that this was Friday, May 1. *Mayday, mayday, mayday* . . . No, it wasn't Dr. Muhammad's beat-up sedan. It was a new pickup truck hauling a trailer, its rear a collage of bumper stickers. I SERVED IRQ. I SERVED AFG. POW-MIA.

Military folk, like a lot of our neighbors.

After a brief pause at Mariam's mailbox, my new neighbors pulled into the driveway where we'd said goodbye, rolling right over the past and my memories. I felt my breath catch. My fists clenched at my sides. I was itching to see their faces. I wanted to know who these infiltrators were. Okay, yes, I knew that they were simply the owners of a new home. (*Mariam's* home.) Her family had sold it; this family had purchased it. Still, I wanted to stop them. The second they opened the front door—a door through which I'd passed nearly every day of my life—the whole thing would be official, irreversible.

What could I do, though?

I blinked a few times at the truck before it disappeared into the detached garage that mirrored our own.

I'd already *tried* to stop Mariam's family from leaving. What I'd tried wasn't crazy or anything. But it wasn't exactly legal, either.


From earliest childhood, I'd spent an excessive amount of time fiddling with computers. As in the actual software on hard drives. It runs in the family; Dad is a professor of computer science. His unofficial job is fixing his department's IT issues. All of his younger academic colleagues are theoreticians without any practical skills. He loves to joke how his job security is dependent on how backward everything really is. Especially infrastructure. He has a point; the Arlington internet hub—as in the actual machinery that makes it all work—is housed in a crumbling cement building that should have been condemned before I was born. "Good thing us old folks know how to repair a toaster oven," he often cracks whenever we drive past it. "It's the first thing you kids will need when your screens go dark." *Hardy-har-har.* Gallows nerd humor from the Muslim tech guy.

On the other hand, that humor has made him something of a lovable dorky legend at work. So when Mariam first told me how bad it was for *her* father, I had a hard time believing her.

She rolled her eyes at first. Then she got mad. "Salma, his name is Dr. Muhammad Muhammad. It might as well be Dr. Evil-Evil. You're so naïve!"

Never mind that he was the best chiropractor in Northern Virginia. Even my grandmother Titi—convinced that a spoonful of honey and nigella seeds can heal anything—swore by his talent. Nobody listened. The depressing truth about the Muslim community, at least ours, is that it sucks at supporting its own. We're either trying to cope with our alienation or debating the legality of something ridiculous, like what qualifies as a "clean sock." I'm not kidding. Our imam might hold the world's record for discussing the virtues of doing laundry. Shoes come off for prayer at *every* mosque, yet somehow we here in Arlington, Virginia, end up with the halal sock police. (Of which Titi is a proud member. So I'm just as guilty of not listening to her sometimes.) All of which is to say that occasionally I'm forced to take matters into my own hands . . . or fingertips, to be exact.

Anyway, Mariam is naïve, too.

Like most non-nerds, Mariam doesn't have a clue as to

how interconnected we all are. Or that there are people—yes, even some who aren't Russian villains—who manipulate search engines. There are even some who do it *legally*, as a job. Yet for some reason we nerds seem to be the only ones who know the truth.

Human beings don't pay attention to truth or logic. They pay attention to Google searches.

While I couldn't hide the Muslim heritage of Dr. Muhammad Muhammad, I could up his game by placing his reputation front and center. The downside: I couldn't tell Mariam, because I had to hijack her router to do so.

In my defense, I'd at least *tried* to guess her dad's username and password. (Isn't it a good thing I can't read the mind of a suburban chiropractor?) Failure to hack in the old-fashioned way prompted me to cross a line I hadn't before: I ventured onto the Dark Web. For better or worse, it didn't take long for me to understand what the benefits were. After I tossed off just a single cursory password-and-username query into this gated netherworld of encrypted networks, a friend appeared to help me: Pulaski88. I was quickly ushered into a chatroom for "ethical hacking"—a forum for the subversive but righteous—and there, under the handle I'll never share, we struck up a conversation. It turned out Pulaski88 was exactly who I was looking for, someone who specialized in accessing "nearby non-criminal hardware."

Long, redacted story short: after I answered some ridiculous questions ("On what planet would you hypothetically live?"), Pulaski88 walked me through what I needed to do to take control of Dr. Muhammad's hard drive—and also warned me of the penalties involved, everything from a class B misdemeanor to a class D felony.

I wasn't concerned. Pulling it off was the easy part.

Once inside, undetected and glitch-free, I tinkered with Dr. Muhammad's meta tags, those keywords that make websites more discoverable. From that night on, whenever someone local searched for a back pain specialist, *voilà:* Dr. Muhammad Muhammad rose to the top. I *did* feel guilty. What I'd done was black hat, criminal. And worse, I'd kept it from my best friend. But it reinforced that invaluable secret: privacy is an illusion. Easily hacked and easily violated. The next morning I covered my webcam with a postage stamp in case anyone out there wanted to snoop on *me*. And full disclosure? Mostly I felt a flush of pride. Mariam's father was briefly the king of the Arlington chiropractors.

My happiest memory from that otherwise grim period was catching him at his phone with a bewildered smile, shaking his head at his sudden rise in internet rankings.

The difficult part? Accepting fate. Boosting his rankings was like rearranging deck chairs on the *Titanic*. A futile, pathetic attempt at stemming the inevitable.

# 2

"SALMA, GET READY. No dawdling. And please wear something nice. Like one of your kaftans."

*Ugh.* Saturday evening, and instead of going out with
friends, I was being dragged to the mosque. During Ramadan.
I don't fast for health reasons, which means that I've always
struggled with the Ramadan spirit. "Mom. Do I have to?"

"For Titi, dear. It'll bring her joy."

*It'll bring her joy.* Titi is moving in with us. Salma! Can
you take the basement and give her your room? *It'll bring her
joy.* Titi would like to go on a walk. Salma! Can you be her
cane? *It'll bring her joy.* Salma! Titi needs another prescription
refill. Can you run to the pharmacy?

Yes, I'm Titi's personal assistant. A full-time joy-maker.
But you know what? Titi deserves it. And if paradise lies at the
foot of a mother, I am quite certain that the key to its highest realm is straight through the heart of a grandmother. So
I forced myself out from under the covers, brushed my teeth,
and jumped in the shower. After battling with my Queen Bey
big curls, I unzipped the hermetically sealed *takchita* that had
been hiding in my closet since last April.

A *takchita* is like a kaftan on steroids. Mine was a vibrant sea of oranges and reds. It would have been gorgeous on some, no doubt—if you had big boobs and wide hips to fill it in, but that ain't happening. Besides, I was more of a tunic-with-leggings sort of girl. I preferred something low-key and comfortable. *Simple.* A double-layered, ankle-length dress is . . . anything but. This particular *takchita* consisted of a cotton undergarment hidden by a layer of silk and sequins, dripping with beads: a fountain of femininity tied at the waist with an oppressively thick made-for-a-queen belt.

As I tied it tightly, I reminded myself of Titi's joy. Then I contemplated the shoes. They matched perfectly with the gown, but those two-inch heels induced palpitations. I, Salma B., utterly lacked the charm and grace of an Oscar-winning actress. Odds were that I would stumble and fall on the mosque's red carpet. Forget it. No way. Mom appeared once again as I finished lacing my cherry-red Doc Martens—Amir's favorite.

"Really, Salma?"

"This dress is ridiculously long. No one will see." Then I smiled sweetly. "It'll bring me joy."

She laughed. "Touché. Now hurry up."

My family attends the local mosque only a few times a year: for *janaza*—the funeral service—when someone dies, the two Eids, and a night or two during Ramadan. It was the grand fundraiser and fancy weekend *iftar* that had us all piled into the minivan and overdressed. When it comes to how my family practices Islam, both of my parents are highly opinionated. Dad is outwardly secular, but as Titi's original joy-maker, he doesn't mind going to the mosque a few times a year. It makes her happy. It's "heritage." Mom is outwardly more observant, but inwardly critical. She's got major qualms with the board of our local mosque. "It's all male and physician dominated," she regularly complains. But she still felt bad for not attending regularly, so going on a night like tonight—holy and charity-oriented—was like double the karmic value.

The funny thing: Mom was born a white Anglo-Saxon Protestant. She grew up not far from where we live now. Her life changed in 1993, the year she received a postdoctoral research grant to study Islamic literature in Tangier. (In her heart she'd dreamed of studying in Tehran—both cities are notorious for producing brilliant authors and poets—but as an American she couldn't if she'd tried unless she was a spy.) Her love of the Transcendentalists, particularly Ralph Waldo Emerson and his poem "Saadi," attracted her to Sufi poetry; her determination to educate herself in a Muslim country brought her to Morocco instead of Iran. By year's end, she'd met my father. She fell in love with him as she fell in love with Islam. Ever since, she's been a proud WASM: a white Anglo-Saxon Muslim.

Of course, she claims she's always been one, her entire life. It just took one step toward Allah for Allah to take two steps toward her.


Amir was waiting for us in the parking lot. He was standing in one of the last empty spots, saving it for my family. Parking is tight on holidays, even though our nice neighbors at All Souls Church share their lot with us. They're Unitarians. (I'm still not sure what that means, but I know they're very welcoming.) They have amazing signs all over their lawn. I've always loved the quotes they display. LOVE RADICALLY. WONDER DAILY.

Amir wore a long tunic, a matching *kufi,* and pressed khakis. He was a gorgeous slender reed.

Me, I was a carrot in a *takchita* and Doc Martens. I didn't care, though. I burst out of the door and ran to him. His parents were already inside.

"*Ramadan Mubarak,* beautiful," he said.

I should have expected he'd add a little compliment to lift my mood.

"*Ramadan Kareem,*" I murmured back.

"*Ramadan Mubarak,*" or "Blessed Ramadan," was the standard greeting. But I love the word *kareem,* for "generous." It rolls off the tongue like a poem. Anyway, it perfectly embodies Amir. I wanted to hug him, but knew better; I didn't want the "aunties"—the older women in the community—to take notice. Funny: he still blushed and glanced around, even a couple of feet apart. Mariam always teased me, *"Man, that brother is shy!"* And she was right; Amir doesn't like being in the spotlight in public. On the other hand, nobody engages in PDA at the mosque—not even parents.

"How are you holding up?" he asked.

I shrugged. "Okay. But I miss you."

"I miss you, too."

He reached out and touched my arm, then quickly folded his hands behind his back. "Well, you know what Mariam told me? There's no point in missing two people when one of them is still here. I'm guessing she fed you that same BS, too?"

I could feel a smile spreading across my face as I stared back into those date-brown eyes. "Yeah. And . . . thank you for—you know—giving me space. I'm better. Ready to exit the scones cave."

Amir pretended to frown. "She didn't tell you to give up scones, did she?"

Before I could respond, Yasmin leapt between us. Amir scooped her up without even blinking, and after a twirl, he set her down lightly on her feet. Even in my crap mood I had to admit that my little sister's hopeless crush on my boyfriend was cute, in its adoring and completely unselfconscious way. More cute was the brotherly way *he* handled an annoying ten-year-old.

"So?" she said. "Can you help? With my project? For Mr. Peck?"

He shot me a quick smirk. "Your Peck project?"

"Yes? Best All-Time American?" Her voice seemed to suggest a silent *Duh*.

Naturally, Yasmin never had any doubts that Amir would recall every moment of her fourth-grade schedule.

"For history class," I grumbled. "Her presentation. She's enlisting extra help. Yours, specifically."

"We-e-ll," said Amir in a slow, drawn-out voice. His eyes flashed again to mine, desperate for any cue to help jog his memory.

*Muhammad Ali,* I mouthed to him.

His face brightened. "Yes! You want me to look at your poster, right?"

Yasmin frowned. "No. I want you to record some music. You know, as a soundtrack for my presentation. We *talked* about this."

I had to laugh. The truth was that I'd also been on Amir to record some music. And to perform live. To share his talent in general. Yes, I know he's pathologically shy. But I also know it "brings him joy." If it took my sister's fourth-grade school project to get him to play in front of other people besides me, then so be it.

I folded my arms across my chest and arched an eyebrow. *You better do what my sister wants,* I told him with my stare.

"It's already done," he said.

"Seriously?" I asked.

He shrugged.

"Awesome!" Yasmin cried, oblivious to my doubts. "Remember: the song is due in two weeks." With that, she fluttered off to join our little sister Hala to stand in line and plate up. Yasmin just turned ten, and this was the first year she had tried fasting for an entire day. Weekends only, but still. She was proud and equally famished. Hala, close in age, who likewise refuses to ever be outshined or left alone, was also "fasting." Or had been since snack time.

"Wow," he said. "That girl is all business."

"Runs in the family," I replied dryly. "I'm assuming you were lying. How long does it take you to write a song, anyway?"

He cocked an eyebrow. "About as long as it would take you to hack into the Franklin computer system—to make sure Yasmin will get an A-plus, song or no song."

I laughed again. "Well played, handsome. Wanna bet?"


Since it was the first week of Ramadan and everyone who was fasting was still adjusting, Amir decided to hang out at my house the next day and watch the Nats game with Dad. His father isn't much of a sports fan, and neither am I. But I'll take any date with Amir, even if it's supervised. Even if I'm basically the third wheel with him and my dad.

Mom, Titi, and my younger sisters were hanging in the kitchen preparing *iftar.*

"Salma?" Mom called before I even made it out of the living room.

I hung my head and turned as she emerged from the kitchen with a large platter of food.

"It would be good to welcome that new family across the street," she said. "Why don't you walk it over?"

I glanced at Amir. He was staring at the TV, furiously pretending to be engrossed. Too bad it was a diaper commercial. Of course, he knew what I knew: that my mother frequently made suggestions that were in fact orders.

I tried not to groan as I took the platter. "Seriously?"

"Yes, seriously," she said. Her hands moved to rest on her hips. Yet another weapon in her arsenal of overused body signs. This one meant: *Salma, the conversation is over, period.*

Amir hopped up. "I'll come with you," he offered politely. "It's the seventh-inning stretch. Besides, I'd like to meet them, too."

I focused on the tray, gripping it like a life raft as Amir held our front door open for me. I didn't need to look where I was going. I could have walked across the street to Mariam's blindfolded. But this was my first time back there. I couldn't bring myself to look up at her house. Luckily, my hands were full, so I didn't have to ring the bell, either.

Amir pressed the button.

I only lifted my head when I heard footsteps.

A middle-aged woman answered Mariam's door. *The new neighbor's door,* I reminded myself. She had a heart-shaped face and soft laugh lines. Something about her put me at ease. I hadn't expected that. With her hand-knitted sweater and pear-like petite frame, she was . . . mom-like. Like Mariam's own mom. Like a dove perched in a nest.

"Hi, nice to meet you," I said. I shoved the plate abruptly in her direction. "Welcome to the neighborhood. This is a gift. From my mom."

The words sounded flat, as if I were reading aloud from a coder's manual.

As she took the platter, I stepped back. Great start. In less than ten seconds I'd made this awkward surprise visit even more awkward.

"Aren't you a dear!" she exclaimed. "Why don't you come on in?"

"Thanks. But you must be exhausted . . . from the move." *I know I am,* I thought. *Exhausted by my pushy mother. Exhausted by standing at Mariam's door without Mariam. Exhausted by Mom's Ramadan generosity. By all of it.*

"Oh, hardly. I insist. I'm Mrs. Turner, but you're welcome to call me Kate." She practically yanked us inside, then steered Amir and me down the hallway. "Come and meet the men. They're watching the Nats game."

"Oh, okay, Mrs. Turner," I said. "But we should be heading back—"

"Kate!" she interrupted with a laugh. "Mrs. Turner is my mother-in-law."

I forced a clumsy laugh of my own and followed her to the back of the house.

There were boxes stacked everywhere. Still, the family room was almost completely set up: brown leather sofa wrapped around the back wall, complemented by a rocking chair with a quilted pillow and a big flat-screen TV—not as big as the one in Vanessa's basement, but a decent size.

Amir's eyes zeroed in on the game. Mine roamed the room. I'd been worried I would burst into tears. Now I just felt oddly detached, as if I were in a dream, or I'd entered some dulled-down alternate universe. Walls once splashed with a haphazard jumble of Mrs. Muhammad's paintings, mostly exotic South Asian birds and verses from the Quran, were now barren—except for three framed documents, all rendered in the same illegible calligraphy. Each was perfectly centered. They looked store-bought. Cheap, even . . . although that was unfair. Point being, I missed Mrs. Muhammad's bohemian flair. I missed the Muhammads. My gaze finally came to rest on one of "the men": a sunburnt middle-aged guy with a close blond buzz cut, sitting on the sofa.

He looked a little older than my dad. If his wife was a dove, then he was an oak. Hairy. Rugged. Thick. A bit too thick in the middle, more sturdy than paunchy, a bottle of beer clutched in one hand.

"That's Kyle Senior, my husband," Mrs. Turner said.

I nodded silently because I still couldn't bring myself to call her Kate, even to myself.

Mr. Turner smiled. "That's me!" His voice was loud and warm. "Welcome! Very pleased to meet you." His eyes stayed on the TV as he waved his free hand at us. I saw that he had a small tattoo on the inside of his forearm. Four tiny digits: 1493. I wondered if that was his unit number. Vanessa's dad, a vet, had a few service-themed tats on his arm.

Mrs. Turner cleared her throat. "And this is Kyle Junior."

Only then did I notice that the couch was occupied. I'd been so focused on the walls that I'd missed the kid in frayed jeans slumped not five feet away. His brown hoodie nearly matched the color of the cushions; it was pulled tight over his forehead. I couldn't see his eyes. He was about our age, skinnier than Amir and clearly just as shy. I didn't blame him for that, though.

"Just Kyle," the boy murmured.

He drummed his fingertips together. His hands were much paler than his dad's. Something else I hadn't noticed: a huge harlequin Great Dane with cropped ears, lying peacefully at Just-Kyle's feet. I broke into a huge smile.

Mrs. Turner caught my gaze and laughed. "Oh, I almost forgot! The most important member of the family. That horse of a dog is Drexler."

I resisted the urge to bend over and pet him.

"I didn't catch your names . . . ?" she asked.

"Oh, I'm sorry!" I quickly apologized. Good thing Mom hadn't come with us. She'd be mortified at my lack of manners. "I'm Salma, and this is Amir."

"Amir, you say?" Mr. Turner asked. He muted the TV and finally turned to us. "Come, have a seat. Both of you." He raised his empty bottle in the air. "Hon, you said you were getting me a new one. Five minutes ago."

"I'm sorry." She hurried to grab the old one from his hands. "And how about you, dears, can I get you some lemonade?"

As I opened my mouth to tell her no thanks, Amir cut in.

"I'm good," he said, placing his hand over his heart, "but I bet Salma would love some. Lemonade is her favorite. Thanks, Kate."

I shot him a quick glare. Yes, lemonade was a favorite. And even though Amir was fasting and was used to others—ahem, me—not fasting, he didn't need to go out of his way to show that or extend our stay. *Hello, Amir? In and out: that was our plan.* But he didn't notice my glare. His eyes were on the TV as he made his way over to the farthest section of the couch, leaving me no choice but to follow. I slumped beside him. I knew he was doing this for my mother, but he could also watch the game at *our* house.

"You know, I have a good buddy named Amir," Mr. Turner said, settling back into his chair. He flashed us a rueful grin. "He lives about nine thousand miles away, though. Where is your family from, originally?"

Amir shrugged. "Um . . . different places?" I knew he wouldn't say more than that.

Mr. Turner's eyes shifted to me. They were hazel, bright. They softened him. Still, his question made me bristle. *Of course a brown boy, a Muslim, wouldn't be local.* But maybe I was overanalyzing. After all, his wife had just invited us inside her home. And if I wanted to wrap up this visit, I should at least try to match his neighborly warmth.

"We were both born and raised right here in Arlington," I said, mustering a smile.

Mr. Turner tilted his head, as if to say *Go on.* Like there was more to the story.

"My mom's side of the family is all from Tennessee," I added. "Nashville. My dad's . . . North African." I almost cringed. I was about to say *Berber,* but Dad would never identify himself as such; Berbers rarely do. Besides, this was not the time to get into ancestry and postcolonial North African politics, or about how Berbers are still fighting to be heard, to be *Amazigh*—meaning "free." The seconds ticked by in clumsy silence.

"Now, that's what I'm talking about!" Kyle Jr. loudly exclaimed.

I shot a puzzled look in his direction. Oh, right. The game.

26

"Thank you for coming by with these gifts," Mrs. Turner said. Sharp lady: she knew it was time to wrap up this supremely awkward meet-and-greet. But then she pulled back the aluminum foil from Mom's tray. Her smile faltered but just as quickly returned. "Wow, these look delicious!" Ugh. She was lying, of course. Not only had Mom gifted them all the good stuff, dessert leftover from last night's *iftar* fundraiser (Titi's finest *ma'moul*, sesame cookies, and date bonbons), I figured I would have to explain each dish.

Amir suddenly tensed up beside me. His eyes widened, riveted by something on TV.

An alert streamed across the bottom of the screen, hashtag #DCterror. The game switched abruptly to a newsroom. My heart began to pound, drowning out the grave voice of the normally goofy local news anchor. But I got the gist—an explosion near the National Cathedral; another on Massachusetts Avenue near the synagogue on Macomb Street; no casualties reported. The screen flashed to an image of a flaming dumpster, accompanied by the bolded words: LIVE BREAKING NEWS—AUTHORITIES CONFIRM TWO EXPLOSIONS IN WASHINGTON, DC. I squeezed my eyes shut for a moment. With news flashes like these, there is a collective holding-of-breath for every Muslim. *Dear God, let it not be a Muslim. Please.* And a prayer: *Audhubillah.* May God protect us all.

With a sigh, Mrs. Turner fell into the rocking chair, shaking her head. "God help us."

Her words echoed my own. I opened my eyes and offered a smile of gratitude, which she returned. I felt a knot growing in my stomach. Time to go. I took a deep breath and stood. "I'm really sorry, but we should be—"

"Of course," Mrs. Turner interrupted, but her voice was soft. She stood as well. "Thank you so much again for the gift. Can I walk you home? I can give you the lemonade to go—"

"Oh, no, thank you," Amir interrupted politely. "That's very kind." Before I knew it, he was up on his feet, too, already halfway to the door.

"We live right across the street," I explained. My eyes flashed to Mr. Turner and his son. Both were staring at the TV, shaking their heads, their faces stony. "It was nice to meet you all." I turned and hurried after Amir.

"It was nice to meet you, too," Mrs. Turner called after us. "Despite the circumstances."

Amir and I didn't exchange a word on the short walk back to my house. There was no need. I knew what he was thinking, and I'm sure he knew what I was thinking, too. Another echo of what Mrs. Turner said, what everyone says. *May God protect us all.*

He paused at my doorstep. "I . . . um, I should practice. With Yasmin's project coming up . . ." He stopped. A strand of wavy brown hair fell in front of his face. He brushed it aside, and looked right at me. "Doesn't it feel weird? Talking like this, like—"

"Nothing happened?" I said, completing his thought. "Yeah. It is. But what else are we supposed to do? Watch the news?" I reached out and took his hand. "Bite our nails?"

I was needling him, and he knew it.

"Funny," he said dryly. "I've switched to the clippers." Nail-biting is Amir's only bad habit. Which I've pointed out many times. Of course, being the mellow guy he is, he just counters with how it's the only thing he does that gets on my nerves, whereas nothing I do gets on his nerves. (Liar, although I can't prove it.) He also claims it serves him well. This is because Mr. Epstein, our music teacher—who "shreds" on guitar (Amir's word)—actually inspects Amir's nails on his left hand, to make sure they're short enough. Apparently this has something to do with crisper tone and faster fretwork.

"Is Sheikh Epstein cracking the whip?" I teased lightly.

Amir shrugged. His smile faded. I reached out and squeezed his hand. "Kidding. Go practice. Wage some beauty. It's exactly what the world needs right now."

He squeezed my hands back tightly. Normally he might try to pull me close and sneak a hug, perhaps even nuzzle my ear, but Amir was fasting and Titi had eyes of a hawk. He leaned in, just a little. "Be good to yourself the rest of the day, okay?"

I couldn't sleep. And after I learned that there'd been a third explosion, near a DC post office, not even being online would offer comfort. I trudged upstairs to warm some milk.

The kitchen light was on.

Mom was at the table, staring blearily at her laptop. "I'm so sorry, love," she said.

"About what?"

"About the world we live in. With the shootings and the bombings . . ."

"You didn't make the world we live in," I said.

She sighed and offered a tired smile. "I haven't made it any better, though. Apart from you and your sisters. Did you see the latest?" She turned her laptop around so I could read the screen.

**AL-QAEDA IN NORTH AFRICA CLAIMS RESPONSIBILITY**

Weird: I'd never even heard of that particular splinter group. Not that it mattered; I wanted to soothe my mother. "Yeah, but I also read that an old ISIS flag was left on the White House lawn, and that there are a hundred other, undetonated bombs out there." I wasn't lying. I *had* read those things. But my mom could never truly parse the differences between internet rumors and what was real. Nor could my dad. I couldn't blame them. They grew up in a different age.

"Thank God nobody was killed," I said, just as Mom said the exact same thing.

She laughed. I returned the laugh as best I could. I knew she wanted to say more, but she was probably worried she would sound either too cynical or too upbeat.

I stepped toward her and wrapped my arm around her shoulder.

"Nobody was killed," I repeated, a whisper in her ear.

In the end, that was all that mattered. The rest was all part of the same giant lie, even though it pointed to the same truth. People were afraid. And on one level I got it. I did. If the narrative of "radical Islamic terrorism" was all you knew—if you lived in that bubble—then your lens was distorted. Trouble is, when people don't see clearly, they don't think clearly. Ignorance warps into fear, fear hardens into hate. But it didn't have to be that way, did it? Didn't some wise person somewhere once say that fear is the first step of wisdom?

# 3

I WOKE UP Monday morning certain I should do something different. I thought of the sign at All Souls Church. LOVE RADICALLY. Maybe this was the way to get into that Ramadan spirit. Yes! Perfect.

Today was a day for radical love. It would have to be. Especially because my EDS—the reason I couldn't fast—was acting up, and that always made me grumpier than usual.

I was first diagnosed with Ehlers-Danlos syndrome when I was five. EDS is a genetic disorder that affects roughly one in five thousand people. So: Lucky me! Basically it means I have more elastic tissue and weaker ligaments than most people. It also means I can wake up feeling extra fatigued and achy. (Like today.) On the other hand, I'm one of the lucky ones. For many, EDS can be degenerative, even fatal. It's why I'm not allowed to play competitive sports. It's also the reason why I spent my childhood glued to my desktop computer . . . and of course the reason that this morning it took me a little longer than usual to get myself ready and down the stairs.

The kitchen was in typical chaos. I sat down and started gobbling my bowl of cereal as quickly as I could. Hala was clearly in a pissier mood than I was. Yasmin's eyes were on her oatmeal.

I wondered what my sisters were thinking. And how much they knew. Mom and Dad had made a point to keep them away from the news all day Sunday. Which I got. It was Ramadan. A month of mercy and peace. And their anniversary.

Mom and Dad got married ages ago during the last week of *Shaban,* the month prior to Ramadan. And then a week later, instead of going on a typical honeymoon, they went on *umrah*—the lesser pilgrimage to Mecca—during the first week of Ramadan. Mom said it was like an Islamic baptism, a divine bath in the ocean of humanity; Dad said it was like a total reboot. They went to the Kaaba, that black cube-shaped "House of God" in Mecca, the directional beacon toward which all Muslims pray. Tradition holds that Adam and Eve built the Kaaba as an earthly manifestation of the heavenly home from which they were cast. The outside is draped in flowing black silk and embroidered with gold verse. The inside is empty, a void. In a way, that's the whole point of Islam—to empty the heart (and mind) of everything but God and love. And to know that the two are one and the same. To feel that awe and to humbly submit to it, with gratitude.

But that was then, in the all-consuming presence of the Kaaba. Here in Arlington, Hala had no gratitude—for anything, especially breakfast. And today was her day "off." Mom didn't want her to fast every day since she's so petite, and besides, she's a third grader. Not necessary. "This bread is burnt," she grumbled.

I wasn't feeling a whole lot of gratitude, either. I stood to dump my dishes in the sink. Dad lifted a slightly blackened slice from Hala's plate. He dangled it between his thumb and his forefinger.

"I know that young people sometimes refer to a failed thing as *toast*," he said in a mock-serious voice. "As an academic, I understand the roots of this symbolism. But I am a stickler for the literal. I believe that toast should be defined as bread burnt to the point of crispiness." He turned to Mom. "Your thoughts, Madame Professor?"

"I concur with your definition of *toast*, Monsieur Professor," Mom said with the same exaggerated formality. She grabbed the offending slice from him. "You, Monsieur, may have your own toast at *iftar*." She walked over to Hala and put a bowl of oatmeal in front of her. "I do apologize for the toast, but these are your options. Eat something, or *you* will be toast!" she said, placing her hands squarely on her hips.

Hala protested, but quickly dropped it when Mom continued to stare her down. She lifted a spoonful of oatmeal to her soured face.

On any other day I would have rolled my eyes and left. But seeing my parents now, united in their corny sense of humor, I tried to imagine them as two lovestruck young pilgrims. I tried to see them in the vast crowd around the Kaaba. I actually *thought* about what our imam said during Saturday's *iftar*, how everything we do as Muslims, whether it is fasting or going on pilgrimage or giving in charity, we do for the sake of emptying ourselves, to rid ourselves of the human ego. Ultimately the only thing that matters is whether we go out into the world with love and light guiding our hearts.

I vowed to approximate some of that feeling today. Or to try.

"Bye, everyone," I said.

"Call Mrs. DLP today if it gets too bad!" Mom called as I moved slowly to the door.

"I will," I yelled back. I got the subtext. Mrs. DLP—aka Lisa de la Pena's mom—and I had an appointment for later in the week. But it wasn't that the EDS was acting up so badly; it was that Mom knew how Mrs. DLP always gave me a mood lift, ever since I'd been first diagnosed. She was practically an honorary auntie.

"Thanks, Mom," I added. "Love you."

"Love you, too, dear."

As I walked outside, I put my game face on. At the very least, I would focus on the positives. I would start with Sunday's scare itself. There's a verse in the Quran that basically says: Each soul is as valuable as the entire universe. All these little universes, living, breathing . . . all had survived. I have to admit that I was also relieved for a selfish reason. Because what *if* those rumors about Al-Qaeda in Yemen were true? Would people think that I had blood on my hands because I was Muslim, that I was somehow complicit? That maybe, even remotely, a part of me sympathized with Muslim asshats?

I thought of something Mrs. DLP once told me, back in seventh grade. *"You can't control other people's garbage. You can only keep your side of the street clean."* Funny: I'd been complaining about some idiotic boys at school after I'd overheard them whispering that EDS was contagious and that I should be quarantined. The stuff of classic middle-school rumors: completely outrageous. It made me laugh now . . . not so much then, though. But Mrs. DLP was right. People would think and say what they wanted to think and say. All I could do was show that my faith, like my EDS, was nothing to fear.

When I reached the end of our front walk, Mariam's front door (*ugh*, the Turners' front door) flew open. Mrs. Turner exited the house with her dog in tow, then cut across the lawn—heading in the same direction as my bus. She looked dressed for morning exercise, in an orange tracksuit that was probably stylish in 1977. *Don't be mean*, I chastised myself. Right. I would resist the urge to wallow in resentment and self-pity, even though a tiny voice in my head kept telling me that Mariam should have been walking across that lawn. Instead I waved and smiled and kept to the game plan.

"Good morning, Mrs. Turner!" I called.

She held the leash tight and took in a deep breath, as if she, too, were mustering a game face for the day. "Salma! Hello . . ." Then she paused. "Are you holding up all right? Sunday was so—"

"Catastrophically awful?" I finished.

Mrs. Turner nodded and exhaled, offering a sad smile. "That's the right way to put it. The weekend went by in one big blur. I never did catch your last name."

"Oh. It's Bakkioui."

"I'm sorry. Bakk . . ." She blinked and shook her head. "I've never been good with foreign names. One more time, sweetie."

I ignored the word *foreign* because it was an honest request. (And yes, in spite of the fact that when it came to Mason Terrace, *she* was the foreigner.) Besides, I'd rather have her ask for a quick tutorial than have her mangle it for the next ten years. "Bak-ee-we," I said. "Rhymes with *kiwi*."

"Bak-ee-we. Right. Not so bad, is it?"

"Nope, it's really not."

Drexler's tail began to wag. He was looking at me, his tongue hanging out, eyes soft.

"Looks like you made a friend," she murmured. "You can pet him if you'd like. Don't let his size fool you. He's just a big baby."

I stepped across the lawn and bent down beside him, stroking the top of his head. He panted in my face, his wet nose nuzzling mine for a second. I giggled and stood, and then froze for a second, struck by Mrs. Turner's makeup. *Wow.* Maybe it was the bright morning sunlight, or maybe it was because I was standing so close to her . . . but she had on a *lot* of concealer and eyeshadow. Slathered on and overdone. Sort of begging to be noticed. But maybe that was her style. I reminded myself not to judge, because being a judgy douchebag was definitely not in the spirit of Ramadan, but she caught me staring and—*crap.* I'd made her self-conscious. She pulled her bangs over her face.

"Well, better be off," she said with phony cheer, turning away. "Drexler loves his walks." With her free hand, she tapped a Fitbit and headed toward the sidewalk. "So do I. Keeps us both in shape. Every morning and every night. Just you and me, ain't that right, buddy?"

My heart sank. I scrambled for a comeback. "Love your tracksuit, Mrs. Turner!" I called.

"Kate!" she corrected over her shoulder. She laughed and waved. "Thank you, Salma!"

I watched her disappear around the bend. Not the smoothest recovery. Not the truth, either. But at least it was a lie that kept my side of the street clean.

A few minutes later, with my mood somewhat improved and my body more or less awake, I reached the bus stop. The usual crew of neighbors and schoolmates awaited, specifically: Jorge Cruz, Aaron Sheppard, Michelle Mayor, and Ava Brown. I stress *neighbors* and *schoolmates*—not friends, not in the same orbit as Vanessa Richman or Lisa de la Pena, perhaps not even in the same galaxy.

Still, love isn't radical if applied only to friends.

I beamed my pearly whites at them . . . for a moment, and then a few more moments. The wait became uncomfortable. Then excruciating. My smile vanished, unreturned. I got a glare from Michelle Mayor. She whispered something to Ava Brown. *Assholes,* I said to myself, even though I knew I shouldn't take it personally. But how could I not? Sure, there was a possibility it had nothing to do with me. The weather *was* dreary. It *was* Monday. So really: no offense.

The bus pulled up and the doors opened. We piled on. I scanned the crowd for a friendly face, only allowing myself to breathe when I spotted Kerry in the rear, an empty seat beside her. Usually I liked to sit up front by myself and zone out to music, but today I could use the company.

She lowered her eyes, clearly trying not to see me.

*Perfect,* I thought. But then she furrowed her brow and looked back up with a smile. Phew. *A friend of a friend is a friend indeed,* I thought, not caring how corny it was. I sat down beside her and began to feel whole again. But just as the bus started up, someone, somewhere, broke the silence with a single harshly whispered word.

"*Mooslims.*"

I slipped my hoodie over my head.

In that moment, I considered bolting. Not to escape, but to tell the All Souls Church that I finally understood their message. An act of love isn't radical. Acts of love happen all the time—in jokes about burnt toast and in promises to write songs and in shouted goodbyes to see therapists. To love radically? That was the ability to love *anyone*. No matter the circumstances. No matter the faith in question.

First period, Pre-Calc (a class I utterly despise) has an added grump-inducing bonus. Michelle Mayor from the bus stop sits next to me. It used to be Vanessa's seat, but Mr. Davis forbade us from sitting next to each other after repeated reprimands to stop socializing. Now she sits in the back.

Michelle is a newcomer; she moved to Arlington last year. She flips her dyed blond hair with the practiced regularity of a religious devotion. Same with the stink-eye she gives me. She used to give it to Mariam, too . . . until, well, now. Mariam and I theorize that her wrestler boyfriend, Chris, might have been the very first person on planet Earth to coin the term "Mooslims." But I've heard him burp more than I've heard him speak actual words in any language, so we could be wrong.

Mr. Davis was organizing his desk, waiting for the rest of the class to shuffle in.

As I thumbed around my bag, searching for a pencil, Michelle started to sling her backpack off her shoulders. But then she stopped. Dramatically. She froze, her posture perfectly straight, to draw attention to herself. Instead of sitting, she marched toward Mr. Davis.

Everyone was staring at her now. The last of the hushed pre-bell conversations fell silent.

Mr. Davis looked up. "Yes, Michelle? Is something wrong?"

"I don't feel safe, Mr. Davis," she announced, as if she were onstage. "You know, with what happened over the weekend." She jerked her head at me. "What with these *jihadis* still out there."

I blinked back. At first I wasn't sure if I'd heard her correctly. Did she just say *jihadis?* The rest of the room was non-responsive. Embarrassed? Unmoved? I whirled around to Vanessa in the back. She was shaking her head in disgust.

"Seriously, Michelle?" she spat. The veins in her neck bulged. "What the hell is wrong with you?"

"Language!" Mr. Davis barked.

I turned to face the front again. My heart began to thump. I waited for him to defuse the situation. And waited . . .

After an eternal pause, he sighed.

"You can go to the office, Michelle. The rest of you, open your books to page one-forty-three."

Michelle hurried out the door and slammed it behind her.

Mr. Davis stood, as if nothing had happened at all.

My mind whirled as I overheard Vanessa whispering obscenities on my behalf. Had Michelle just been punished? Or had Davis just given her a free pass to skip Pre-Calc because of *me*—because she thought I was one of "these jihadis"? Mr. Davis's tone was unreadable. Which scared me. He could have stuck up for me, could have made this a teachable moment. He could have talked about the facts.

Fact one: the authorities were still investigating. Fact two: *jihad* is misunderstood and abused by Muslims and non-Muslims alike. Fact three: the only jihad I was guilty of was an internal one: the battle of the *nafs:* higher vs. lower self, consciousness vs. ego.

*Those* were the facts. And higher-self Salma—the girl who makes way too many excuses for others—wanted to take Michelle down with a love-bomb tackle, roll her around in a big bear hug. (Radical love.) But my lower self—the one that always tries to get its way—was more than ready to bitch her out. Wasn't that Mr. Davis's job, though? Not the bitching, but the handling, the "adulting"? Wasn't *he* supposed to reach for his higher self and deal with Michelle's offensive behavior in a meaningful way? Didn't he at least feel responsible to talk it out?

He shot a surreptitious glance at me.

I sat up and opened my hands, silently telling him: *Yes? Say something!*

In response he pushed his glasses up his nose, turned his beady eyes on the whiteboard, then scrawled away, oblivious—or pretending to be oblivious.

I couldn't decide which was worse: faking that he didn't care or truly not caring.


As soon as the bell rang I gathered my belongings and bolted out the door. Vanessa was calling my name, but I kept walking. She wouldn't give up, though. She ran to catch up to me in the hallway.

"Hey," she said breathlessly. "What do you think you're doing?"

I dropped my shoulders. "I'm sorry. That was lame. I just—"

"Needed to get the hell out of there?" she said, finishing my sentence.

I nodded.

Vanessa cracked a mischievous smile. "Please," she said, patting her cargo shorts. "I get it. So, look, I was going to save these to get out of his next exam, but now I'm thinking we could use them to make a point." She pulled out a bright purple pack of grape-flavored gum.

I stared back, not following. "Um, how?"

Her eyes widened. "Wait, you don't know about Mr. Davis's aversion to grape flavors?"

If Vanessa devoted even a tenth of the time to schoolwork that she devoted to digging up dirt on the teachers at Franklin—or useless information like gum flavor preference—she'd be a shoo-in for valedictorian. But she was obsessed with the personal lives of the staff and administration. They were a constant source of outrage, fascination, amusement, and horror . . . and even, in some rare instances, envy. It was a good thing she wasn't into blackmail.

"It's like he has an allergic reaction or something," Vanessa went on, unwrapping a stick and shoving in into her mouth. "It makes him nauseated. He'll vomit. I'm serious. It happened two years ago. My older brother Luke was there." She stopped chewing. "What?"

My nose wrinkled. I was actually with Mr. Davis on this one. With my sensitivity to synthetic smells and tastes, that gum smelled like bad cotton candy left in the sun.

"Yes, I know it's gross." She giggled and shoved the gum back in her pocket. "But here's my plan: I'll bring these to the next class with Davis. And I'll tell everyone but Michelle. I'll make sure everyone starts chewing at once, and he'll barf. She'll be *so bummed* not to be in on it."

Now I had to giggle, too, even though I would probably

barf. I didn't doubt she could pull off her plan. No doubt she could get the very same people who had stayed silent moments ago to go along with her. Vanessa transcended cliques; it was one of the things I loved most about her. Then again, her only other school-related passion was throwing parties, either at home or at her family's place on Lake Arlington. Wherever her parents *weren't*, Vanessa *was*. Hosting for everyone.

She locked arms with me and steered me toward our lockers. "But listen—" She stopped mid-sentence. "Oh crap! It's Monday."

"Meaning?"

"Duh, I've got gym!" She shoved her textbook into my hands. "Would you hold on to this until later? I need to get to Ms. Wallace early, before class starts. It's track week and there's no way in hell I'm going to do any actual running."

I arched an eyebrow. Even kids who've never had Ms. Wallace knew that she made *"no exceptions for anyone!"* Anyone on the Franklin premises would have heard her shriek these words at one time or another. Plus, rumor had it that she'd eaten several office passes in front of horrified students— literally chewing and swallowing—and that her husband had left her for another man. The rumors came from Vanessa, of course. But Mariam had been there to corroborate. . . .

My throat tightened. Mariam should be here now, too. I needed the bright side of our moon.

"What?" Vanessa asked, peering into my moistening eyes. "You're not worried about me, are you? Salma, please. I'm the only case where Wallace makes *one exception*!"

I had to laugh. The impersonation was dead-on. Maybe she *had* started blackmailing the Franklin grown-ups. Or more likely inviting them to her parties. Radical love, Richman-style.

Stupidity is one thing. Vandalism is another. Nobody had ever defiled my locker before.

I saw the graffiti from down the hall. And of course, people saw me seeing it, so they averted their eyes and cleared the area. Such courtesy. Now I was alone with this lovely little message. *Two* messages. Some bigot with the artistic skills of a toddler and the intelligence of a primate had scrawled in indelible black marker RACE TRAITOR and TOWEL HEAD GO HOME.

This was a first. I'd gotten plenty of nasty looks and whispers, but nothing written. No lasting, visible, inscribed articulation of the thoughts behind the fleeting glances and mutterings. Rage welled inside me. At least it was tempered by the desire to laugh at the idiocy.

Seriously: race traitor? I don't know what that means. To look at me, you'd say I was as white as Michelle.

So . . . what, then? Good luck pinning me down. Dad's side is an enigma. Yes, he's North African, Berber—Riffian to be exact—but he looks white, specially with his red hair.

Mom's even more complicated. A few years ago she took a swab test from one of those ancestry sites. Conclusion? She's a global hybrid: Scottish, German, Irish, Scandinavian, Eastern European, Greek, 1 percent South Asian. And she looks even "whiter" than I do. She's so white that the DAR keeps soliciting her to join them. Yes, *that* DAR: the Daughters of the American Revolution. But why wouldn't they? Her mother, my grandma Thiede, had been a member; her side of the family has a veteran in every generation dating back to the War of Independence. And while most in the DAR are like Grandma

Thiede was when she was alive—a high-society Southerner who promoted patriotism and general do-goodery—a few of them also promote waving the Confederate flag in the name of "heritage." To this day, Mom fantasizes about joining just to be a secret progressive among them. She once even prepared a lecture for the DAR about the forgotten history of American Muslims in our armed forces.

I scowled at the graffiti. *Bet you'd be shocked to learn about that, you assholes.* Whatever. The race thing made no sense, but TOWEL HEAD GO HOME was truly moronic.

First of all, I didn't wear a scarf. Well, unless Mom made me.

Secondly, hijabis got *style*. Why don't others see that? Of course, the question was as stupid as the graffiti itself.

And the GO HOME part! *Go home?* If by "home" they meant "go to a different country," then sorry, buddy, but no can do. I was born and raised here. America *is* my home. If they meant "go home" in a literal sense, then hey, I'd gladly oblige and skip the rest of this gloomy piss-poor day.

It's true that I share some fundamental beliefs with the billion or so Muslims out there. But scratch beneath the surface and things get complicated. Real quick. Besides, Islam is not a "foreign" religion by any stretch. Nearly a third of the millions of slaves dragged here from Africa *were* Muslim. Of course, acknowledging that piece of U.S. history required a little honesty and intelligence.

I took a deep breath.

*It's your senior year, Salma. A lot is riding on this.*

I fought to stay calm, sensing people returning to the hallway. I could feel the presence of multiple eyes staring at my back, my locker, my space. My gaze wandered to a black

Sharpie I kept on the top shelf. Impulsively I grabbed it. I wouldn't call what I did next Zen doodling; I hardly felt mindful and composed, but I did feel as if I were in a different state of consciousness. I even managed to forget about all the curious stares.

Within seconds I transformed the slurs into a jumble of tiny swirls and butterflies. I was particularly proud of how I used the "R" in "RACE" to create half of the biggest butterfly of all.

Butterflies are a long-held obsession. I *wear* the obsession. Mom gifted me an open, spiral ring set with a tiny hand-carved butterfly the week I was first diagnosed with EDS. We'd just returned from the hospital. I was five years old and a sobbing wreck. (A suspicion I've never shared with her—not that she would confirm it anyway—I actually think she picked the ring because she mistook the butterfly design for a ribbon tied into a bow. She wanted me to view my condition as a gift. I was "stretchy!" She used that word a lot in the early days.) Since then it had gone from barely fitting my thumb to tightly squeezing my left pinkie.

Over the years, the butterfly has come to signify more than "turning my EDS-frown upside down." Mom's words again. Truly awful: a shocking low for her. But maybe even then she knew that one day I'd see kinship in the butterfly-as-caterpillar, how it's a lowly pest in its first form, yet all about the possibility. How the caterpillar embraces the dark, wrapping itself in a chrysalis of solitude, then morphs into a new entity—a majestic, winged beauty . . . how could anyone not be enraptured? And do you know how that happens? The morphing part? Through cannibalism. Self-destruction. The caterpillar turns into a stew of enzymes and literally feasts on its own body, following a genetic instruction code that scientists call "imaginal discs." In simpler terms, it means that a worm (no bigger than a speck of dirt) dares to imagine a higher existence.

In simplest terms, though, it means that butterflies give me hope.

On my way to my next class, I kept my head down. I turned down a stairwell just to avoid the crowds; whatever, I'd take a different stairwell back up. I couldn't help but contemplate how lame humans can be compared to other life forms. Especially when I heard someone yell, "Bet she's got a bomb in there!"

I almost laughed again. Then a heavy hand shoved my backpack.

Off balance, I tumbled down the last few steps and crashed to the linoleum floor.

I wasn't hurt. Only shocked. Numb. Besides the outrage and humiliation, I felt instant panic. Crap. My computer. I flung my bag around and checked my baby just in case. Solid. It was fine. This could have been bad. It had sensitive material on it. Like proof of my hacking into Dr. Muhammad's server. . . . I raised my eyes, hoping to see if the asshat that did this to me had the balls to stay, but he or she didn't.

No one stuck around. The bell rang and people were scurrying to class.

As I tried to stand, my left knee buckled. There was a loud pop, followed by an intensely sharp shooting pain up and down my left leg. I winced and collapsed onto the steps. Shit.

I knew exactly what was wrong. It wasn't the first time I had laterally dislocated my patella.

Now I wouldn't be able to get onto my feet without help.

I forced myself to take a few deep breaths. Overall, for me, EDS isn't that big of a deal. I've gotten used to—or at least learned to live with—the constant anemic headaches, lethargy, and random bruising. Sometimes, just for fun, I even enjoy grossing others out with my super bendy fingers, curling them backward and saying, "Oh, my fingers!" I would have liked to gross out the jerk that pushed me. Or showed them the middle. Whoever it was. I doubt I'd find out. The hallway and stairwell were deserted. Not only had I been shoved down the stairs and abandoned, I'd been injured. But maybe that was the point.

Of course it was the point.

A lump began to lodge itself in my throat. I sniffed and concentrated on breathing, barely noticing the approaching footsteps until they pounded with urgency. I looked up. It was Vanessa—followed by Lisa, in gym shorts. In an instant they were crouched down beside me, out of breath and faces creased in concern. Vanessa handed me a bottle of water. I took a big sip, then wiped my face.

"Are you okay?" Lisa whispered. She gave me a cursory once-over, the way her mom did whenever I arrived in her office and wasn't feeling right.

I shrugged, not wanting to cry in front of them.

They flashed an unreadable look at each other.

"You don't look okay," Vanessa murmured. "Let me take you to the nurse. Then you should go home." She slung my bag over her shoulder, while Lisa pulled me up.

With my arms around both of their shoulders, I winced and forced myself to put one foot in front of the other, then drew a shaky breath. "Thanks. But . . . um . . . how . . . ?"

I wasn't sure how to ask the next question. But it didn't make sense that Vanessa and Lisa were together right now. There were friendly, but they weren't friends. There was no tension or negativity between them; they just had their own scenes. I happened to be the one tiny sliver of overlap in the Venn diagram of Vanessa Richman and Lisa de la Pena—in the same way that I was friendly with Kerry Morrison, but only hung out with her when Lisa was around. It would be weird if Kerry and I suddenly appeared out of nowhere, as if she were the Boots to my Dora.

"Instagram," Vanessa said in the silence.

I stopped hobbling. "What?"

"Someone . . . ," Lisa began, then bit her lip. "Someone took a picture of you from the top of the stairs, like they knew it was going to happen. Like they were waiting for it. And they posted it. Immediately. I'd just changed into my gym clothes when I saw it." She glanced at Vanessa.

"And I was coming down the hall, and she showed it to me," Vanessa continued. "And so we both went to Ms. Wallace."

"Get this," Lisa chimed in, gently ushering us down the hall. "Ms. Wallace actually said—well, more like screamed in front of the whole class—'What assholes!'" She and Vanessa exchanged a quick awkward smile. "She told us to go find you and see if you needed any help."

"So that's what we did," Vanessa said, matching Lisa's movements. "Rushed, actually."

I nodded. We shambled toward the nurse's office in si-

48

lence, heads down, creating a wall between the world and us. Not that any wall was necessary; the halls were empty.

"You know what you need?" Vanessa whispered. "A snuggle with Thomas."

Lisa smirked. "Is Thomas some sort of weird code name for Amir?" she asked.

Even I had to laugh at that. A tear fell from my cheek. "He's my cat," I breathed.


Vanessa was right, of course. A snuggle was just what I needed. A few hours later, I was in bed with our ancient Devon Rex.

Mom grew up with all kinds of pets, but Dad is allergic to animal dander. The story goes that she was willing to sacrifice pets to marry him. On their fifth anniversary he surprised her with the gift of a furless hypoallergenic kitten. So Thomas has been a Bakkioui longer than my sisters or me. It's hard not to get jealous, unless we have him one-on-one.

As he padded over my stomach, rearranging himself for another nap, I almost felt normal. My leg was elevated on a throne of pillows. It had stopped throbbing. Injury-wise, I'd had plenty worse. Hopefully at my next PT appointment I'd get rid of my clunky metal brace and upgrade to a sleeve, something fancy like the Pro-Tec Gel 400. I already knew from the EDS blogs that it was super-sleek, lightweight, and supportive—and, most important, available in my favorite color: indigo blue. I also knew that it was expensive. I made the mistake of mentioning this fact to Dad, who snapped that insurance would pay for it, and that I had to "stop looking up prices online."

Realizing that he was slightly hangry, Dad apologized and

kissed me on the head. "You deserve a Ramadan treat." After that, he left me in my room with Thomas. He'd settled; he started to purr. The sound grew and filled the room, loud and slow and rhythmic. I kissed his wet nose. Mom once told me that Sufis liken the purring of a cat to *dhikr:* divine remembrance. It's a balm. It can heal. The Sufis were right, and Mom was right, and Vanessa was right. I *was* healing. But I wondered if I could heal in a place where I didn't feel safe.

There was a knock on my door. "Salma?" Mom asked.

"Come in."

She entered slowly, smiling at the sight of the cat and me. "Salma, about school tomorrow. I am happy to drive—"

"Can't I stay home?" I interrupted.

She shook her head and sat on the edge of the bed. "You can walk just fine."

"I'm not talking about that."

"I know," she said.

"Do you have any idea how—how . . ." I was about to say *how messed up Franklin is*. But I needed Mom to hear me, to know that I wasn't being hysterical. "How Franklin can be so nasty?"

She swallowed. Then she stood, avoiding my eyes. "I do. But not everyone at Franklin is the same. It's up to you to prove the nasty ones wrong."

I scowled. Time for one of her go-to mantras. *Salma, it is your senior year.* Or *Salma, please take your behavior seriously.* Or my personal favorite: *Salma, we don't talk about money, but if you're going to receive tuition benefits, then you'll need to maintain a four-point GPA through graduation.*

So I waited. She didn't say a word, though. I should have

been relieved. I wasn't. I was angry. The longer I waited, the angrier I became. She reached for the door.

"How?" I shouted. It was loud enough to wake Thomas; he jumped off my stomach. "How do I prove them wrong?"

"Salma . . ." Mom drew a shaky breath. "Stand up for yourself and your culture."

"My *culture*? It's the same as theirs! It's fucking Franklin High School!"

She blanched at the F-word. At least that was something. I wanted more, though. I wanted her to call me on it. I wanted her to yell back. To be not broken. Wasn't I the one with the injury?

"Turn it around, Salma," she said. "Turn it around." She sniffed and shut the door behind her.


I waited another hour before I gave in to the temptation of FaceTiming Mariam. But screw it. I felt justified. She'd made me promise I'd resist for her sake, because free video calling was illegal on her end, whatever the platform, even Skype. (Needless to say, my attempts to instruct her on how to circumvent this failed. She was hopeless. *VPN, girl! It's easy!*) Maybe it was a mistake to wait. It was past midnight her time. I was almost positive she wouldn't pick up. I listened to the dial and waited for video.

Audio came on first. "Mariam?!"

"YOU!" she shrieked in delight. In that moment, her face filled the screen.

I hadn't seen her since we'd said goodbye.

In a way it was lucky the sudden lump in my throat kept

me from talking. I couldn't tell her what happened. Best not to. Besides, she looked so happy. Why ruin a glow I missed so much? I kept my brace and crutches out of frame.

She got right into it, jabbering away. Everyone was well. Her father was finally happy. His new practice was kicking ass. It was apparently much easier to fast in a Muslim majority country. Not that I would know either way. "And no idiot bigots! Only rich people with back pain!" Her new school seemed cool. Well, with caveats. "Weird, though, like . . . linguistically. My teachers are from Scotland, and Australia, and New Zealand, and I can't understand them. My math teacher is the worst. He's a Kiwi and sounds like a rugby player who got all his teeth knocked out. I'm like, 'Wait, we're speaking the same language, aren't we?' Oh, get this: I'm a total anomaly. All the kids here ask me to talk 'American.' "

When she finally took a breath to pause, I wasn't sure what to say.

In the silence, she sighed. "Problem is, I've got nobody there like you. I never will."

It was an offhand line. But it was exactly what I'd craved to hear. Our moon was still full.

Luckily, before I could start bawling, she was off again on another tangent. I forced myself to recover. Her only real complaint—aside from the lack of an insta-friendship with a Salma B. clone—was that there weren't any boys as cute as Amir.

"Or as funny," she lamented.

The old Salma B., her Mason Terrace BFF, was back. I smirked into the phone. "Give it time. At least another week. Want me to hack the school database? Maybe I can find a boy you missed."

52

"You know, there is this one teacher . . ."

"Mariam!" I laughed.

"I'm kidding. That's super-haram."

We hung up promising to check in with each other through any means (legal or illegal), at least twice a month. *"Until the future."*

This actually used to mean something. It meant Boston. Mariam had applied to BU; I applied to MIT. Vanessa . . . well, Vanessa wasn't sure she was ready for college. She wanted to take a gap year. Amir, of course, took his sweet time agreeing to the "plan," but eventually he did—thanks to Epstein, who reminded him that the New England Conservatory of Music had a top string program. The latter point appealed more to Epstein than Amir, because I think Epstein secretly wants to be a teen again. But whatever, it worked. Amir applied. There was a plan. We were supposed to stay together.

Later I found out that Mariam already knew what happened. And that Amir had told her. *And* that they had conspired with Vanessa, who then conspired with Lisa, to plan what followed next.

At 12:04 a.m., Amir texted with a cryptic message:

> I'm asking you a favor. The sucky part: You need to go upstairs and open your front door.

Seconds later, I heard a car outside. It loitered for a minute, then sped away.

I was touched, intrigued, but also mildly annoyed. Amir

knew the nature of my injury. He knew what he was asking. This was going to be a pain in the ass. Well, a pain in the leg.

On the other hand, everyone was asleep.

Slowly, cautiously, I limped upstairs.

When I opened the door, I found a vase of fresh flowers on the stoop: a bouquet of lilies and baby's breath. The fragrance filled the hallway. Once I managed to close the door, I allowed myself to take a deep intoxicating whiff. It was only when I opened my eyes that I noticed the small card strung around the vase.

---

WITH LOVE FROM MARIAM, VANESSA,
DORA AND BOOTS, AMIR, AND EDWARD NORTON

---

My phone dinged: another text from Amir.

Tomorrow morning I'm asking you one more favor.

I didn't even realize I'd started crying until a tear splashed on the screen.

Ready for it. Thank you.

In a delirium, I hobbled into the kitchen to set the flowers down. My mom had left her laptop open on the table, which was unusual for her. I touched the pad to revive the screen.

There I saw an unsent email in progress to Principal Philip.

*I am writing on behalf of my daughter, who was attacked on the Franklin premises. I am outraged that I haven't heard from you. We are not litigious,*

*though in this case we certainly have every right to be.*
*Above all, I am deeply shocked and saddened. Your*
*silence signals tacit approval of bigotry at your school.*
*My daughter's pre-calculus teacher enabled a fellow*
*student, Michelle Mayor, to*

That was all.

It was enough. I wiped another tear away. Mom wasn't broken at all.

I WASN'T SURE what to expect the next morning. The muffled purr of cars pulling in and out, the thump of doors closing—these noises generally don't register during breakfast, as it's the only time Mason Terrace ever consistently has traffic. So when I opened the door to hobble to the bus, I was genuinely surprised to see Amir's white Volkswagen Jetta. I giggled like one of my sisters. I couldn't help it. He stepped out of it with a big fake show of being gentlemanly.

He placed his hand over his heart and bowed. "Here I am, at your service."

"Okay, I get you're being ridiculous," I said. "But this is totally out of your way. And don't you usually practice oud right now?"

Amir waved his hand dismissively. "Not an issue," he said.

That was BS. He loved his oud like I loved my computer.

"Your bag and crutches, my sweet?"

I concentrated on not blushing or acting like a middle schooler (failing) while he threw my stuff in the trunk. The next thing I knew, he was sweeping me off my feet—literally—and carrying me over to the car. When we were both inside, he handed me a fresh double latte with extra whipped cream. My favorite. I brought the warm cup close to my face. It was sugared *kareem*. It woke me up.

I reached forward with my left hand, interlacing my fingers with his. "Do you have any idea how perfectly your name fits you?"

"Not until you came along. What's a prince without a princess?"

I blew him a string of kisses.

"That's all I get?" he teased.

"Hey, we're right in front of my house. Titi could be watching. Besides, wouldn't that break your fast?" I gently responded.

As we pulled away, Amir flipped on the radio. Coldplay's "Hymn for the Weekend" was playing. It couldn't have been timelier. Maybe he'd arranged this, too. The ride was a blur, though I was very conscious of how he dropped me off all VIP-like right in front of the school.

I smiled as he sped off toward senior parking. And I kept smiling. All morning long, even at Michelle and Mr. Davis. My mom might have been angry, was right to be angry—and I was grateful for every scathing word of her note—but right now, today, she would have to harbor that indignant rage for the both of us. For better or worse, Amir had sent me into school loving radically.


Fourth period, I heard my name crackle over the loudspeaker: "Salma Bakkioui."

It was Mrs. Owens, of course. Still, I winced. My name

had never been among those called out during the school day. Plus, she always called me "Salma B." Why the sudden change? It sounded so official, so . . . well, plain weird.

"Salma Bakkioui," she repeated. "Please come to the principal's office."

I ignored the puzzled stares as I crutched out of the classroom as fast as I could, wondering why on God's green earth *I,* of all people, was being called to the principal's office. But then I relaxed. *Mom's note. I bet I'm getting an official apology. Now, that would be civil.*

"Hi, Mrs. Owens," I said, breathless from the hurry. "Um, you called my name?"

She lifted her head slowly. Her eyes seemed to scroll up to mine, then flash away, her perpetually bright smile pained. Honestly, she looked sick, as if she were battling a stomach flu. It occurred to me suddenly that I'd seen this nauseated expression of hers before: in eighth grade, right after the mass shooting in San Diego. And a few other times in years past . . . I'd never put two and two together—maybe I hadn't wanted to, maybe I'd been too young and naïve—but now the reason was crystal clear: she couldn't bear to be near me whenever there was news about atrocities committed in the name of Islam. How long would it take her to get over this latest one?

Actually, why did I even give a shit? I would be graduating soon. It was *her* problem, not mine. Principal Philip would make everything better.

"I'll walk you in," she mumbled. She stood and turned quickly, maybe to avoid my glare, and led me to the conference room next to Principal Philip's office—where she closed the door behind me. No one was there. I sat and waited.

My phone buzzed with a text from Amir.

> I heard your name. What's up?

> You know my mom. Tiger on the inside.

> I bet she was so pissed off.

> Still is. Complained too. Directly to Principal Philip.
> Can't wait to see Michelle eat her words.

> Take a picture for me?

> Damn right I will.

I heard footsteps on the other side of the door.

*Finally. Put on a smile, Salma, accept their apologies with grace.*

The door creaked open.

Two police detectives entered. They wore matching dark suits—business suits, not cop uniforms—badges clipped to their breast pockets, American flag pins on their lapels. The first was tall and slender, but well built. He looked like someone who competed in triathlons. In the middle of his chin was a prominent dimple. The second was older, a bit disheveled, like he'd been staring at a computer screen for hours on end through his thick glasses. He didn't greet me with a partial smile like the younger detective. Instead he grabbed a seat and pulled a notepad out of his pants pocket.

The door swung shut. I felt the room shrink and my temperature soar. I was expecting to feel relieved. Instead I felt ambushed. As we sat there in silence, I kept wondering why no one else had been invited to join us. Specifically Principal Philip. I'd been called to see *him*. Yet here I was, alone with two strangers. My thoughts raced into the past, scouring memories, chasing down any tension I'd missed between us. Nothing. None of the awkwardness I'd just experienced with Mrs. Owens.

Sure, Principal Philip had asked a few dumb questions about Islam over the years. And yes, he made no secret of his admiration for Robert E. Lee. Neither bothered me. Plenty of ancestors on my mother's side admired Robert E. Lee, too. I remembered once, freshman year, Mariam grumbling about his insensitivity after a mass shooting in a church. He'd made a big stink at an assembly over changes at the Arlington House—Robert E. Lee's nearby historic estate and Franklin's go-to field trip destination (naturally) . . . something about how its curators had exploited a tragedy to "disrespect the General." I could even picture the ugly sneer on his face as he'd said those words. *Disrespect the General.* But I couldn't recall why. And right now, with law enforcement officials sitting directly across from me, it didn't seem to matter much anyway.

The younger detective cleared his throat. "Thanks for taking the time out of your school day to come and talk to us. You're under no obligation to stay, but we wanted to ask a few questions."

"Um . . . okay?" My voice was shaking.

"This is just a routine check," he said. "I'm Detective Tim McManus, but you can call me Detective Tim. We're pleased to meet you . . . Salma, is it? Can I have your full name?"

I took a breath and focused on speaking without fear. "Salma Dihya Bakkioui."

"Salma Dihya Bak-kee . . . yee," he said. He flashed a quick smile, acknowledging that he might have mispronounced it. "Pretty name. I don't mean to alarm you, but the school received a bomb threat. Can you open your laptop, please?"

At first I didn't understand him. I must have misheard. I

tried to follow a line of logic given the words that he'd just uttered. His tone was inscrutable. A bomb threat? Wouldn't they have cleared the premises? We had lockdown drills to train for this sort of thing. And why was he smiling? Why did he compliment my name, knowing he couldn't even say it properly? My eyes flashed to the disheveled older cop, who leveled his glasses at me. I stared back for a moment, unnerved. There was no emotion I could see in those fixed, dark eyes. *The Silent One,* I named him. I had no choice; unlike his counterpart he seemed to have no interest in introducing himself to me.

"No problem," I finally managed. "I have nothing to hide." I reached for my computer case, but Detective Tim darted forward and put his hand over mine.

"I'll get it."

Frozen, I watched as he reached in and removed my darling, my precious, my *baby.* Nobody, not my parents or sisters—not even Amir or Mariam—dared to handle it without specific permission. Detective Tim withdrew and flipped it open on the table so that the screen faced me, then began to tap on the keyboard. A Quranic verse appeared as wallpaper. He rotated my computer so the Silent One could view the image. The Silent One jerked his head in a sort of code language I recognized from the longtime partners on *Law & Order: SVU.* At least that's how my brain interpreted it. Olivia Benson was my hero.

"What does that say?" Detective Tim asked me.

"It says, *'Hasbunallahu wa ni'ma'l wakil.'*"

"In English."

" 'God is all we need. What an excellent Guardian is God.' At least that's what Titi taught me."

He traded another glance with the Silent One, who shrugged noncommittally, then jotted something down in his notepad.

"Who is Titi?" Detective Tim asked.

"My eighty-two-year-old granny."

He frowned at me. "This is serious. I'd prefer less sarcasm."

"About *what*?"

"This friend 'Titi,' the person who taught you this phrase, is . . . ?" He left me to fill in the blank.

"I just told you," I snapped, shifting in the chair. "She's my granny. If you don't believe me, call her. Or call my mom. Or my dad." My voice rose. "This is serious, right? I want to talk to them. *Now*."

"Absolutely," Detective Tim said. "You can call them in one second. . . ."

He slid my computer across the table to the Silent One, who in turn inspected it. The sudden soft buzzing of a text made Detective Tim stiffen. The Silent One sat up, too. Like a pair of synchronized robots, each pulled a smartphone out of his inside jacket pocket. They glanced at their screens, glanced at each other, and shoved the phones back inside. What was going on? If they wanted to know what I was up to online, they would have done one of several dozen things—beginning with actually *touching* the keyboard. Just as I was about to demand what the hell was going on, the Silent One ripped a page out of his notebook, crumpled it, and tossed it into the recycling bin. Then he closed my computer and gently slid it across the table to me.

"Well," said Detective Tim, "we appreciate your time and cooperation. Sorry to interrupt your school day."

I glanced between them, then pushed myself away. My leg was throbbing. My EDS was making me even *more* irritable than the situation warranted. "So can I go?" I grumbled.

"Yes. Oh. One more thing. I just wanted to ask you about a boy named Amir."

"What about him?"

Detective Tim leaned in. "He's your boyfriend?" he asked, close enough that I could smell his aftershave.

I leaned back. "What do you care?"

"I'm sorry; I don't, really," he said, withdrawing. "You're right. It's not my business. Just gauging how well you know him. Are you aware that he's in touch with people overseas?"

"I . . ." I bit my lip. Instead of answering right away, I stared at the floor, afraid of what I'd do if I looked into his face. "Yes," I said finally. "Amir is a musician. He Skypes with other musicians. It isn't easy to find a community of world-class oud players in Northern Virginia."

"A community of what players?"

My jaw tightened. "It's an instrument. Google it."

"Are these friends in Morocco?"

I paused, baffled. "I . . . um . . . maybe? Mostly the United Arab Emirates, I think?"

"But your parents met in Tangier, correct?"

"Yeah, I'm sorry." I shook my head. "What does that have to do with Amir?"

"Nothing. You were with him last Sunday, May third."

It was a statement, not a question. My pulse picked up.

"Sunday? Yes. At my house, the neighbors . . ." Now I was frightened. In seconds, Detective Tim's stream of non-sense had somehow suddenly brought us to the day of the bombings. The room spun as the headline from Mom's computer flashed through my mind.

## AL-QAEDA IN NORTH AFRICA

"Something wrong?" he asked.

I nodded furiously. "Yes. I told you that I wanted to leave, and I told you that I want to call my parents. I'd like to do both now, please."

Detective Tim smiled again, as he had when he'd butchered my name. "Of course, Miss Bakkioui."

This time he pronounced my name flawlessly.

With my jaw hanging open, he and his nonverbal partner left the room.

# 5

I STEWED ALONE for what felt like hours, though it was less than four minutes. I knew this for a fact because I held my phone in my hand and stared at the screen the entire time. Still, I didn't make the call to my mom, the one I desperately wanted to make, precisely because they had given me permission. I would be strong, stronger than them, just as Mom advised. To use her sad cliché, I would turn this around. I would resist them in any way I could. *The nerve. Treating me like a damn criminal! Here! At Franklin!* I was proud of my restraint (even as I was losing it) when Principal Philip finally appeared.

He opened the door and held it for me.

"Thank you for your cooperation, Salma." He spoke in a monotone. "You can go."

Funny: he'd used the same word that they had. *Cooperation.* I couldn't think of anything lower on my list of priorities. I'd come here for *contrition*—his, specifically—for a formal apology over how I'd been attacked and ignored. Instead *I'd* been treated like a suspect . . . in what, though? Had there really been a bomb threat? If so, he had bigger problems than me. Neglecting a bullied Muslim student with EDS was one thing; neglecting the entire school would surely drown him in a flood of lawsuits and get him fired. None of this seemed right. I tried to meet his eyes. He avoided mine, just as Mrs. Owens had.

"Is that it?" I asked, giving him one last chance. Only then did I realize how desperately I wanted him to explain himself, to tell me he was sorry, to confess that he had no control over the situation. *Anything.* Maybe he was simply following the police's orders; even saying that would have helped. It was a feeble excuse, but a plausible one. He just needed to offer it.

At a loss, I finally demanded, "Are we in danger?"

"No, it's . . ." He shook his head. "There is no danger. It was a misunderstanding."

"Is that it?" I repeated.

He nodded stiffly and gestured for me to leave.

Well, then. The world had lost its mind. Without another word, I stormed—okay, limped on crutches—out of the office . . . past him and past Mrs. Owens, then out into the hall toward the exit. It would have been a gloriously defiant departure had I been able to shove open those heavy doors at the school's main entrance. But of course I was denied even that small victory, thanks to my bad leg. I whacked the automatic door opener with a crutch. I envisioned Mrs. Owens's sickly tight-lipped smile in place of the blue button. This was the same woman who'd doted on me when my EDS had acted up in the past. Who congratulated me semester after semester for making the honor roll! I'd taken her basic human decency for granted. Principal Philip's, too. In their silence and in-action, they were no different than the idiots who'd shoved me down the stairs and posted it on Instagram. What did they think was going on? What about the words he said at commencement every year? "We thrive together thanks to a social contract built on trust." Apparently that social contract wasn't so binding.

My thoughts were at a fever pitch when a hand suddenly pulled on my shoulder.

I whirled around, livid. "Leave me alone!"

It was Amir. He stepped back.

"Oh my God, I'm so sorry, Amir," I whispered. "I didn't know it was you—" A lump lodged itself in my throat. All of a sudden I was crying.

"What happened?" he whispered. "Are you okay?"

I shook my head and sniffed. "Just take me away. Anywhere."

"Good timing," he said. "No one will notice if we leave now, anyway. It's lunchtime."

"It is?" I hadn't even noticed.

Amir whisked me away. No questions asked. We hopped in his Jetta and sped toward the Beltway, fortunate that neither of our afternoon teachers consistently took attendance, and even if they did, we'd get home in time to erase the automated school-to-home absentee messaging service. Ha-ha! Screw you, Franklin.


Mariam always thought that Amir was quiet because he's shy. And he is on some level, yes. Still, she never quite got it, got *him*. The truth is that he just prefers to listen instead of speak. It's no great secret or mystery: you can't be such a talented musician unless you are a listener first. But there's something more, too—something Mariam might have even known on a subconscious level, but that I never realized or understood until Amir and I got together. It's the unspoken fear all brown-skinned boys share. Especially Muslims. Most days it barely registers. But it never truly goes away—the fear that a stranger will always assume the worst, that you should never attract attention to yourself . . . that your survival depends on being as close to invisible as possible.

Of course, right now, Amir was just being a good boyfriend. After all, he knew *me*, too. He knew how much I needed silence. I didn't care where we were going. All I wanted was distance. Distance and highway hypnosis. And gradually Amir's presence, combined with the blur of passing cars, helped my mind disconnect from the massive shit sandwich the day had served. Sure, we all have to eat one from time to time. But today was some kind of Bonanza All-You-Can-Eat Special.

As we rolled over the Fourteenth Street Bridge, Amir finally took a deep breath. "Are you feeling any better?" he asked.

I pulled my good leg off the dashboard. "Yeah, a bit."

He reached over and stroked my cheek. "What happened, *habibti*? I'm worried."

*Habibti.* My love. I took a deep breath. Those words. His voice. *Kareem.* He was always *kareem.*

"Yeah, so . . . I'm actually not sure. But I *think* that someone called in a bunk bomb threat, and even though the cops knew it was bunk, they decided to interrogate me anyway. One of the few token Muslims. And Principal Philip was totally cool with it, because he knew it was a fake." I scowled at the glistening tree-lined Potomac, once again parsing the horrific and nonsensical sequence of events. "You know what? Come to think of it, for all I know, there *was* no bomb threat.

Maybe they just made one up so they could ask me about May third."

I glanced at Amir, who was silent. He gripped the wheel tightly. A rare display of anger.

"What?" I asked him. "What is it? Were you questioned, too?"

"No," he said. "I wasn't. But before you ran me over in the hallway, I overheard Chris and Michelle, laughing their asses off. Chris was giving props to Warren. You know, his older brother. He said, and I quote: 'Warren's got the mad prank skills. He shut down the whole Metro once.'"

I clenched my fists. That figured. I'd heard rumors about Warren over the years, mostly through Vanessa, although I barely remembered him. He graduated when I was in eighth grade. Same year that Vanessa's older brother graduated. Warren had been a big shot at Franklin, a star quarterback. (Cornerback? Something.) The story came drifting back, how Vanessa once told me that he'd gotten a full ride at Virginia Tech, but his scholarship had been revoked. . . . He'd gotten arrested, hooked on opioids, and was now sharing a bedroom with his younger brother. Knowing Vanessa, this pathetic tale was probably true. It almost made me pity Chris. Almost. I was about to open my mouth to say that I could forgive an idiot drug addict for doing something idiotic and drug-induced—if that's what had in fact happened—when Amir nudged me with his elbow.

"You know what I think?" he murmured. The cloud over his face had lifted. The darkness melted into a smile as he pulled to a stop at a red light.

"That we should find Warren and beat the crap out of him?"

He shook his head. "Too easy. I think it's time to initiate Project Mayhem."

"Ha!" I laughed out loud in spite of myself.

I wanted to kiss him then, kiss him like I had that first night . . . kiss him in honor of our special movie. It figured *Fight Club* brought us together. I mean, what a deranged film. Not a single ounce of typical romance. Maybe that's why atypical romance had ensued. There we'd been at Vanessa's, all those months ago, publicly glued to the screen and secretly glued to each other. Glued to the silly empowerment and the absurdity of the plot. Why *wouldn't* two nerdy Muslim teens love a film about a gang of disaffected white men, led by a mentally ill insomniac, all pummeling each other in basement fights while secretly plotting to destroy civilization?

I leaned forward and fake-punched his arm.

"What can I say, Amir. You met me at a very strange time in my life."


Once Amir took a right onto Constitution Avenue, I knew exactly where he was taking me: the Smithsonian's Butterfly Pavilion. It was only a few weeks ago that I suggested we go there for my eighteenth birthday. I guess he's bumped it up on the calendar, thinking, quite rightly, that a day spent in a garden could undo a morning trapped in hell.

The Natural History Museum's only live exhibit was practically empty of other humans. Amir and I were wonderfully alone in that tubular, climate-controlled room with a hundred or so free-flying goddesses. Or gods. I'm not *that* talented of an amateur lepidopterist.

My eyes immediately zeroed in on the Blue Morpho. It

has topped my "must-see" list for ages, and since I don't have any international trips in the foreseeable future (they live in various South American countries), I was overcome with total euphoria. I crushed Amir's hand. "I know, I know," he whispered, slipping from my death grip. "I see her, too."

We crept closer to the exotic plant where the Blue Morpho was resting—motionless, her wings fully extended. I inhaled deeply. I absorbed every inch of her delicate glory. Her dark-as-night frame, her spider-thin veins. And what a color, a blue to which all blues aspire, so irresistible you want nothing more than to fold yourself up into a microscopic ball and fall inside.

Then, just like that, she collapsed her wings, revealing an earthy-brown underside. Another blink and she was blue again.

Brown. Blue. Brown. Blue.

Up and away she flew.

I turned around and stood toe to toe with Amir. "Thank you . . . for this . . . for you . . . just what I needed." I slipped my arms under his and tucked my thumbs into his back pockets.

He pulled me close. "Anything for you, Salma."

"Anything?"

"Anything."

*Wow. Anything? Okay, Amir . . . you've got me. Hooked. Like a moth to a flame. Ready to melt.*

Just then a group of loud-mouthed visitors in hideously matching T-shirts burst into the pavilion. DC tourists. You gotta hand it to tourists: they always know how to screw things up. We flopped down on a nearby bench.

"So," I continued. "If anything truly means an-y-thing, then let's go to Manu National Park. Peru. It's a Mecca for butterflies."

"Why wait?" he said. "My private Jet . . . ta is at your service."

"That pun was worthy of my dad in its lameness."

"Then forget the Jetta," Amir said. "We should get out of here. Why don't we go to the UAE? We could take a gap year. Work. Study. Whatever."

I laughed again, but I felt his dark eyes on mine. He wasn't smiling anymore. He was serious.

"Dubai has the largest butterfly garden in the entire world," he added.

"I bet it does. And the tallest building and the biggest mall. Sorry, but an über-conservative, fake-ass, *dunyawi* playground for the ultra-rich doesn't appeal to me."

Amir pulled his hair up into a topknot, slowly, as though he was calculating the pathway of least resistance. He's allergic to confrontation, anything that might upset his super-mellow, slightly hippie-hipster vibe. But he wasn't going to let this go, either. Quiet or not, he's as stubborn as I am.

"We don't need this shit, do we?" he asked softly. "Dubai is an open society, Salma. There are women in miniskirts and ladies in *burqas*. And there's a lot more to it under the radar. Trust me, okay? I know a ton of people who moved there. They can finally breathe. What does Mariam say? I bet she loves it, right?"

I opened my mouth, and then closed it. The rowdy tourist group had snaked its way over to our corner. I didn't want to argue with an audience. Besides, he was right, sort of, which pissed me off. Not the being-right part, but the Mariam-liking-the-UAE part. At least that was the vibe she gave when we Skyped.

He slouched down, resting his head on my shoulder. My

gaze fell to the ground. A dead butterfly was lying in the shadows, wings torn. Torn like me. Between places, people, myself.

I rested my head on his. Amir had a built-in positives-only compass, which I usually appreciated. But none of this Dubai talk was in "the plan." A plan he swore to long before the Mariam saga. And even though her parents were now promoting their own new plan (one which involved Mariam staying "local"—aka "in Dubai"), I still hadn't relinquished my plan. Boston could still happen.

The crowd passed. Amir stirred to life.

"Look, I know you have strong feelings about your plan, but trust me, it's worth postponing," he said, sitting up again. "NYU Abu Dhabi has a hackathon. A hackathon, Salma!" His face grew serious again. "Please, just don't write it off. Life here isn't all rainbows and butterflies."

My gaze returned to the dead butterfly. Even in death, the creature was striking. Her struggles to achieve a higher existence were totally worth it. But . . . *Rainbows and butterflies? Come on, Amir. You're better than that, and I'm not that naïve.* I can be, I have been, no doubt. But the stairs incident was different. Being interrogated by the police was different. My cushy, middle-class, suburban, I-can-pass-for-white, privileged bubble had been totally popped, along with my patella. Maybe Amir's could stand to be popped, too.

"I know it isn't all rainbows and butterflies. Those cops asked me about you."

He tilted his head. He almost seemed amused. "They did?"

"Yeah, apparently they feel it necessary to monitor you and your fellow oud nerds. It's a better use of their time than, say, questioning Warren about a bomb threat. But you know what? I live here. And I *want* to live here. That just wants

73

to make me rub my home in their faces. Let them monitor all they want." I let out a short bark of a laugh. "Trust me, neither of them is Olivia Benson from *Law and Order: SVU.*"

Amir chewed his lip, absently staring off into space—maybe into the abyss of worrying about being watched, or maybe into some imaginary bright future where ignorance wasn't an issue. Then his eyes met mine and softened. "Yeah . . . screw them all. Let's get you one of those frappy-dappy drinks you love and head back. It's nearly three."

I reached for my crutches. "Okay. I have Titi duty, anyway. She wants to bake for *iftar.*"

"Full-time joy-maker?" he cracked lightly. "But . . . Salma?"

"Yeah?"

"What else did those cops say? Anything I should worry about?"

"They didn't say anything worth repeating," I grumbled, angry at myself for bringing it up. "I'm sorry. Really, it was nothing."

"You sure?"

"Yeah. But, Amir, you know what? You can skip the coffee. Just get me home."

He grimaced and turned to the exit. "No problem."

As we drove toward my house, I couldn't shake the terrible aftertaste of being treated like a suspect. Of being lumped in with terrorists like Al-Qaeda in North Africa and a sleeper cell from Syria. And although the facts still weren't known, the rumors persisted—in the news and now in my school. One news show even suggested this was the work of Shi'ites of Hezbollah, which was really weird because attacks in the West almost always come from violent jihadist Wahhabi types, hardcore, nonthinking literalists who claim to be Sunni, but betray all that is Islamic and hate everyone who is not "one of them"—Muslim or non-Muslim alike—as *kafirs*.

Like me. I'm such a kafir—loving my Sunni, Shi'ite, Sufi, and non-Muslim brethren alike. Finding validity in all their truth claims (because ultimate truth can't be claimed).

Oh my God. Listen to me. The facts aren't known and even I am echoing what the talking heads are saying—the one thing that holds all these groups together, that they're "Mooslim."

*Astaghfirullah.* I just wish we could take all the crazy terrorists and strident puritanicalists—no matter what tradition they betray—and drop them off on a remote island. Leave the rest of us—as in the 95 percent of the people in this world who are normal—the heck alone.


I had hardly been home for a millisecond when Titi looked up from the bay window and frowned. "Bad day, *habibti*?"

I left my bag by the front door and collapsed on the cushion beside her.

"No, I'm okay."

"Truly, Salma Dihya?"

I'm a bad liar and Titi knows it.

"Fine. You're right. I had a horrible day, and my leg is aching."

She tapped my knee and smiled. Her English isn't great, but over the years we have managed to patch together a common language.

"Really, that's okay, Titi. You're the one who deserves a massage."

She batted away the suggestion. I lifted my leg and placed it in her lap. Being Titi's joy-maker has some pretty sweet upsides. As her hands worked downward from my knee to my ankle, I studied the hard lines around her smile. I wish those wrinkles could speak. I wanted them to take me back, across time and space, to Titi's past. To the land of her childhood, stories about saints and djinn. Strange how at certain times, stories you've heard a million times can feel both wonderfully near and painfully distant.

Like the story of my middle name. Titi had insisted upon it when I was born, a title and talisman she's hung over my head ever since. Always invoking it.

*Salma Dihya, Salma Dihya, Salma Dihya.*

Dihya was the feminine face of the *Amazigh,* "the free people," as Titi and Dad would say. Back in seventh-century Algeria, she was so badass—a freedom-fighting warrior, a Jewish queen from the Djerawia tribe of the Zenata Imazighen, and (according to some) a sorcerer. But sorcery aside, she's enough of a hero that others claim her: Muslims, Berbers, Zionists, French colonialists, Arabs . . . as an Arabized Berber, Titi grew up under colonial rule. Her best friends and neighbors came from every faith and background: all different, all North African. For her, my middle name was meant to celebrate the beauty of those differences, to transcend identity politics. To Moroccans like Titi, Dihya was always a symbol of something greater. She was aspirational. A call to be brave and noble, to love those who love you . . .

Once more, I thought of Mom's computer screen.

**AL-QAEDA IN NORTH AFRICA CLAIMS RESPONSIBILITY**

I owed Amir an apology. He was only trying to be helpful today. To connect me with me. And then on our way home, I was being so mental, so stuck in my head, that I forgot to say our ritual goodbye.

I whipped out my phone and texted.

> My dearest fellow Norton nerd: I'm really sorry. I was just so mad. I wanted to murder someone and you were only trying to help. And the stupid thing at school is done. Let's have a do-over. ASAP.

I looked up at my grandmother. "Thank you, Titi. Do you want to bake now?"

Titi smiled. "I do. Titi's scones . . . better than Mom's."

*Better than Mom's.* Yep, that's Titi. Proving her own skills in the kitchen—American-style.

As I was about to slip my phone back into my pocket, it buzzed with Amir's response.

> Was I asleep? Was I sleeping? My house. Sunday. Yours forever, Tyler Durden.

Later that night I almost began to remember the pre–May 3 Salma Dihya Bakkioui. Almost.

First Vanessa texted to make sure I was okay. When her face appeared on my screen, I nearly burst into tears. But I quickly got control of myself and replied with a "thanks, yes, fine," and even threw in a couple of heart emojis (which I hate), while the memories flooded back: the shove, the cold floor at the bottom of the stairs, how I'd felt tossed aside like garbage. But I could fight back. I wasn't alone at Franklin. Vanessa had my back. Amir had my back.

Next Mariam texted, completely out of the blue, with a

bunch of ridiculous photos. Apparently for the hell of it she'd gone to a local Dubai salon and asked for a Gulfi makeover— fake eyelashes, painted eyebrows, penciled-in lips. She looked amazing. Like a brown goddess. But she'd also superimposed a photo of me right next to her, same deal. I must say, her Photoshop skills were improving. (Of course the ironic do-over was gorgeous on her, the fake one on me, not so much.) I looked like a hooker. Which was the point. Her final text:

> Can't wait for u to meet my new imaginary friend.
> Don't judge her because she's a prostitute.

I laughed out loud. Girl has always had a wicked sense of humor.

Your sister misses you, I texted back. I resisted adding: *Badly.*

On a whim I decided to venture again onto the Dark Web to see if I could somehow track down a free flight to Dubai. Maybe I'd play hooky for a week. But I quickly forgot about running away when I found a message waiting from Pulaski88. I hadn't visited his forum since "the operation" (his words).

> **Pulaski88: Haven't seen you around. Worried you got caught hijacking that chiropractor's router? I can recommend some lawyers in your area.**

I smiled as my fingers flew over the keyboard in response. I'd been wondering about him.

I had a hunch that he was a resident of Pulaski, Virginia: a tiny town I happened to visit last fall when Mom insisted that we at least *tour* the campus at Virginia Tech. On our way out, a tire blew; the nearest town was Pulaski; the grizzled mechanic there replaced our tire free of charge. I guess they breed altruism in that part of the state. The symbolism of *88* was more of a mystery. Eventually I figured it was a nod to his own talents as a math whiz. (Hackers are like rappers that way, alas.) Thanks to Mr. Davis and one of his many tangents, I knew that eighty-eight was an "untouchable" number, though I couldn't remember why or even what "untouchable" meant, math-wise. Not that it mattered. Pulaski88 was saying that nobody could touch him as a hacker.

So I did what came naturally: I teased him. Why did he have such little faith in his own instruction? Or was it that he was worried I might surpass him in his hijacking abilities? That the student would become the master?

**Pulaski88: Dig your attitude. Do you have another operation in mind?**

**Me: Destroy a piece of corporate art and trash a franchise coffee bar.**

I'd typed the response immediately, almost without thinking. It was a direct quote from *Fight Club,* one of its more absurd lines.

**Pulaski88: Operation Latte Thunder has been done before.**

My smile widened. Too bad Amir wasn't here to share this moment. I suddenly imagined Pulaski88 looking like Edward

Norton. I saw him sitting in a dark room, his haggard face lit blue from a desktop screen, smiling back with a bruised lip and black eye.

Me: A DDoS has been done before, too, but that hasn't stopped anyone.

Pulaski88: Is that what you have in mind? What's the target?

Me: No target. But I'd love to bring the asshats at my school to their knees. They deserve their own shit sandwich.

As soon as I hit Send, I felt a twinge of regret. It was a joke. I'd never risk anything as destructive as a distributed denial of service, a cyber-attack that would take Franklin offline—an attack I could probably execute, given its simplicity. But my new friend might not get that I was blowing off steam.

Pulaski88: Guessing you're not serious.

Me: Never serious when I'm here.

Pulaski88: Good. That means that you already know the first rule of ethical hacking. Never be serious. And the second rule of ethical hacking is . . . ?

I laughed out loud for the second time that night.

Me: Never be serious.

# 6

AMIR HAD NO idea how good he had it at home. As the youngest of five—and the only boy, stress on *boy*—he lived in a paradise that amounted to minimal parental supervision. When he came over to my house, it was a family affair. Forget an unannounced visit. We'd never even tried, because I could foresee exactly what would happen. Both of my sisters would suddenly appear to fawn over him, followed by Titi, who would plant herself like a tree between us (because Amir "brought her joy," of course)—then Mom, who would ask me to do some kind of chore, but not before calling Dad to come home early from work to join the fun.

*"Oh, hi, Amir! We had no idea you were coming over! What can we feed you? Do your parents know you're here?"*

And I had it better than most. Mariam hadn't even been allowed to date.

So the Saturday afternoon silence was . . . lovely. (As in: the opposite of what you'd experience upon opening the door of the Bakkioui household.) I found myself tiptoeing as I followed Amir inside. I didn't want to disturb the quiet. Mr. Ammouri was up on the second floor, fiddling around in his office, while Mrs. Ammouri was at the store, shopping for her upcoming trip.

Amir had four older sisters, who had all flown the coop. I had gotten to know the younger two, Mona and Manal, but the older two lived halfway across the country. One of them (I can't remember which because they all had "M" names) was expecting twins. Twin boys. And that's who his mom was shopping for. She was going to visit for an entire month—to put the finishing touches on their nursery and, I assume, to celebrate the entrance of these first grandbabies into the world. It was kind of cute. From what I'd gathered from Mom over the years, Titi had been the same way with me.

As always, visiting the Ammouris felt less like hanging out at my boyfriend's home than visiting a spa. The design was sleek and modern. The lighting was soft. The residents' personal boundaries were respected. The only things missing were mud baths and new age music.

We headed straight for the living room, where Amir eyed the family film collection.

His mother had arranged all the DVDs in chronological order on a floating TV console—I'm guessing from Crate and Barrel. She shopped there a lot. *"Amir, I CAN'T order living room furniture online,"* he'd quoted (or made up) in a dead-on impersonation. *"The joy of shopping is SURPRISE."*

Another thing I loved about the Ammouri family: they were normal.

The Bakkioui family took no joy in shopping. They took no joy in surprises, really. Rules were paramount—set by Mom, approved by Dad, and enforced by Titi.

Rule #1: The TV is for watching sports, PBS, or whatever Mom (and Mom only) deems "not rubbish." Mom and Dad both police our screen time but don't really censor what we read. It's an intellectual snobbery thing. They're always parroting, *"Kids, if you're bored, then you should read."* Printed words. Anything. Even "the obituaries" (Mom's joke). Mom thinks her Sufi humor is hilarious, the whole contemplate-your-death approach to true living. One night over winter break I made the mistake of arguing to her that as family we should watch *The Walking Dead*—you know, instead of reading—because "nobody does death better than zombies." Needless to say, she didn't find my humor quite as hilarious as her own. She even tried to block AMC but didn't know it comes with basic cable.

Amir, on the other hand, can access eight zillion premium channels. His living room is a temple to entertainment, the massive TV a digital idol. Hence Mom's opposition. In her not-so-humble opinion, TV is short for "Time-sucking Vortex." A vortex to infinite *ghafla:* Quran-speak for heedless soul draining. (No use arguing that watching Norton was a *qualitative* time suck. So, too, *The Walking Dead*.) But no matter the time of day or night, Amir had the living room all to himself. That's what you get when you live alone with two loving parents who are in de facto parenting retirement.

"I can't choose," I mumbled. My eyes roved over the dizzy blur of titles. "I guess you weren't kidding the other day about ordering his entire filmography."

"Kidding? About Norton?" He flopped back onto the couch. "That would be sacrilege. Besides," he added, "how else am I going to pass the time while fasting?"

Yes, Amir even uses religious terms to mock his devotion to entertainment, at least of the Edward Norton variety.

"Go with your gut," he went on. "With whatever makes you happy." He started a drum roll on the coffee table.

At the sudden noise I glanced toward the hallway. Force of

habit. I knew the racket wouldn't disturb his father. Recently Mr. Ammouri had suffered some hearing loss, but he was too proud to consistently use his hearing aids. Amir grumbled that it was "denial" about getting old, though honestly part of the reason Amir had so much freedom (he's said so himself) was *because* his parents were old.

*Tap . . . tap . . . tap, tap, tap.*

Amir's drum roll grew louder, faster. Leave it to a musician to make a coffee table sound like a real instrument. I would have laughed if it weren't so irritating. I needed something to throw at him.

"Okay, okay," I said, turning around. "Wait one sec. . . ."

I hesitated. There was a piece of furniture I'd somehow missed in our single-minded Edward Norton mission—a gaudy, brightly woven Middle Eastern floor pillow. But how? I'd never seen it before. Faux coins dangled from the trim. It definitely wasn't Crate and Barrel. I bent over and picked it up. Or tried.

"Heavy," I grunted, attempting to hurl it at Amir's head.

He ducked, laughing. "Hey, watch out! Could be valuable. That's Dad's. He just got it out of the attic. I think he wants to sell it on eBay. Or maybe that's Mom's wishful thinking."

"Part of his GTFO plan?"

Amir's smile wilted. "Don't get me started. He's got cash and passports stashed. I'm serious."

*Ugh.* I shouldn't have opened my mouth. It was Mariam's fault. It was Mariam's *joke.* Back when she still believed that she was here to stay. When we all believed.

I sank down beside Amir, trying to ignore the emptiness in my chest. I wanted her to be here. I wanted to hug her and then punch her and then hug her again. I could hear her voice, dripping with sarcasm; I could see her shaking her head at me with her crooked grin. *"Salma, this isn't about Islam or America. Every chiropractor on planet Earth has a GTFO plan."*

Too bad the joke wasn't funny. Not when it came to Amir's dad. He had already gotten the F out of one country. Amir's oldest sister was just a baby when Mr. Ammouri packed up the family and left Syria. He'd been smart; he knew the inherent instability of dictatorships. But he paid a price for that wisdom, forced to watch from afar as civil war tore his birthplace to pieces and set everything ablaze: people, places, history. Amir once told me that he'd never seen his father cry, really weep, until he realized he couldn't go back to Aleppo to bury his own mother. . . .

I sighed. Loudly.

Amir leaned close. "Hey, don't worry about the Dad thing," he murmured. "I tease him all the time. Like: 'Yo, Dad, if you want a safe place to hide your money, try my pocket.'"


We settled on *American History X*. Or we tried. The movie stopped seconds after we loaded it. As in: black screen. The DVD player, the TV, the modem: all of it was unresponsive. Dead, actually. Amir stood up and frowned. Then he stepped toward the hall.

"The lights went off," he said.

It was still sunny, so I hadn't noticed. But he was right. The air conditioner had stopped humming as well. Birds chirped outside.

Amir glanced out the window. "Wanna get some fresh air? We can sit in the hammock."

I stretched my neck. "Yeah, that sounds great, actually. It might help with this lovely little headache that has creeped up on me."

"EDS?" he asked, turning toward me.

"Honestly, I have zero clue. Sometimes my condition is that mysterious."

He stood and placed his hands on my head. "Poof. Be gone, shitty headache."

I laughed, closing my eyes while his callused fingers rubbed my temples. "Man, I wish it were that easy."

"Me too." His voice was light and tender.

My eyes still closed, I stood and hugged him, resting my head on his chest. "This especially helps," I whispered. He was taller than me, tall enough that when I stood next to him my ear was at the level of his chest. I listened to his heart. I felt the rhythm.

"Good," he whispered back.

I stayed there, wrapped inside his arms, wanting to say more . . . to tell him I loved him, but my mouth remained closed. On one level, I almost didn't need to. It was like he was saying it to me. And I to him, without vocalizing it—

A floorboard creaked at the top of the stairs, followed by footsteps.

We jumped apart. Amir's dad appeared in the hallway as we settled back into our adjacent spots on the L-shaped sofa. He looked as if he'd just woken up from a nap. His graying hair was rumpled, his blue dress shirt untucked. But he flashed a bright smile when he saw me. "Salma! How are you?"

"Hi, Mr. Ammouri."

I smiled back. After a few awkward seconds I began to twist my butterfly ring in obsessive circles around my left pinkie. (My version of Amir's compulsive nail-biting.) When the silence became painful, I grabbed a magazine from the glass coffee table. Big surprise: Amir's mother didn't subscribe to *The Hacker Quarterly* or *Phrack*. I feigned interest in the *New Yorker*. No way would I ever get used to a parent who rarely supervised. The Bakkioui family had ruined me.

"No power down here, either?" Mr. Ammouri asked.

Amir shook his head.

His dad peered up at the dead hall light. "How's the knee, Salma?"

"Better," I said, as loudly as I could without shouting. "I have PT early next week."

"Oh, good. Mind if I steal Amir to check on the circuit breaker?"

"No! I mean of course. Not at all." I put the magazine down and glanced at Amir.

He'd already started chewing his thumbnail. I got why: he wanted some alone time with *me*, but now his dad needed *him*, and he was pissed about it. Not at his father per se, just about the timing of the power outage. I was bummed, too. Alone time in the hammock would have been nice.

Mr. Ammouri frowned. "*Ya'llah*, now. Upstairs."

"Salma, you didn't hack into our electrical system, did you?" Amir joked under his breath.

I couldn't help but laugh. His father laughed, too. Amir arched an eyebrow at me, a sad twinkle in his eye. His father hadn't heard a word; he was only laughing because I was laughing.

All at once I felt a pang of guilt. Here I was having fun at his expense—a guest in his house intent on making out with his son.

"You know, it could be a fiber cut?" I suggested, raising my voice a little. "It's funny that most people don't know about this, but my dad told me that there's this whole system of wires underground that are totally unprotected. . . ." My voice trailed off.

Mr. Ammouri patted Amir hard on the back. "You two are such comedians," he said.

He hadn't heard a word of what I'd said, either.

Amir shrugged. Our eyes met. This time, there was only sadness. The twinkle was gone.


It didn't take long for Amir and his dad to conclude that there was absolutely nothing we could do except to call the power company. Now it was just a matter of waiting around for the technician. With his workday shot, Mr. Ammouri used the opportunity to become our third wheel—planting himself in the middle of our hang time. On the other hand, he was standing in front of the fridge, taking out leftovers. Like me, Mr. Ammouri can't fast. He's been a diabetic all his life. Anyhow, the cool thing about Syrian food is that a lot of it doesn't need to be reheated, especially the dips. Amir excused himself for a second and ran upstairs.

My eyes bulged when he returned with his oud.

Okay, *this* was a treat. Totally worth a power outage and loss of Edward Norton binge-watching. I could count on one hand the number of times I'd seen Amir play—and all were in the early days, when he was still willing to operate outside his comfort zone to win me over.

"You're really going to play for us?" I asked.

"Well, I have to run my material for Yasmin's project by *somebody*," Amir replied dryly, avoiding my eyes. "And if I'm going to conquer my stage fright, this is a good first step."

I had to laugh. "Oh, I get it now. This is a directive from Sheikh Epstein."

Mr. Ammouri glanced over at us from behind the kitchen island, confused. "Sheikh who?"

"MR. EPSTEIN, DAD," Amir answered loudly.

Mr. Ammouri shook his head, confused.

Amir put his oud down and walked over to talk to his dad. "Hey, Baba, it's just us." He spoke sweetly, deferentially, *kareem*. "Turn your hearing aids back up."

His father flashed me a grin, like a naughty schoolboy. I chuckled as he reached behind his ear. He must have known that Amir had confided in me that he'd developed a habit of turning his hearing aids down—or off—when Mrs. Ammouri was around.

"So who's this sheikh?" he asked.

"Epstein, Dad," Amir said, lowering his voice now. "My music teacher. I told you: he wants me to get in the habit of playing more in front of people." Amir returned to the sofa and slumped down in the cushions, picking up the instrument and cradling it in his lap. His hair flopped in front of his face. "I also told you that Salma here thinks that I revere him like a guru. Keep in mind that this is an adult who wears tie-dyed ponchos. But, like you said, Salma is a real comedian."

I had to laugh again. "Touché," I whispered.

Leave it to a smart-mouthed musician to play a coffee table like a drum *and* to make his girlfriend take back everything she'd ever said about the dorky teacher who kept stealing away our time together. The piece that he wrote (for my sister, no less) was . . . strident. Repetitive. Deliberately so, in the best and catchiest way. It sounds absurd, but it *was* Yasmin. It was also Yasmin's subject, Muhammad Ali. It was defiance with a bounce. Best to leave the descriptions there; it's impossible to do justice to the haunting beauty of an ancient instrument played live.

Even the shape of the oud recalls some long-forgotten era when music was something sacred: a time before recordings, when music could *only* be enjoyed live, for a lucky elite. Its body is like a hard-boiled egg cut in half, though the inlay on the flat part is what makes it special. It's much more ornate than what you see on a lute or guitar. At least Amir's was. Also, the end of the neck—the piece with the tuning pegs—skews at an odd backward angle. Like a guitar with EDS, the way a person can look when a limb is removed from its socket. But in the case of the oud, it's a more sensible design; the player doesn't have to reach too far to make any adjustments.

As Amir played, I snuck a quick glance at his father. Mr. Ammouri's eyes were closed, brow furrowed in concentration. He was fighting to listen. I prayed he could hear what I heard—

Amir abruptly stopped.

Someone was pounding at the front door.

"Dad!" Amir shouted.

His father's eyes popped open. He gathered himself off the couch and hurried, discombobulated, to answer.

Amir flashed a sad grin. "Oh well."

I blew him a kiss. "Thanks for playing that for me," I said. "Yasmin will love it. *I* love it."

He blew one back. "I'll send it to Yasmin tonight. If the power comes back on."

A moment later Mr. Ammouri returned with a man in gray coveralls and a utility belt. I was honestly tempted to take advantage of the distraction to sneak off with Amir. But the man's profile caught my attention. He smiled politely and began to survey the room, checking out the power outlets. My eyes narrowed. There was something familiar about that smile. I stared, rudely—worse, *knowing* it was rude—but unable to help myself. I knew this technician guy. He was solid. Muscly. That sunburned neck . . . My eyes zeroed in on the small tattoo on his left forearm: 1493.

"Mr. Turner!" I said out loud.

He turned and met my gaze, then broke into a smile and straightened. "Salma!" He removed his cap, revealing the telltale buzz cut. "Well, I'll be."

"You two know each other?" Mr. Ammouri asked.

Mr. Turner nodded. "My family just moved in next door to the Bakkiouis," he explained, "and Salma and your son . . ." He paused. "I take it Amir is your son?"

Mr. Ammouri nodded.

"Yes, these two, you see," Mr. Turner continued, "they were kind enough to deliver a housewarming gift to my family. You've done a fine job raising him."

Amir's own smile grew strained. Few things made him more uncomfortable than being complimented as if he weren't present. It was a mark of his *true* shyness, the natural flip side of wanting to remain invisible. I knew this for a fact because my parents and Titi did it all the time. He began backing toward the hallway, clutching the oud against his chest.

"Please, I don't mean to interrupt," Mr. Turner apologized. "Keep playing. My son Kyle is a musician, too. So I get it. Practice. Practice. Practice. It's good discipline, too." He raised his voice again. "So where's the router?"

Mr. Ammouri motioned him back toward the hall. "This way . . ."

"Good to see you, kids," Mr. Turner said. Then he paused. "Can I trouble you two for a favor?"

I glanced at Amir and nodded reflexively, at a loss.

"Kyle Jr. is transferring to Franklin High on Monday," he explained quietly. "It's hard being the new kid and he's never been to a big school before." He bit his lip. "It's just . . . He's homeschooled. We've moved around a lot. I'd be grateful if you could keep an eye out for him. It puts my mind at ease knowing he has such good neighbors at his school. Good kids."

I wasn't sure what to say. Amir was silent, too.

"Of course," I said as politely as I could.

"Thank you," Mr. Turner said. "I really—"

"Can I pay you by check?" Mr. Ammouri interrupted. "We rarely keep any cash around."

Mr. Turner flashed a big smile. "We'll bill you, sir. You don't have to worry about that at all right now. I'm just here to fix your problem." He turned away from us.

"My dad's not kidding," Amir grumbled to me. "He doesn't know how to use an ATM card."

I tried to laugh, but I felt a little queasy as Mr. Turner followed Mr. Ammouri upstairs. Mr. Turner's manner was so plainspoken and earnest. He probably wouldn't have thought of me as a "good neighbor" if he could see inside me right now, stewing with a litany of whiny complaints. My lower *nafs* was being a total jerk. Here was a decent non-Muslim actually wanting his kid to *hang* with the Muslim kids, seeing us as a way *into* the Franklin social scene—and yet my antisocial, I've-got-my-own-crew self was shutting the whole thing down. *Does that mean I have to be Kyle Jr.'s friend? Does that mean I have to introduce him to my friends? Do I have to invite him to Vanessa Richman's parties? What if he's a jerk? Do I have to report back to you?*

Maybe he'd just forget about it. Or maybe I'd just have to avoid all three Turners. As these uncharitable thoughts began to fester in my mind, the house whirred to life. Power restored.

# 7

I WAS GRUMPY Monday morning. Amir had driven early to Franklin and Mr. Epstein. Here I was, lurching out of the house to take the bus.

Apparently Amir's tie-dyed sheikh had phoned the Ammouri family last night. The reason? To ask if his favorite oud player would be willing to help out with an upcoming "gig"— the word Amir actually used—and maybe perform a song with Mr. Epstein's nerdy all-teacher band, "Public School Funk-a-Delic" (the name Amir actually quoted). Good thing Amir hadn't seen me cringing. The upshot? He and Mr. Funk had to rehearse, and the only time that could possibly fit both their schedules was first thing in the morning. My door-to-door school chauffeur service had come to an end.

*Astaghfirullah*—may Allah forgive me—I shouldn't complain, especially this month. Besides, even though it had only been a week since "the accident," I'd followed the initial orders: rest, elevate, ice. My knee was less swollen. The pain was subsiding. Tomorrow I had a PT appointment with Mrs. DLP, and I was confident she'd let me ditch the crutches.

Furthermore, Amir has been nothing short of awesome this entire week. He'd gone above and beyond with his piece for Yasmin. And yes, credit was due to Mr. Epstein. As much as I made fun of the guy, I knew that Amir was lucky to have a mentor like that, to have someone so invested in his talent. I also knew that it wasn't luck. Amir *deserved* it. If Mariam had been the bright side of the Salma-Mariam moon, then I was the lucky one; Amir was the sun—more radiant than ever.

And yet the crap mood persisted.

Mostly it was because once again, I had to share the bus with Michelle Mayor. Whatever. At least she'd kept her mouth shut since that horrible day. There was also an upside: now Vanessa and I were able to sit next to each other again in Davis's class. (Apparently socializing in Pre-Calc was preferable to fearing one's neighbor.) As long as Vapid Barbie left me alone, I would let sleeping dogs lie. Besides, I could tune her out. Outside, balancing on the left crutch, I reached into my knapsack pocket for my headphones. Ah, the many miracles of recorded music: unlike the days of the original oud, I could create a wall of sound between the world and me.

My fingers came up empty.

*Shit.* Yasmin must have taken them to listen to Amir's piece. Why in God's name she thought it was okay to take my stuff without asking was beyond me. Injured or not, I'd made it clear to her and Hala that I'd kick their little butts if they did . . . whatever.

Onward.


Halfway down the block, I spotted two teenagers turning the corner from Oak Street.

I squinted in the morning sunlight. Was that Michelle?

Yep, definitely. She was walking shoulder to shoulder with Chris.

As they approached, I remembered Amir's expression when he told me he'd seen them laughing after I'd been questioned by those asshole detectives. It suddenly occurred to me that the bomb scare at school could have been *their* idea. I'd be willing to bet on it. I could see them planting the idea in Warren's drug-addled brain, getting him to call the school and the police from an outside line, all to heap suspicion on me. It would be typically thoughtful of them, considering everyone's valid fear. Considering there had really *been* a terrorist scare, along with what we heard on the news every night—considering that the authorities were still hunting for domestic operatives. And even though the facts still weren't known, the rumors about "radical Islamists" persisted.

Michelle and Chris drew closer.

My eyes flashed from one to the other. The yellow stripes in his bright red polo matched her chemical hair. Both looked colored in by a giant crayon. What were they doing here? She lived in the opposite direction, near the bus stop. Chris didn't even ride the bus . . . but when Michelle's stare locked with mine, my breath caught in my throat. In that instant I knew exactly why they were here. Their leering smiles were unambiguous.

They were here for me.

But how did they know I would be back on the bus? Or had they been doing this every morning, waiting for my return? Stalking me in hopes of catching me alone?

"Hey, Bak-ew-wee!" Michelle yelled.

I turned in the opposite direction—back toward Mason Terrace—and picked up my pace, thrusting my crutches forward, then swinging my legs in unison. The goal was to keep away. Period. If I could maintain the distance between us, I could get within screaming distance of my house. Thrust, swing; thrust, swing . . .

"Bak-ew-wee!"

*That's not my name, assholes. Rhymes with "kiwi," remember?*

Thrust, swing; thrust, swing . . .

"Salma!"

Her tone was darker now. My pulse ticked up a notch. I paused and fumbled for my phone. My fingers shook as I speed-texted Amir. Maybe he hadn't started his lesson yet. Maybe I'd get lucky and he'd see my barrage of messages.

Hey.

Really wish you could magically appear on my block right now.

Michelle, Chris stalking me.

Seriously. If you can, COME!

No response.

Scared. Pls txt

Still nothing.

"Hey, ISIS!"

In spite of being afraid, I almost laughed. Really? Did people still say that? *Yeah, okay, Michelle. You got me. I'm, like, totally the biggest fan of public beheadings. Good thing I'm not wearing one of my ISIS pins.* HOORAY FOR SLAVERY. POLYGAMY RULES. Or maybe something her boyfriend would appreciate? Like a black-flag version of that idiotic Confederate bumper

sticker on his Dodge, with a substitute for the word *South:*
THE CALIPHATE WILL RISE AGAIN!

"Hey, Salma, where's your immigrant boyfriend?" Chris shouted.

I glanced over my shoulder.

He was in the lead now, walking with a stiff gait. He looked robotic. Barbie and the Bot. Coming to get me. What a way to start the day.

I turned back to my phone. Seven forty-six. Amir was one minute into his lesson, which meant he'd probably muted his phone. He always silenced it in the presence of Sheikh Epstein.

"SALMA!"

Two voices together. Were they jeering in unison? All at once I realized I was shaking so badly that I couldn't move forward. Mason Terrace was in sight. Mason Terrace . . . where *I* lived. Where *I* grew up. *Mine.* I'd traveled to and from this cozy little suburban cul-de-sac ten thousand times or more. Never once had I felt scared. Not when I was three or five or fifteen. Michelle and Chris were claiming my turf as theirs. In that moment I saw the bright green lawns and spring flowers and cookie-cutter homes for what they really were, a beautiful dream of security dreamed by and for cookie-cutter types.

"Leave me the hell alone!" I said out loud.

Bad idea. I'd pissed them off. I knew this because I was no longer listening to the quiet rage bubbling in my head, but to footsteps pounding on the sidewalk. They were running toward me. They sounded like a steel-toed army. I closed my eyes and held my breath and wondered how much time I had. I wondered what it would feel like to get kicked from behind. Or to be hit in the back of the head. Or to eat cement.

(Probably worse than eating linoleum.) And the tragic irony was that I was well on my way to recovering from the last—

"*Leave. Her. Alone.*"

The world came to a screeching halt. Three words. Shouted from nowhere.

I nearly fell as I spun around. My new neighbor, Kyle Turner Jr.—the homeschooled interloper who'd moved into Mariam's home—had sprinted to place his body between mine and theirs. Michelle and Chris froze. They gawked at him. I couldn't blame them for gawking. I was their mirror image. I watched Kyle's lips move but with the blood rushing in my ears, I couldn't hear what he was saying.

Was this really happening? Was this the kid whose dad had asked me to look out for him? This skinny and pale savior, this valiant hero cloaked in nondescript jeans and a hoodie? He couldn't have looked more anonymous. Like he'd deliberately dressed to go unnoticed. Shit, I would have done the same thing if it were my first day at a new school. He turned to me. His eyes were twitchy. I wondered if he was as scared as I was. In a way, that made him even braver.

"Are you all right?" he asked.

I opened my mouth to answer. I couldn't form words. I might as well have stepped off a roller coaster; everything had turned to Jell-O. I blinked.

"She's fine," Michelle barked in the silence. "Right, Chris?"

I peered past Kyle. Chris was nodding, though his face was red. The veins in his neck looked as if they were struggling for space in all that bulk.

"I asked Salma," Kyle stated in a calm voice. "Not you."

Michelle snorted and tossed her hair back, revealing a tiny silver crucifix dangling above the neckline of her spaghetti tank. I nearly burst into tears. I'd never noticed that she wore a necklace before. (Why *would* I have noticed?) Maybe it was new. But Grandma Thiede wore a silver necklace just like Michelle's. My heart squeezed. She would have howled in disgust. Or worse. Grandma Thiede was both fiercely protective and a devout Christian: one who'd never once questioned or disparaged her daughter's conversion to Islam, one who'd loved her Muslim daughter and grandchildren until the day she died.

"What are you staring at?" Michelle spat.

She was close enough now that I could smell her body lotion, sickly sweet and antiseptic. Just like that cop's aftershave: toxic, from my perspective. It suited her perfectly.

"If you don't want to see my boobs, you better go back home. I'm not wearing a burka. We don't have Sharia law here, in case you haven't noticed."

*What the . . . ?* The very last thing on my mind was Michelle Mayor's cleavage. My heart was still beating fast, but her stupidity somehow eased a little of the fear. This was starting to feel like a bad comedy skit. "I—I was looking at your necklace," I stammered.

Michelle's eyes darkened. She inched closer. "You got a problem with it?"

"No, I just . . . my grandmother—"

"Hold on," Kyle interrupted. He leaned in, stretching out his arms to prevent her from getting within punching distance. I wondered if she saw what I saw, if it was maybe intentional on Kyle's part: he'd made himself into a human shield that formed a cross. With his bony wrists jutting from worn hoodie sleeves, I glimpsed a tiny string of digits on his left forearm: 1493. Tattooed, same as his father. Maybe it was some family thing? Solidarity with Dad's army unit? The family that tattoos together . . .

"Look, I'm new here," Kyle said to Michelle. "And I'm a Christian, too. But if I belong, so does Salma. Muslims, Christians, Jews: we're all Children of Abraham."

I tilted my head.

*That* was unexpected.

Michelle glanced at Chris, who had a deer-in-the-headlights look.

"Are you a meth head?" he asked.

With a sigh, Kyle relaxed and dropped his outstretched arms. "No, I'm not. But I have a question for you. Why are you picking on your neighbor?"

Chris blinked a few times. "What's it to you?" The Bot didn't even sound angry anymore. Just baffled. I was, too, to be honest.

"Because *I'm* her neighbor," Kyle said.

"Then get with the program, dude!" Michelle shouted with a big fake smile. "Tell her to get out of your neighborhood and go the fuck home."

"She is home," Kyle replied softly. "And so am I, and so are you. We all live here. Together. And we have more in common than you think. If you call yourself a Christian, read your scripture."

He straightened. I hadn't realized how tall he was. All of a sudden, he seemed to be towering over the two of them. They backed away. Or maybe they didn't. Maybe I just desperately wanted them to retreat. Time seemed to freeze . . . until Michelle burst out laughing. The sound of it was shrill, forced—as phony as her chemical odor. It trailed off awkwardly, like air escaping a balloon. I almost felt sorry for her. Kyle had reversed the spotlight and made *her* afraid. She almost looked human. Almost.

"We're all People of the Book," Kyle said in the same calm tone.

*He's homeschooled,* I added. Maybe out loud. I can't be sure. I was definitely thinking it, rudely, even though I knew that wasn't fair. Even though I knew homeschooling could be legit.

"Okay, I don't even want to know what Kool-Aid you're drinking," Michelle said. She grabbed Chris's arm, yanking him down the street. "Have fun with your new boyfriend, Salma!" she shouted over her shoulder, returning to her over-inflated self. "Does Amir-the-queer know? Or is it a three-some?"

The moment they vanished around the corner, Amir's car screeched into view.

I nearly dropped the crutches. He threw the driver's-side door open, not bothering to close it. Kyle stepped away to make room as Amir ran straight to me and swept me into a hug, crutches and all.

"I'm so sorry I didn't get here faster," he murmured. "What happened?"

Good question. I had no clue. In the span of maybe two minutes, I'd gone from fearing for my life, to thanking the Lord, to ducking insults, to hearing what sounded like a church sermon from . . . my neighbor. The boy who lived in Mariam's house. I suddenly realized I was staring at him again. Kyle must have noticed, because he cleared his throat, then shifted on his feet and stared at the sidewalk.

"Some kids were bullying Salma," he said. "Kids you know, I'm guessing?"

Amir nodded, holding me close. "Assholes. They looked like they were in a hurry to get away."

Kyle shoved his hands in his pockets. "I just hope they hurry into the light," he replied.

His voice was so quiet that I barely heard him. One of Michelle's phrases made an abrupt and unpleasant reappearance in my mind: *Kool-Aid.* My new neighbor had a conversational style that was . . . unusual. No wonder his dad wanted us to look out for him. On the other hand, he had no trouble handling a confrontation. *Astaghfirullah.* What was my problem? This perfect stranger had just rescued me. Now I was being just as judgmental as Michelle. I pushed Vapid Barbie from my mind. She would not poison me.

"Thanks for sticking up for Salma," Amir said.

"It was the only thing to do," Kyle replied, heading back toward his house.

"You need a ride to school?" Amir called after him.

Kyle shook his head. "Thank you, no," he answered. "My dad sometimes works the evening shift, so he lets me borrow his truck."

My legs still shaking, I slipped into the Jetta, happy to be safe. Happy to have Amir. But as I settled in, something occurred to me: I didn't remember if I had actually thanked Kyle. I'd definitely felt gratitude. But in all the madness, I wasn't sure I had uttered the words out loud.

I unrolled the window. "Hey, Kyle?" I yelled.

He didn't so much as flinch.

"Kyle!" I shouted, louder.

Then I saw it: the white wire. It hung from the back

pocket of his jeans and snaked its way up to his ears. I slumped into the window frame. I thought again of his dad's concern as I watched him vanish around the corner. *A kindred spirit,* I thought. Doing what I'd planned to do all along this morning, putting an invisible wall between the world and him.

# 8

EXISTENTIAL *MEH*. THAT'S how I felt for the rest of Monday. The feeling carried over to the following day, as if a physical weight were holding me down. It double-sucked because I had Pre-Calc. Which meant I had to see Michelle. Again. Luckily, Vanessa was still back where she belonged, in her old seat. Michelle no longer sat to my right. That was the good news.

As class settled in, Vanessa leaned over and tapped my shoulder. She had a note. I snatched it up before Mr. Davis could see us. When I unwrapped the crinkled paper a stick of purplish gum fell onto my lap: About that near death experience yesterday. Here are your options:

Retaliation—you, me, gangster style

Double date @Lake Arlington with Dora and Boots

Lower-self Salma, my vengeance-seeking *nafs*, wanted nothing more than to go full Durdenesque on the world and circle option one. But when I glanced back at Michelle, and took in her fakeness and her stupidity, I knew it wasn't worth it. Nope. I would be out of Franklin very soon. Best to lie low, ignore, even if it truly sucked. I grabbed my pencil and bubbled in option two, adding a long overdue rider: *putt-putt challenge!*

I folded the note and shoved it back in her hand.

A few seconds later Vanessa whispered out of the corner of her mouth, "Right on."

Mini-golfing for three—Vanessa, Mariam, and me—was once a time-honored tradition. But since Amir and I had become, well, *us,* the tradition had fallen by the wayside. Mariam's departure put a full stop on it. Which wasn't right. Putt-putt was still *our* thing. Always had been, always will be. I knew that Mariam wouldn't only approve of this plan; she would insist that Vanessa and I play in her honor.

Teaming up against Dora and Boots would be an added bonus. Miniature golf is the only "sport" I'm decent at, and I'd relish the opportunity to lovingly kick butt against Lisa, who's a real athlete. I could even tease Mrs. DLP with it in my next therapy session.

All of a sudden, Mr. Davis cleared his throat and whirled from the board. At first I thought he'd somehow caught us passing a note. "I'm sorry," he muttered, shuffling quickly to the door. "I need a five-minute break—"

Before anyone could even react, he'd vanished into the hall. The door swung shut behind him.

In the quiet that followed, people began exchanging glances with one another. Except for Vanessa. She kept staring at the board, a Cheshire Cat smile on her face. She blew a bubble with her gum. When it popped, I sniffed . . . and nearly wretched. The room stank of something powerfully familiar: cotton candy left out in the sun. And it dawned on me that every single person in class, except for Michelle and me, was chewing gum, too. . . .

*Oh, my—*

I laughed out loud and clamped a hand over my mouth. Granted, I was about to puke. But I hadn't felt this happy in, well, far too long. Without turning her head, Vanessa extended a low fist across the aisle toward me. I bumped it with my own. Everyone was smiling at her now. Everyone was blowing bubbles and giving her the thumbs-up. Everyone but Michelle, who glared around the room, equal parts baffled and pissed off.

*Vanessa, you are my hero.* I didn't think it was possible. But the girl was a genius. She'd actually done it. She'd pulled off a two-pronged prank of vengeance in one masterstroke— supplying just enough gum for all but Vapid Barbie, and just enough to drive Mr. Davis right out of the classroom.


Unfortunately, at the end of the day, Vanessa's "vintage" 2005 Buick LeSabre also reeked of foul grape chewing gum.

I tried not to hold it against her on the drive up to the lake. But I couldn't disguise my relief when I opened the door. I lunged out, taking a deep breath of . . . *Uh-oh.* The air was stagnant, humid. The lake was like glass. The sky was not; the clouds were gray and thick. A thunderstorm was on the way. Sure enough, as if to confirm, there was a faint and distant rumble. I turned around. Vanessa was still inside, rummaging through the glove compartment. As it turned out, Kerry and Lisa had other plans. (Which sucked.) But if it rained, at least we had a better chance of finishing a game with two players instead of four.

"Good thing we didn't check the weather," I said dryly. "We might want to start before it pours."

"Just a second," she stage-whispered. After removing a ziplock bag, she climbed over to the passenger side and stumbled out, kicking the door closed behind her.

"There's a more effective way to exit."

She shrugged, unfazed. "The driver's-side lock is stuck. It won't open."

"Point taken." Vanessa's ride was like my body: a bit worse for wear, a little unconventional, but functional. Able to go from A to B. I could see now that her baggie contained a few telltale brown cubes. *I should have known*. . . . She unzipped it with a flourish, unleashing an extremely pungent mix of chocolate and marijuana. Before I could say a word, she popped a brownie into her mouth.

"Wan-one?" she half-articulated, holding the bag wide open.

"Is it medicinal?" I joked.

"And you've known me for how long?"

I laughed. "I could ask you the same question."

Twenty minutes later I was balancing on my good leg, holding a crutch over my head and stretching my back. I could hear Vanessa moaning.

"Enough, my one-legged wonder. Make. Your. Shot."

I set the ball down on the green and practiced my shot, zeroing in on the perfect angle. "Prepare to get your ass kicked, in three . . . two . . ." I held my breath and swung. The ball glided straight through the tunnel, past the sand trap, and stopped just short of the hole. Vanessa booed.

One swing later the course was hers. She hilariously imitated my every move—from the prolonged stretch, to the slow and methodic setup, to the whack-and-miss. Not surprisingly, her execution was equally as . . . well, awful. On hole six she hit the ball so hard she nearly struck an elderly couple who were quickly catching up to us—the only other people dumb (stoned?) enough to come out for mini-golf on a day when thunderstorms were practically guaranteed.

"SCORE!" Vanessa yelled as the ball ricocheted off the windmill and shot toward them. "I mean, FORE!" She dropped the rent-a-club and covered her bloodshot eyes with her hands.

I watched, grinning, as the ball sailed over their heads and landed in an artificial mini-pond, green with algae. The woman straightened, puzzled. She glanced toward the splash, then shrugged and concentrated on the next putt. I started laughing.

There was another rumble of thunder. Vanessa dropped her hands and blinked up at the sky. The clouds were turning a sickly mushroom gray.

"You can look now," I deadpanned. "It missed, but that lady might be onto you."

Vanessa laughed, too. When she fixed her stoned gaze on the couple, though, her laughter faded. She turned back to me, suddenly somber. "She's never going to stop, you know."

"I know. They're catching up. It's about to start pouring—"

"No, not *her*," Vanessa interrupted. "Michelle. And her Douche-Lord boyfriend. I mean, I get your strategy. I know you like to fly 'under the radar.'" She made air quotes, then bent down to pick up her club. "But you've got skills, Salma. And I know you know I know."

"Eloquent," I cracked. She was right, though. She had me, too. And to be honest, at this particular moment I was surprised she'd remember a conversation we'd had four years ago, let alone four minutes ago. But it was one of our first. I was *such* a nerd then, with even fewer friends than I have today. So when Mrs. Duffner made me Vanessa's tech buddy in computer class—aka her free *sabilillah* tutor (though Duffner wouldn't put it in those terms)—I bragged a little about my budding "under the radar" hacking skills. Using those same dorky words. Thereby being as on-the-radar as possible.

"Are you thinking of the latest Unicode virus?" I teased, knowing full well she'd have no idea what I was talking about.

"Unicorn virus?"

I smirked. "Close enough. It's the character-encoding system for writing in any language. I could send Michelle and Chris a Trojan horse. Shut down their phones completely." I sighed, ruminating over all sorts of malicious pranks I'd never pull. "Or send them both forty nonreturnable pizzas . . ."

"Are you hungry?"

"Are you stoned?" I answered automatically.

We both giggled. She dropped the club again and started rooting through her cargo pockets.

"Here," she said, handing me her phone. "I'd gladly be the front for this Unicorn thing. You know, just in case it can be traced. It's for a good cause."

Small raindrops tickled my nose. I reached out and squeezed her hand as I shook my head. "Nah. But thanks. You better put your own phone away, though. That model iPhone isn't waterproof. And . . . as much as I want to ditch Mrs. DLP today, I probably shouldn't. I'll have my mom come pick me up. She'll give you a ride home, too."

Vanessa smiled and squeezed her eyes shut, tilting her face toward the rain. "Nah. I'll just stay with the car until this brownie wears off."

Mom dropped me off curbside since we were running so late. She also very thoughtfully decided not to ask why Vanessa had chosen to hang out alone at a mini-golf course in the middle of a thunderstorm. I wondered how much she really knew or suspected about Vanessa. Maybe she just knew I needed all the good friends I could get right now, so she focused on the weather. The rain was intense but quick. The skies were already clearing by the time I hobble-hopped to the front door.

I took a quick second to collect myself. Miss Clementine Watkins, Mrs. DLP's shrunken post-retirement-age assistant (not nice but accurate), loathed disruptions. And tardiness. I was already guilty of the latter. So I held my breath as I opened the door . . . Ever. So. Slowly.

Luckily, she was on the phone, so she couldn't verbalize her displeasure. Instead she lowered her bifocals and leveled a glare at me that spoke volumes. I flashed a lame *I'm-so-sorry* smile, then crutch-tiptoed past reception toward the Treatment Room, making sure to be extra quiet. But it wasn't for her sake. I had to pretend to sneak up on Mrs. DLP. It wasn't a choice, really; it was a silly ritual that dated back to when I first started seeing her. I would enter the Treatment Room, clasp my hands (perpetually cold) over her eyes, and shout "Gotcha!"

Predictable and corny, yes—and useless, considering I had to first put my crutches away to pull it off. But after all these years, she still begged for it. She was the only grown-up I knew who sat with her back to an open office door. Mrs. DLP was a proud, self-proclaimed comic book nerd. Her office walls were plastered with life-sized posters of Marvel's finest. Black Panther. Spider-Man. The Wasp. According to her, the Wasp would have no trouble sitting with her back to a door, either. . . .

"Gotcha!!"

With a laugh, she flicked my frigid hands away and spun around.

"Hey, girl!" Her wide brown eyes fell to the crutches, and then to my knee. The smile quickly fell from her face. "Lisa told me what happened," she murmured in disgust. "The whole thing. But I had to see it to believe it." After a moment she lifted her head. "I am so, so sorry, Salma B."

"I'm fine, really," I lied. "It's nothing. Stupid kids. Every school's got 'em." I tried to laugh, hoping she'd laugh in return. She didn't. As if to agree with my general disappointment, my knee began to throb. (Perfect timing, considering where I was.) I didn't need another glum and outraged grown-up in my life. I needed the fun-loving auntie-by-proxy who always made me giggle, who managed to make me forget about my EDS even while she was working overtime to ease the symptoms.

"You doing okay?" she asked me pointedly.

I slumped down in the chair, suddenly exhausted—from my chronic disease and from everything else. "I've been better," I admitted. I winced slightly and leaned forward to massage my sore knee.

"Did Franklin punish the creeps who did that to you?"

I laughed again, miserably. "Not yet. It's not exactly at the top of Principal Philip's agenda."

She frowned. "Wait. Let me understand you, sweetie. There haven't been any repercussions?"

"No, because they don't even know *which* creeps did it. I mean, I have my suspicions, but I don't have any actual proof. Not that Principal Philip is even interested in finding out . . ." I shoved the memory of those two detectives from my mind; I didn't want to get into it with Mrs. DLP and have to relive that whole surreal nightmare. "Anyway, the only proof that it even happened is this." I got out my phone and leaned forward to show her the photo that had been anonymously tossed up on Instagram. There I was, in an agonized heap at the bottom of a Franklin stairwell. Even looking at it now, for the umpteenth time, I found myself silently asking the same questions: *Who does that? Who can live with being that cruel? Who sleeps at night after pushing a girl down the stairs and sharing a photo of it?*

Mrs. DLP's eyes turned to slits. "So nobody knows who did this to you," she said quietly. "And there's been no follow-up from the school. None whatsoever."

"Not that *I* know of," I grumbled.

She sat up straight. "Is there anything else?" she whispered.

I swallowed. She took a deep breath. And in that moment, her eyes opened wide once more: a pair of glittering brown butterfly pupae emerging from their chrysalises. Maybe it was some sort of Reiki treatment to absorb my pain and send me light, but it wasn't New Agey phoniness. Not from Mrs. DLP. Everything about her was 100 percent genuine and authentic; this was how she showed me that she was present, every part of her being—for me, here, now. Then again, the window to her soul was always open. I doubt she could draw the curtains even if she wanted to. My own soul was locked in a vault. But in moments like this, she always knew how to crack it open.

"Salma, anything you say here stays here," she gently prodded. "You know that."

Without warning, the floodgates burst, and out it came—chronologically if not coherently—the whole story about hearing my name over the loudspeaker, about the apology that never came, about Detective Tim and the Silent One, about what happened earlier this morning with Barbie and the Bot, about how my new neighbor swept in and de-escalated the confrontation with his brave and strange behavior . . . about how I was worried for him now because he'd taken a stand against Franklin's Grossest, its Alt-Right fringe.

Until I'd said that last part out loud, I hadn't even realized how I felt, myself.

Out of breath, I stopped talking.

Mrs. DLP sighed. "Let me tell you something, Salma B. Well, two things. The first: you're the only patient I've ever had I've approved of as a friend for my daughter. A real friend."

I stared at her. "Whoa. Seriously?"

"Seriously. And I see plenty of her teammates."

My eyes fell to my lap. Lisa had always been a jock. It made sense; Lisa's mother was in the best shape of any human being I'd ever known, young or old, male or female. I'd always been fairly certain that Kerry and I were Lisa's only two non-jock friends. Truth be told, I'd had a hard time not feeling resentful every now and then. God (and Mrs. DLP) had gifted Lisa with all the collagen and energy I would never have, times twelve. *All work is easy work* was their mother-daughter mantra. Literally. I was certain I'd be hearing it more than once today. . . .

"The second thing is that Principal Philip won't get away with this," Mrs. DLP said. "I promise you. He's a bigot, plain and simple. He's just better at hiding it than most. It's how he's kept his job."

I sniffed, still staring down at my legs, at the soreness inside them that never fully disappeared. "What do you mean?"

"In practical terms, I mean he'll be hearing from me—and from several other members of the faculty—at the next PTSA meeting. This isn't the first time he's turned his back on a student." Her tone softened. "And don't even think about asking me who that student is, because like I told you, anything anyone tells me here is strictly confidential. I know you, Salma B. You're a nosy one."

At that, I had to laugh.

"You probably know what I'm about to tell you," she added.

" 'There's no time like the present and no present like the time,' " I quoted.

"Smart girl. And all work is . . . ?" There it was: the mantra. She waited for me to finish.

"Easy work," I repeated dully.

"Salma, look at me."

I lifted my head.

"I want to tell you something." Mrs. DLP leaned forward and laid her hand on mine, tapping my butterfly ring with her forefinger. "I know how strong you are. The truth? You're stronger than I am. What you told me about being worried for this boy who moved into your friend's house . . . You are a special sort, Salma B. In your shoes, I wouldn't be as strong. I wouldn't be thinking about my new neighbor's safety. For all my lecturing, that's a fact."

I swallowed hard. "So now what?"

"That's easy," she said, her smile returning. "Now I help you get stronger." She patted my hand and stood, nodding to the row of stationary bikes. "Let's start simple, with quad sets and heel slides and leg raises. Then we'll move on to a little cardio. No negotiations, Missy Miss."

I was spent after two minutes of biking. Lame, I know. Mrs. DLP clucked her tongue as my legs slowed to a stop and the machine quieted.

"What's up, Salma? It's on the lowest resistance. I know you can do this. All work is—"

"Don't say it," I groaned, cutting her off.

"Then don't make me say it!" she shot back with a laugh.

I wiped my forehead with the towel hanging from the handlebars. "But should I be doing this so soon after the accident?" I asked, trying not to sound whiny. "I mean, it's not like I'm training for the Olympics or anything."

She snorted. "Please. Everything you want is on the other side of that pain."

Now I was annoyed. Her platitudes echoed Mom's. *"The*

*only way to ease your pain, Salma, is to accept it. The Prophets knew pain, a lifetime of pain. It's a path to clarity, to a sound heart. That's a blessing.*" Enough already. Why do adults have to lay it on so thick? I was seventeen. Enlightenment wasn't my goal. An occasional win in mini-golf was enough for me.

Mrs. DLP tapped her foot. "Haven't got all day, cupcake."

I pushed out my bottom lip, pouting.

"Ha! That worked when you were five, Missy Miss. But it won't work now." She smiled. "You're tired. But you've got this. I know it . . . and *she* knows it."

She pointed at a poster of Wonder Woman.

*Seriously?* If Mrs. DLP was hoping to motivate me, it wasn't working. I hadn't even seen that movie, for one thing. Plus, I couldn't get past that woman's skimpy attire. It's not like Hollywood has superhero men traipsing around in their undies. (Or do they?) Whatever. I lived in the real world. And while it may be true that God blessed us with pain, he hasn't blessed *me* with any superpowers. Mrs. DLP must have caught me glowering, because she reached into a nearby cabinet and pulled out a brand-new Pro-Tec Gel 400—metallic blue with black bands and reinforced stitching for extra support. And unlike my brace, it was sleek and light, everything a girl with EDS and a butterfly obsession might dream of. I knew the brand because, nerd to nerd, she knew *me*. She'd pulled this same trick on me the last time I'd had a knee issue (with the other knee, six months ago).

Now it was useless trying to hide my smile. Honestly, Mrs. DLP had her own superpowers; she was telepathic. She dangled the encouragement in front of me like a buttered scone.

"If you do this, Salma B., you can leave behind the crutches and the brace. You can ride a bike again. You know, come to think of it, that's a great idea. You should do some biking this summer—"

"Got it," I grunted. I shut my eyes and envisioned a different sort of hero. I envisioned Dihya. She wore a red turban and a matching robe. Undies were not part of her equation: my secret blow against Mrs. DLP's Marvel Empire. I laughed.

"What's so funny?" she asked.

"Nothing," I said, eyes still closed, still on Dihya. I forced everything else out of my mind. I focused on Dihya's face, her dark eyes and the indigo tats on her cheeks and her forehead, images of the land and the sky—sacred, but also practical, like code. Protection from nefarious forces.

On the ride home, Vanessa texted. I shifted in my seat so that Mom wouldn't see what she'd written.

> Good news: Found Michelle's info and Chris.
> Ordered 40 pizzas.

I burst out laughing. Then my phone buzzed a second time.

> Bad news: She wants revenge 4 what I did 4 u.
> Check this out. Isn't that f'd up?

Attached was a screenshot from Michelle's Instagram account. It was a flyer. A challenge, actually, called "Punish a

Muslim." Apparently May was an unofficial monthlong holiday devoted to punishing Mooslims. A time when oppressed white people got to push back, stand up against their civilizational foe. It got all cheerlead-y, too. "Do not be a sheep!" "Fight back!" "Protect your people!"

My phone buzzed a third time, another screenshot:

10 points: verbally abuse a Muslim or vandalize property

25 points: pull off head scarf

50 points: push a Muslim down the stairs

75 points: beat a Muslim up

100 points: burn a mosque

200 points: kidnap, torture, and kill a Muslim

500 points: bomb Mecca

Nice. Thanks to me, Michelle was racking up major points. I could live with that, though. I'd expected that. What sickened me more was how much attention this flyer had garnered. A total of 978 viewers had liked it. Vanessa texted again: Hey, you there? You ok?

I shot off a quick reply: Here. Fine. Sort of. Wish I had a magic wand. It's time to rid the world of these evil people.

I added a montage of emojis. The cursing emoji. A poop-faced one. A string of flexed biceps. Anything to vent.

At the stoplight Mom lightly tapped me. "Such a busy social life," she teased.

She probably assumed Amir was texting me love notes. I couldn't bear to look her in the eye, or even respond. I turned my phone off and stared through the window. It was still raining. A drizzle, not a downpour. But the clouds were darker now. Hungrier. They threatened to swallow the day and the light that remained.

# 9

VANESSA'S TEXTS REMINDED me of something: I still hadn't thanked Kyle for what he did for me.

It wasn't as if I'd been avoiding him. Or procrastinating. I just hadn't seen him. On the other hand, two days had passed since he'd stood up for me. Now it was Wednesday, and I still hadn't made the effort. Even if "kindred spirit" was pushing it in terms of what I knew of Kyle—and I had to keep telling myself that I didn't really know anything at all—he'd gone above and beyond. Good people deserved goodwill. There was one thing I *did* know: he'd done more than I would have done. Maybe a part of me just wanted to prove to myself that Mrs. DLP was right, that I could be strong. So after the final bell on Wednesday afternoon, I waited near the doors to the parking lot until I spotted him.

Like everyone else pouring out of Franklin, he'd yanked out his phone. He was in a hurry, too. I watched as he jabbed at it and brought it to his ear—an actual call. Should I just let him go? Ironically, without the crutches, I was slower now. Mrs. DLP's sleeve was much more comfortable, of course. . . .

No. I would do this. I owed him.

Steeling myself, I snaked my way through the crowd. By

the time I caught up with him, he'd reached the driver's-side door of the Turner family pickup truck. Luckily, he didn't get in. He was still talking. I hung back to give him some privacy. I hated when people (i.e., every single member of my family) eavesdropped on my conversations. But he spoke so loudly that I couldn't help overhear.

"No. I am n-n-not getting *involved*," he said, stuttering slightly.

Sounded heated. I backpedaled a step. Maybe now wasn't the best time after all.

"It wasn't like that." He took a long breath. "Bakkioui was in trouble. It's over."

*Bakkioui?* I froze in place. I was . . . Bakkioui. For a second I wondered if he was talking about someone else. But what other Bakkioui would have been in trouble?

"Of course I know!" he hissed, agitated. "If anything, Dad—just listen. I know what I'm doing." Kyle winced. He held the phone away from his ear, his body tense, and then brought it back. His free hand tapped nervously against his pants.

"Yes, sir," he said, his voice quieter. "No . . . yes, yes, sir. Right away."

He jammed his phone into his pocket.

A school bus behind me started its engine. Instinctively I ducked down behind the nearest car, a tiny VW Bug; I didn't want him to think I was spying. (Because I was.) Bad move. A sharp twinge shot through my newly recovered knee, so I kept going, plopping down on my skinny butt. As the pain subsided, I held my breath. Had Kyle turned? Had he seen me? I waited while the cars nearby roared to life along with the bus. I couldn't stay hidden for long. As carefully as I could manage without putting undue weight on my knee, I used the VW door handle to hoist myself up.

Only then did I sigh in relief. The truck was already pulling out of the parking lot.

I leaned against the hood of whoever's Bug this was, its blue metal hot from a day in the sun. I tried to make sense of what the hell had just transpired. Why had he been so defensive? And was he really talking about me? He must have been, but why the last name only? No one did that, except for Ms. Wallace at roll call in gym class. And, of course, Barbie and the Bot . . . but they did it to dehumanize, to emphasize the foreignness of the sound, to stamp me as the enemy—

"Enjoying the view?"

I jumped back. *Amir.*

"Jesus, you scared the shit out of me."

He laughed. "I realize you hold me in high esteem, but *Isa?* A bit much, don't you think?"

"Ha, ha," I grumbled. My legs were still wobbly. I leaned against the hood again. "Your dad's right. You're a real comedian."

"And awesome and handsome and profoundly humble. So, mind if I ask why the sudden fascination with Mrs. Owens's car? You want me to get rid of my Jetta, right? You're trying to send me a message that my ride is an embarrassment?"

I immediately backed away from the hood. I had no idea it belonged to Mrs. Owens. Just what I needed: her to catch me and suspect I was up to no good. "I was—um, watching Kyle."

"Clocking the neighbor who valiantly rescued you?" Amir teased. "Should I be jealous?"

He was trying to snap me out of whatever funk I was in,

to get me to laugh, but I was shaken. "I don't know how valiant he is after all."

Amir's smile faded. "What do you mean?"

I replayed the incident for him in real time: explaining exactly what happened, and exactly what I heard. Word for word. When I finished, he sighed.

"Salma, come on."

"Come on, what?"

"You know what I think?" he asked gently. "Kyle's dad is probably worried Michelle and Chris are going to find him and beat the shit out of him. I'd be worried about the same thing in Mr. Turner's shoes. No wonder he was pissed off. He doesn't want his son, the new guy in school, playing hero."

I frowned. That was a very good point. It was also one that hadn't occurred to me.

"Fine. But why did Kyle call me Bakkioui then, like *they* did? Isn't *that* strange?"

"He's a military kid. It's probably second nature." Amir took my forearms, spinning me toward him, so we were face to face. "How about this? From now on, nobody else gets to rescue you except me, okay? It will make life much less complicated."

I found myself smiling back. Maybe I'd overreacted. It wouldn't be the first time. Exhausted, I rested my head against his chest and closed my eyes.

"Wanna hang out at my house for a while?" he murmured. "We never got to finish our Edward Norton marathon. You'll have to listen to me practice, though."

"Practice for what? Yasmin did her presentation today. . . ." I felt another pang of guilt. I still hadn't told Amir how beautiful his piece had sounded on my headphones.

"This is for the *gig*," he clarified.

I laughed. "Please don't use that word," I said.

He laughed, too. "Fine. For my epic world-debut oud performance at the Black Box with Public School Funk-a-Delic."

"Much better." I leaned back and looked up at him. "Wait, Mr. Epstein's band is really playing at the Black Box? That's so cool." This time I wasn't poking fun at Amir's guru; I meant it. The Black Box was one of those old-school DC clubs, legendary for breaking bands that went on to stardom or at least cult status. Maybe Mr. Epstein wasn't as dorky as I'd made him out to be. No, of course he was. You only had to look at his egregious wardrobe choices. It was one of the reasons I secretly liked him.

"So is that a yes?" Amir asked, his brown eyes filling mine.

I sighed and slumped back against him. "I can't. I have to wait for Hala and Yasmin. Dad's taking Titi to a dentist's appointment. You don't know how lucky you are that your sisters are older."

As soon as I got home I headed straight for the sofa. In another hour my sisters would shatter this beautiful silence. My eyelids closed instantly. My body seemed to melt into the pillows. I hadn't realized how sore my knee was from my little hiding stunt in the parking lot until the weight was removed and I could stretch my leg straight. The pain went away. . . .

After God knows how long—it felt like an instant—I jerked awake. I glanced at the clock: quarter to four. No sign of my sisters. The house was eerily silent. After rubbing my eyes, I sat up and looked at the hall tree. The only bag that hung from the hooks was mine. Now I was wide awake.

"Hala?" I shouted. "Yasmin?"

Nothing. Not a peep. Ignoring my sore knee, I checked every room in the house. Including my own. Then I messaged Mom. Hala and Yasmin not home yet. Change of plans?

Her text bubble instantly loaded: No. They should be there. No after school.

By the time Mom arrived home twenty minutes later, I'd moved beyond regret to worry. I rushed to the front door. "I'm so sorry, Mom. I didn't mean to fall asleep. I was just so tired and—"

"Shh." She rested her computer bag down by the hall tree and rushed to me. "Hon," she said, lifting my chin. "You did nothing wrong. Nothing. Understood?"

I nodded and bit my lip, but looked away. "But what if they came home and then left? Or what if they never even got to the front door or onto the bus—"

"Stop," she said. "I called the school. I spoke to the bus driver. Your sisters were on it. They're probably at the playground. It's a gorgeous day. I'm sure they lost track of time."

I nodded, feeling my throat tightening. If Mom could hold it together for my benefit, I could hold it together for hers. She removed her work flats and slipped on her Chacos.

"And you know how convincing Hala can be," she added, forcing an easygoing tone. "If they are not at the playground, they're at a friend's."

Maybe they were. Hala was annoyingly clever, and Yasmin would go along with whatever scheme she cooked up. Both also played their cuteness to their advantage to get away with just about anything. Like, for instance, shirking schedules.

Going to the playground with no advance warning. Driving me crazy with some excuse they would no doubt make up on the spot . . .

I heard Dad's car pull into the driveway.

Mom headed for the door. "Stay here with Titi. Dad and I will canvass the neighborhood. You'll see. It'll be fine. Just fine."

*Two "fines,"* I thought. She was clearly talking to herself more than she was talking to me. Nothing felt fine about this. But I kept quiet.


One hour and fifty-three excruciating minutes later, I decided to stop looking at the clock. Even cuddling with the cat wouldn't take the edge off. I'd been lying on my back in the cushioned bay ever since Dad and Titi had arrived, Thomas on my stomach. I'd imprisoned him there. As Minister of Calm, his presence was sorely needed. But the longer the wait, the weaker Mom's theory about Hala and Yasmin was becoming. My mind was on an endless treadmill of "what-ifs," none of them good. Especially now that I had seen Michelle's Instagram challenge.

*What if someone took it seriously? What if something really bad happened?*

I squeezed Thom. Hard. He squeaked in disapproval. I finally released my death grip, and he jumped off my stomach, making his way toward Titi. She sat cross-legged on the floor clutching her small *tasbih*, her string of prayer beads. Ninety-nine in total, each bead corresponds to the ninety-nine names of God. One by one, they fell from Titi's grasp. I wondered if she was thinking what I was thinking: One of God's names is *al-Waajid,* the Finder. God would find them and bring them home, wouldn't He?

The front door swung open. Titi and I jumped up.

Mom and Dad stepped inside. Empty-handed. Grim.

"Anything?" Mom asked.

I shook my head.

She glanced at the clock, and my eyes instinctively followed. Quarter to six. Her face twisted with agony. Without a word, she and my father headed straight for the kitchen phone. I guess they were moving to Plan B: Treat this like the emergency it was. Phone the police. Put out an Amber Alert. Plan C wasn't too far off: Panic. I'd already beat them to it. I stood up. My knee buckled, and in that instant, the room spun. It felt as if the entire world were suddenly squeezing my waist. *I'm going to vomit.* Titi gaped after me as I clutched my gut and bolted for the bathroom, slamming the door shut.

False alarm. Nothing came up but bitter bile.

I ran the faucet and splashed cold water on my face. After that I rinsed my mouth, trying to ignore my haggard reflection.

When I finally returned to the living room, Titi was standing at the window, weeping. I wanted to console her, but I couldn't. I couldn't even look at her. I felt oddly detached, as if this were some dream from which I couldn't shake myself awake. This couldn't be happening. Not to us. Not to my sisters.

*"Ya'llah, Salma Dihya. Salma Dihya . . . ya'llah."*

She clapped her hands and turned to me, teary eyes wide

and elated. My breath caught. She was *smiling*. She wept with joy, not fear. I hobbled to her side and nearly collapsed; there, outside, was the sight I'd longed for. My sisters. Relief washed over me. They weren't alone. Mrs. Turner, holding Drexler on a leash with one hand, led Hala and Yasmin across the street with the other.

"Mom! Dad!" I shouted, limping slightly to the door. "They're home!"

The entire family burst outside. I stood there for a moment at the threshold of the open doorway, watching. My parents went straight for the girls and swept them up in hugs; Titi went for Mrs. Turner. After clutching Mrs. Turner in a tight embrace, Titi kissed her hands and mumbled Lord knows what in Riffian.

"Oh, hello, good evening," Mrs. Turner mumbled stiffly. She managed an uncomfortable smile. Drexler, in contrast, was wagging his tail vigorously.

"Thank you, thank you, missus," Titi mustered in her heavily accented English.

Our neighbor drew away from my grandmother, clutching the leash with both hands behind her back. Mom and Dad finally let my sisters go. Hala and Yasmin had been silent; only I could see their faces were streaked with tears. I stepped forward. Mrs. Turner turned to Mom and Dad.

"Hi, you must be the Bakkiouis. I'm Kate Turner, your neighbor. I found your girls when I was walking Drexler in the woods around back." She squared her shoulders and tightened the length of the dog's leash. "Took a bit of cajoling, but I finally got them to come with me. Hope that's all right."

In a rush of relief and gratitude, my parents spoke over

each other, a near-hysterical jumble. Then they both laughed. After a clumsy pause, Mom reached forward and extended a hand.

"Thank you for finding my babies. They were . . . in the woods?"

"Yes." Mrs. Turner shook hands quickly and let go, clutching the leash again. "Pretty far in, too. They didn't tell me why. I'm just glad they're all right." She was already back-pedaling across the lawn. Clearly she just wanted this little incident—whatever it was—to be over. "And please, no need to thank me. I know you would have done the same for my boy. Have a good night." She turned toward the street. Drexler's collar jangled as he shook himself and followed.

"Please, why don't you come in," my mom called after her. "I can make you some tea. It's the least I can do."

"Oh, no thanks!" she replied without looking back. "That's awfully kind of you, but I'm already running behind schedule. Kyle Sr. likes his meals right on time." She let out a little high-pitched laugh. "It's easier that way, you know— early to bed, early to rise. Next time, maybe." She waved goodbye over her shoulder and hurried into Mariam's house, shutting the door behind her and Drexler.

*Their house,* I reminded myself. *The Turners' house.*

Amir was right. I'd been foolishly paranoid this afternoon. I made a promise to myself right then and there that I would thank Kyle no matter what, even if I had to go over in person tomorrow.

Meanwhile, Mom had turned to the girls and assumed the position: arched brows, hands on hips. An epic tsunami of a scold was coming their way, and no matter how high Hala turned up the cuteness or how sad Yasmin pretended to be, nothing would stop it.

"What in the world were you thinking?" she barked. "We spent three hours looking for you. Three hours!"

Dad gently whispered something in her ear. She nodded begrudgingly and turned back toward the house. I sighed, wanting to chew them out myself. On the other hand, at least they were home. . . .

"My little pumpkins." Dad stepped forward. There he went, buttering them up. Something about his accent and the hint of French could charm anyone, especially his girls. "You are not in trouble. No, no. Just tell us what happened. *S'il vous plaît?*"

Yasmin opened her mouth, but started to cry. Mom stopped and glanced over her shoulder.

"Let's get back inside," Titi said. "Where we belong," she added pointedly.


At the dinner table, during *iftar*—between Yasmin's heaving sobs and Hala's halting additions—parts of the story finally emerged.

It all started right before final period, the big moment: History with Mr. Peck. Yasmin was so proud of her "Best All-Time American" poster that she'd unveiled it in the hallway to show her friends. (I couldn't blame her; she'd re-created in grays and blacks the classic 1965 photo of Muhammad Ali, standing in the ring over Sonny Liston at the moment he won his second world championship. It was spectacular by any measure. *I* would want to show it off.) She was taking it out of her cubby when several boys crowded around her. They snatched it from her hands. Within seconds, her prized work was on the ground, crumpled and ruined.

I kept glancing between Mom and Dad. Their faces were blank masks.

"Is it completely destroyed?" Dad asked in a low voice.

Yasmin was weeping again; she couldn't answer. Hala left the table and went to the hall tree to retrieve the poster from Yasmin's backpack. Or what was left of the poster. There was a jagged hole where Ali's face had been. The famous quote, carefully stenciled in 1960s-style font, had been ripped in half and covered in dirty footprints. *Float like a butterfly* was illegible; *Sting like a bee* was missing completely. It was pitiful.

"I chose that quote because of you, Salma," Yasmin choked out. "After what happened. Because you love butterflies."

I shook my head and seethed. My left fist clenched, turning the flesh around my pinkie ring a bloodless white. I looked to Mom.

"I'm so sorry," she said, her lips quivering. "You don't deserve this."

Yasmin wiped her nose. "I got scared. I mean, after what happened to Salma, I thought . . . I mean, I took Hala . . ." Her throat caught. She sniffed, unable to finish.

"Where was Mr. Peck during all this?" Mom demanded.

The girls shrugged.

"Was he in the classroom?" Mom pressed.

"I don't know," Yasmin finally answered.

"What do you mean?" Dad asked.

"I mean I *don't know*," she snapped.

Mom drew in a sharp breath. "Don't worry about that.

We'll be in touch with him. But why didn't you come home? Why were you in the woods?"

Hala looked to Yasmin, who spoke quickly. "We were hiding. I was worried they would follow us. Anyway, I thought we might as well practice if it's true. . . ."

Now *I* couldn't keep quiet. "Practice? For what? If what's true?"

Yasmin stared at her feet. She wouldn't say, but she seemed more nervous than embarrassed.

Hala slipped her hand inside Yasmin's. "You know, if we have to run away," she whispered. "All of us. They said they were coming for us."

Mom's hands flew in the air. "*Who* said that?"

"The boys," continued Hala. "They said that the government was going to round us all up into re-portation camps. We didn't want anyone to know where we lived." She frowned. "I'm sorry, Mom. I didn't mean to scare everyone—"

"What kind of camps?" I interrupted.

Hala and Yasmin both blinked at me.

"Deportation," Dad said, his voice lifeless. "That was probably the word."

"*De*-portation," Hala echoed, emphasizing the first syllable. "Right."

"Monsters," Titi whispered. She wasn't being superstitious or allegorical. She was speaking truth. My mind flashed to the last time I'd run away from "monsters." Eight years ago? Mariam and I were about Yasmin's age, having a sleepover at her house. We started joking about spending the night in those same woods, and the joke morphed into a dare, and the dare morphed into reality—the way it always seemed to go with us. We climbed out of that tiny basement window, running into the canopy of trees and bushes . . . and literally at the exact moment the pitch darkness swallowed us whole, several creatures screeched. We screeched, too. We booked it back to her house, diving headfirst into the basement, nearly pissing our pants from laughing so hard. *"Mason Terrace has a monster infestation!"*

Funny how our imagination soothed us. How we felt safe pretending that feral cats or raccoons (or whatever) were monsters. The way children do. Except . . . the boys who'd bullied my sisters weren't make-believe. They were monsters by definition. Predatory. Inhuman. I pitied them. Had they meant what they'd said? Had they even *known* what they were saying? I doubted it.

"Deportation is not going to happen," Dad murmured. "Ever."

Nobody said a word. There was nothing to say. Under the table, Titi tugged on her tasbih.

# 10

MOM ORDERED A day off. She and Dad called in sick, for themselves and the rest of us. We *were* sick. We needed time to get well, family time. A day to stay put and lounge in our jammies. I had a hard time even getting out of bed.

Vanessa texted to see how I was doing.

> U ok, Salma B?

Amir had probably told her what happened last night. And Vanessa had probably told Dora and Boots, because a few minutes after Vanessa's text, I got a giggly and nearly incomprehensible video message from the two of them, which (I think?) was supposed to be an infomercial parody. "Hi, we're team Kick Ass [laughter] . . . call one-eight-eight-K-I-C-K-A-S-S when [snorting, giggling, something indiscernible] . . . because some asses need kicking. Seriously, girl, we've got your back and whoever shares your DNA. Love you, Salma!"

I sighed. It was sweet, if a little over-the-top. It also made me wonder what else was swirling in the ether. No doubt someone, somewhere—with a posse, too—was laughing his or her ass *off* at my expense.

I could barely muster the energy to respond to her text beyond a cursory:

Ok thx, Nessa—c u tmrw. I'll explain later.

Their videos, their texts, it was all really sweet and certainly helped to soften the blow. But I wanted more. It wasn't enough to call Domino's or screw with someone's iPhone. I wanted payback.

For a moment, I considered chatting with Pulaski88. He'd probably have some ideas in terms of revenge. But who was the culprit? Michelle, Chris? I doubt they were hanging around the middle school. Did they have younger siblings? Unrelated minions?

My stomach rumbled. My brain felt foggy. If I was going to have any executive functioning powers, I needed to eat.

When I emerged from my bedroom cave, I found Dad sitting on the living room floor playing cards with Hala and Yasmin. Mom was still asleep. I caught a glimpse through the kitchen window of Titi in the backyard. She was doing laundry, her way. Old school. She refused to use the dryer. With Titi in charge, our sheets and clothes smelled like the great outdoors. (And occasionally *looked* like the great outdoors: I'd once found pigeon turd on a favorite pair of jeans, an unfortunate discovery I kept to myself.) So when the doorbell rang, I just assumed she'd accidentally locked herself out of the utility room again. But opening the fridge, I saw that she was still outside.

*"Mon amour?"* Dad called from the living room. "Please? We're playing Demon's Pounce."

I hoped it wasn't Amir. He should have been at school. Then again, my next-to-perfect boyfriend had a habit of popping up unannounced. It would be just like him to ditch to make sure my family was okay, bring flowers. I walked toward the door, stopping to look at myself in the mirror. I was in baggy sweats and an old VANDY FOOTBALL T-shirt, not my ideal Amir outfit. The oversized top had sentimental value—it was a relic of last summer and our last visit to Grandma Thiede in Nashville, the last time we ever saw her. None of us knew at the time that her cancer had returned . . . although maybe she'd had a hunch and spared us. As always, a lifelong Vanderbilt cheerleader through and through, she gave us ridiculous football gear. I wondered how she would react if she knew what had happened to her granddaughters. She'd be at our door as well. She'd also be at Franklin's door, dressing down the faculty in that gorgeous Southern accent. I missed that accent. It was molasses laced with arsenic.

Screw it; Amir would just have to see me in my current state. I tied my hair back.

By the time I opened the front door, whoever had rung had left. Waiting on the steps was a wicker basket. I reached down. On top of a plaid handkerchief was a gray envelope.

*To the Bakkiouis.*

I peeked under the cloth.

Cookies! I scarfed one down, dripping crumbs as I opened the letter.

*Dear Neighbors,*

*Kyle Sr. and I are thinking of you.*
*Our family is so relieved that your darlings are safe*

*at home. Please know that we are always here for you, for anything at all. I am glad they met Drexler! He's always here, too, if they want to visit. I'm home nearly all the time. Except for our hour-long walks—8 a.m. every morning!*

*Yours truly,*
*Kate Turner*

*P.S. The cookies are nut-free and half the sugar. The daffodils are from our yard. Freshly picked! Enjoy!*

Freshly picked, indeed. I remember when Mrs. Muhammad planted those flowers. She never picked them. They lasted longer that way. Growling, I glanced between the opened envelope and the note. I'd assumed the envelope had been printed electronically. But Mrs. Turner had handwritten everything. She was quite the perfectionist. Verging on anal-retentive? It was like calligraphy . . . had *she* made those prints on their walls? Was she actually more like Mariam's mom than anyone knew? Maybe. Every letter was precise and uniform: down to the tiniest flourish. I shook out the crumbs.

Okay, from this angle I could see that her handwriting wasn't *that* perfect. No way could she have done those prints on the wall. (A weird relief.) She also gripped the pen too hard. Aggressively. The paper had been punctured in a few places.

I closed the door behind me.

"Who was it?" Dad asked.

"Our neighbor, Mrs. Turner," I said, handing over the basket and the note to Dad. "She brought us cookies and—"

"Wait, *what?*" Hala interrupted. "Cookies?"

She and Yasmin slammed their cards down. In an instant they swarmed Dad like vultures, giggling as he removed the cloth. They looked so happy. It should have made *me* happy. But watching their eager hands dart into the cookie pile just made me queasy. Clearly, yesterday's events hadn't affected them as much as they had affected me. They were past it. I envied them, honestly. For them today was turning out to be just a free day off.

Dad looked at me. "You already ate one, didn't you, *mon amour?*" he teased.

Unconsciously I reached to wipe my mouth.

"Don't worry," he added. "You concealed the evidence."

At that, I mustered a laugh. He patted the space beside him. I sat.

"The note, Dad." I made sure to shove it into his hands. "Read it."

After skimming it twice, he sighed. "*Masha'Allah.* We are fortunate to have such good neighbors."

"Yeah, but . . ." My voice fizzled.

I knew why I felt guilty and conflicted. Mrs. Turner had rescued Yasmin and Hala from their hiding place in the woods. I still hadn't thanked Kyle Jr. for standing up for me to Barbie and the Bot. On the other hand it wasn't for lack of trying. I'd attempted to thank Kyle Jr. Instead I'd overheard an over-heated conversation that made no sense. Why would Kyle's father ask Amir and me to befriend his son, and then scold that same son for *"getting involved with Bakkioui"*? My mind flashed to the way Kyle Jr. had spat out our name, pronouncing it flawlessly, but with an undeniable harshness—

"Salma?"

Dad was staring at my hands. I was clutching a throw pillow. I let it drop into my lap.

"It's strange. Give me that," I grumbled.

"What's strange?" Dad pressed.

"The letter. Them." I could feel my father's eyes still on me, disapproving. "Okay, *strange* isn't the right word. . . ." My voice trailed off. It *was* the right word. I just didn't want to get into the Kyle Jr. incident. Or non-incident. No doubt Dad would echo what Amir had told me: I'd overheard something I shouldn't have and taken it totally out of context. It probably meant nothing. Probably.

"*Haram alaik.* Just yesterday—"

"I know, I know." I stood, tossing the pillow back on the couch behind me. "Your girls are all home. Safe and sound." *Astaghfirullah.*

"They are," Dad agreed, his voice sharp. "Thanks to Mrs. Turner."

My shoulders slumped. What was happening to me? I longed for Mariam. I longed for Vanessa. I longed for anyone whom I could make understand. Pulaski88 maybe?

Dad reached over and squeezed my fingers. "Why don't you split these flowers in half and give some to Mom?" he murmured. "And the rest to your grandmother. It will bring her joy."


It was a beautiful spring day, clear and windy. The linens flapped in the breeze. Titi sniffed the daffodils and smiled. "Give these to your *ummi,*" she said, handing them back.

"No, no. Those are for you!" I said, kissing her on the cheek and heading inside.

140

"Go rest!" Titi admonished.

Not a bad idea. I'd just sat down on the porch and was about to eat one of the cookies I selfishly hid in my pocket, when I heard a car pulling into Mason Terrace. Even from back here, I knew exactly where it was going: Mariam's driveway. It was like an alarm bell; in the madness of last night, I'd forgotten about wanting to apologize to Kyle. But I could also tell from the sound of the motor that it definitely wasn't the Turners' pickup truck. I ducked around the corner of the house to take a peek. Long experience had trained me how to hide in the front yard shrubbery. But that was innocent waiting—usually for Dr. and Mrs. Muhammad to leave, so I could sneak over to Mariam's and interrupt her homework on a school night. Now I was hiding to spy. But on whom? And what was I even hoping to learn?

A shiny blue Mercedes pulled into the Turners' driveway. Fancy, something even I knew, though I am clueless about cars. The guy who emerged looked fancy, too. He was tall and slender, in a blue power suit, his thick gray hair perfectly styled. Handsome. A little like George Clooney, in fact. He left the engine running and the driver's-side door open. As I stared at him, Mr. Turner burst out of the house. His eyes swept the street as he approached the car. Mr. Fancy climbed back in behind the wheel and closed the door. Mr. Turner walked briskly over and hopped in the front passenger side. Now I couldn't see a thing; the windows were tinted. But a few seconds later, Mr. Turner hopped back out. He was holding a leather briefcase, also fancy. He hurried back inside the house just as quickly as he'd exited it, without so much as a wave or a smile or a goodbye. Mr. Fancy backed up and peeled away.

I didn't even realize I was holding my breath until I exhaled.

Okay . . . what was that all about? I brushed the crumbs off my face. But even as I wondered, I felt ashamed, spying on the neighbors while snacking on the goodies those same neighbors had gifted us. Mrs. DLP was right; I *was* nosy. The roar of Mr. Fancy's engine faded. The better question was: Why did I care? Lower-*nafs* Salma answered quickly. *Maybe because no one around here drives a Mercedes like that. Maybe because nobody around here pulls up, drops off a briefcase, and leaves in under thirty seconds. Maybe because nobody around here would get in someone's car without saying hello first.*

Maybe Mr. Fancy was paying the friendly neighborhood electrician for a repair in cash.

After all, Mr. Turner billed his clients. He'd said so himself at Amir's house.


Upstairs I found my parents' bedroom door closed. I knocked cautiously.

"Yes?"

"Hey, Mom. Can I come in?"

"I don't know; can you?"

I frowned. Mom got grammatical under two scenarios: grading time or when she was frustrated. Often they went hand and hand. Opening the door slowly, I presented her flowers, palm outstretched. She flashed a tired smile from the unmade bed, her de facto home office. Thomas sat purring on a pile of rumpled blankets by her feet.

"Sorry," she breathed, closing her laptop. "Come and sit.

Where did you get those?" She tried to shove aside files and papers to make room for me.

I settled in beside Thom. He nuzzled his head against me. I ran my fingers over his warm scalp. "From the Turners," I said. "They also brought some cookies."

She closed her eyes and took a deep breath, barely appreciating the flowers, which she typically loved. Mom liked daffodils the way I liked lilies.

"You okay?" I asked.

"I'm tired," she grumbled. "In more ways than one."

"Because of fasting? And yesterday?"

She wrinkled her nose. "Yes, plus the lackluster response I'm getting from Franklin Middle. Mr. Peck is being responsive—he feels awful, said he would have intervened had he not been down the hall copying lessons." She drew a sharp breath, running her fingers through her short blond hair. "At any rate, he's giving Yasmin an A-minus, the grade she likely would have earned had this not happened. He saw the drafts, knows her record." She mustered a smile for my benefit. "He said that Amir's song was a nice touch."

"I'll tell him," I said quietly. "So, that's sort of a happy ending, right? But you still seem annoyed."

She sighed, turning her attention back to her computer. "I just wish I knew who those kids were. I'd like to talk to their parents, one on one. But Mr. Peck won't give me their names. He said his hands were tied, citing Franklin's new privacy codes."

I wasn't sure I understood. "So wait. Mr. Peck knows who did this but won't tell you?"

Mom nodded. "Precisely, which is why I emailed Principal

Philip. Several times. His response was . . . pro forma. Curt. To the effect of: Franklin is a place where everyone's concerns are taken seriously. The subtext was clear. He wants me to drop it."

"Figures," I muttered. Mrs. DLP's words echoed through my head. *He's a bigot, plain and simple.*

Mom stared at me. "Why do you say that?" she asked.

Crap. I shouldn't have mentioned it. I'm awful at filtering, always letting things slip out.

"Salma?" she said, her voice stern and focused. "Did Principal Philip say something to you?"

"Um . . . not really. No. I mean, I was called into his office last week. I thought he was going to apologize for not following up with the kids who'd pushed me down the stairs. Instead he wanted to see if I was behind some stupid prank. It was a phony bomb threat, so there were even some cops. But nothing happened. He was just rude. . . ." *Shit. Stop, Salma. If you tell her now, she'll totally freak out. She'll press for details. You'll spill the beans on the whole day. Aren't you working toward more privileges? More time with Amir?* "Anyway, it was . . ." My voice trailed off.

"Salma?"

I focused on the cat so she couldn't pry anything more out of me. Yes, last Tuesday was awful. But that was then. Right now, my sisters were the ones being bullied. Full stop.

"Honey, you didn't finish your thought," she prodded.

"Uh . . . sorry. Brain fog." She'd have to believe that one. With EDS it's pretty standard. I snuck a peek to study her expression. She looked as if she was trying to connect the dots.

"So let me see if I have this right," she said. "The police came to school, because of some sick prank, and Principal Philip was rude to you. Did he think you were behind it?"

I shook my head. "No. He said it was a misunderstanding. He was just . . . rude. That's all." All of that was true, at least.

With a sigh, Mom opened her computer again. "You know, I've heard whisperings from other moms that he plays favorites."

"Yeah, Mrs. DLP said the same thing," I murmured. "Sort of."

"It could also be an institutional reflex. Protect the institution at all costs. It's poppycock." She reached for her glasses. "Speaking of ossified institutions, I've got nearly a hundred exams to grade and an article to finish. The one on Malamatiyya poetry."

*Poppycock? Ossified?* I cracked a half smile. Sometimes Mom's sharp tongue sounded more nineteenth-century London than twenty-first-century Arlington. "The Malama-whatta poetry?" I asked.

"Rabiah, Hafez . . ." She rattled off a half dozen more names I'd never heard, presumably dead Sufis. "God's unruly friends," she explained, maybe forgetting my habit of tuning her out when she got all academic on me. "Those who challenged the various paradigms of their day, political, theological. They saw virtue in rebellion and following the unorthodox path."

I leaned over to kiss her, then stood. Thomas hopped off the bed with me.

"Interesting," I said. Little did she know that I found her words to be more inspiring than interesting. She had planted in my brain a desire for vigilante justice. My own approach to "convalescing."

Back in my cave, basement door locked, I whipped out my dual iPads and mounted them to my laptop for a triple monitor setup. The more surface area, the better. I had Mom's words to thank. It was time for some virtuous rebellion, to follow the unorthodox path. Nearly everyone viewed me as a pariah anyway, thanks to my faith. It was time to embrace the pariah I really was, thanks to my computer skills.

The plan? To dox the principal. I would not sit around while Mom wrote strongly worded letters and Mrs. DLP raised a stink at the next PTSA meeting. That was all well and good. But it wasn't enough. If there were parents who really wanted to oust Philip, they needed irrefutable proof of his bigotry. And I could hand it to them. Anonymously, of course. Doxing was the perfect solution. The approach is simple—hack into someone's private files (or photos, but I wasn't interested in accidentally discovering something *that* personal). All I needed was an offhand comment, something offensive and racist. Written by Philip.

As I sat at my desk investigating Franklin's firewall, a tingling sensation coursed through my fingertips—part EDS, part adrenaline. I set up a triple VPN to secure my presence and tunneled my way into the school's network. If anyone at Franklin found out what I was up to, I would be expelled in a heartbeat. It was best to follow one of Pulaski88's fundamental principles: When ethically hacking, time was of the essence.

Thankfully, Franklin isn't exactly the Department of Defense in terms of security. In under ten minutes, I had access to everything Philip had access to. I scoured his email for anything I could use against him, but it was the usual boring school administrative stuff. But then a new email popped up in his inbox.

I squinted at my laptop screen. The subject line read: Podcast 32 ready to air. The sender was a media group: the Family First Coalition. I was tempted to look at it, but if I clicked on the email it would no longer be bold, no longer appear as unread. Fine. If I couldn't find some dirt on Philip, the very least I could do was locate the names of the punk-ass middle schoolers who'd put my sisters through hell and dox them. In person.

It was surprisingly easy to find them. All disciplinary incidents are recorded in the same database; I soon had access to their records, their grades, their daily schedules, even their after-school schedules. School had just gotten out, and both of these douchekins had Arcade Club at four p.m. It was perfect. Resisting the urge to do anything extra—say, changing all their grades to Fs—I powered down my laptop and called Amir. I told him I needed his help, a ride to school for a little payback. I told my parents that the best way to convalesce was to get a frappy-dappy. I promised them that Amir would have me back before *iftar*. *That* part was true, at least. After that I changed my outfit.

## 11

———

BY THE TIME Amir arrived, I was pacing the sidewalk, debating whether to call on Dora and Boots. Charge the middle schoolers with a posse of my own, care of 1-888-KICK-BUTT. No, this was my burden. This was family business.

Outfit-wise, I'd gone full Tyler Durden. Like I'd come out of the *Fight Club* hole. The activist geek was out in the open now: black Doc Martens, matching black jeans, black T-shirt, thick eyeliner.

In other words, I didn't look like myself. And Amir knew it.

Windows down, car in park, he flashed me a sad smile. Even though he'd agreed to pick me up, I hadn't shared the full plan. The plan to find the kids who'd terrorized my sisters; scare the living daylights out of them; void their Instagram points with some points of my own. Mutual Edward Norton fetish aside, I could tell that Amir wasn't digging my vibe.

Whatever. I was pumped and ready to go.

"You're only going to talk to them, right? Nothing crazy?"

*Talk? Nothing crazy?* Did he even hear himself? I had every right to go crazy on those obnoxious little twerps. Then again, Amir was Mr. Kareem. He couldn't help himself . . .

so I bit my lip and nodded. "Of course," I said, clicking my seatbelt.

Amir bit his nails. I could tell he was thinking something he didn't have the nerve to share.

"What?" I groaned.

"Nothing." He slid the gear shift into drive. "It's just . . . getting soft isn't the worst thing."

We drove in silence the entire way to Franklin. Only when we turned the corner into the school parking lot did Amir shake his head and put his foot on the brakes.

"Amir—"

"Salma, wait." He pulled the key from the ignition and shifted to me in his seat, his dark eyes on mine, serious. "Just listen to me. I talked to Mr. Epstein about what happened. He's not happy about it. He thinks the 'Yasmin B. Incident' is an opportunity. He used those words. He and Mr. Peck and a couple of other teachers are planning a sit-down with Principal Philip. There's a laundry list of issues. Did you know that Philip has threatened to suspend anyone who participates in gun-control walkouts, you know, like the one that went down at T.C. Williams?"

I shook my head. Sadness washed over my body, an invisible weight. It pushed me down into the seat cushion. My little sister's name was now a label, a catchphrase for an agenda. Exposing the unspoken bigotry at Franklin was a positive thing, yes . . . but it had nothing to do with what really happened to Yasmin. The person. The ten-year-old girl. The human being who'd been scared into the woods. The student who'd had her work destroyed.

"Amir?" I heard myself say. I turned to him and laid my hand over his. "I'm not going to wait for some 'Kumbaya' moment that might never come. I know Mr. Epstein cares. I know he's a good guy."

"Exactly, so—"

"So let me finish. Yasmin isn't his sister. She's *my* sister. I need to do something about it."

Amir stared out the window, gnawing on his thumbnail, avoiding my eyes. "Do *what*, though?"

"Something that will help my family," I said, unbuckling my seatbelt and opening the door.

"Salma, wait." He reached for my shoulder. "Listen. I get it. I do. Just . . . I'm worried, okay? I don't want you to get in trouble. I don't want to give them more of an excuse to hurt you."

"But this isn't about me." I turned around and shook free as I pushed myself out of the car. "If you're worried, then don't stick around. Seriously. I don't want you to feel you're complicit in something you don't agree with."

I left the car as fast as I could without limping, making a beeline for the front entrance. I winced with each step, but my back was turned. I didn't want him to see that I was in any pain. Because he could sweet-talk me . . . he could get all *kareem;* he could convince me to see some sunny way to fix things. Amir *was* the sun. And I needed that. Sometimes. But right now *I* was the darkness of the moon, hidden from the light, and right now that was exactly what I needed, too.

The metal doors slammed behind me. My boots clomped in rhythm down the sterile cinderblock and linoleum hall. Conveniently, Dylan Douchebag and Aaron Asshat were both signed up for Thursday's Video Arcade Club. Room 401: the middle school computer lab. As I passed the main office, I saw that the door was ajar. Principal Philip was standing in front of Mrs. Owens's desk, discussing something. Both of their heads were down. Since they didn't look up, I gave them the finger.

Childish, yes, but cathartic.

I picked up my pace. It was sort of perfect that I'd teach them a lesson *here*. I'd taken Cybersecurity Club with Mrs. Duffner in that exact room several years ago. I turned the corner separating Franklin High from Franklin Middle—

And I barreled straight into Sheikh Epstein.

Papers flew, scattering to the ground in a flurry. He immediately apologized and bent down to pick up his music sheets. The sheet nearest my foot was marked *No Woman, No Cry. Amir for Salma*. I bent down and handed it to him, my heart suddenly racing. I could feel my cheeks getting hot.

"I'm, uh, I'm so sorry," I stammered. "I wasn't watching where I was going."

We stood up at the same time. I saw now that Mr. Epstein's usually serene face was creased with concern. There were dark circles under his eyes. His short, thinning hair was messier than usual.

"You don't have to apologize," he said gently. "For anything. You and your family are *owed* an apology. Several, in fact. And you're—" He broke off as he took in my outfit. "Salma . . . you're not alone. Just, please, promise me that you won't do anything that might get you in trouble."

*Trouble.* It was the exact same word Amir had used. And in the same way: code for the right deed with the wrong execution. I blinked at him. All at once I burst into tears.

"I won't," I croaked. The words stuck in my throat. "I promise."

"Glad to hear it." He reached out and patted my shoulder.

I wiped my eyes. No doubt I smeared my ridiculous makeup all over my face. Still, I forced myself to return his gaze. Amir was right. Because somehow his sunlight had reached me anyway. I saw it right now. It was reflected in Mr. Epstein's weary face, in the compassion he couldn't hide.

"Thank you." I sniffed. "For, um . . . actually, never mind. Probably best if you don't know."

Mr. Epstein smiled. "Hey, I'm just glad you ran into me. Feel free to run into me whenever you need to. I'm happy to wear kneepads."

I laughed through my tears at his dorky joke.

"Bye, Mr. Epstein," I said, then turned and shambled toward the exit.

I suppose I should have known all along that my revenge plan was a fantasy. I felt regret and relief in equal measure as I rehashed it in my mind one last time before letting it go. Step one: remove Aaron and Dylan from room 401. Step two: pin their scrawny necks against the wall. Step three: scream *"Fayn kayn l'bit del'ma?"* angrily, emphasizing all the scary guttural letters and gesturing wildly. Step four: leave them soaking in their tighty-whities, sopping wet. The beauty of it was that *"Fayn kayn l'bit del'ma?"* wasn't a threat. It literally means "Where's the restroom?" in colloquial Moroccan Arabic. A good phrase in case they did, indeed, piss themselves. . . .

What wasn't a fantasy? Amir.

He was still there, in the parking lot, sitting in his Jetta. Waiting for me. I'm sure there were a million things he'd rather be doing. Like getting in a Ramadan nap. Yet, in spite of everything, he was still there. In spite of the fact that if I'd gotten in trouble, he would have gotten in trouble, too.

I opened the door and slid in beside him. "I didn't do it," I whispered. "I . . ." My throat caught, and I couldn't go on. A tear rolled down my cheek. Without a word, he reached for my hand.

I held it tight in return. When my breathing evened and I managed to collect myself, I finally let go. "There's no way I could ever let anything happen to *you*, too," I choked out.

He leaned over and kissed me on the cheek. Then he started the engine.

We drove in silence, and the dark cloud slowly lifted. Ten minutes later, when we pulled onto Mason Terrace, I felt like myself again. I even felt *good*. My knee wasn't throbbing. I vowed not to entertain any more revenge scenarios. I would stay off my screens and be with family, spend time with my sisters, bring Titi joy. But as I climbed out of the Jetta, I spotted Mrs. Turner leaving her house with Drexler. She shuffled out their entryway, paused, and answered a phone call. When she got off, she immediately sank down, sitting on the last step. She buried her face in her hands while Drexler sat there, sniffing the air.

"What do you think that's all about?" Amir asked.

I shook my head. "Not sure. Why don't you go in and say hi to my family? I'll see what's up with her."

"Cool."

By the time I made it across the street, Mrs. Turner was patting her eyes with a handkerchief and looking up to the sky, lost in thought. She seemed . . . overwhelmed. Broken. The way Mom and Titi had when it seemed we would never find Hala and Yasmin again.

"Hi . . . Kate," I said, forcing myself to use the name she insisted upon. "Is everything all right?"

"Oh!" Her face flushed. She hadn't even noticed I'd been standing there. "I'm fine, dear."

"Are you sure?"

"Oh, yes. I just need to hurry back inside. I forgot to pack Mr. Turner's dinner. He's got the late shift and I completely forgot." She stood up, turning toward the door. "Sorry, Drexler. Your walk will have to wait."

I stepped back a bit. Mrs. Turner clearly didn't want to talk about whatever was really bothering her. And this was the best she could do—under the circumstances, whatever they were—without telling me that it was none of my business. I knew I shouldn't pry. But I wanted to help her, to repay the favor she had done for us. The many favors. Drexler tilted his head up at me, his droopy brown eyes seeming to reflect his owner's sadness. "Um . . . Mrs. Turner?"

"Yes?" She was so distraught that for once she didn't even insist on being called Kate.

"I'd be happy to take Drexler for a walk. He can hang with us, too. Until you get back."

Her worried face softened slightly. "Oh, I couldn't trouble you—"

"It's no trouble," I gently interrupted. "You would actually be doing *me* a favor. By letting me thank you for what you did for my sisters."

A fleeting smile crossed her face. "Well then, thank you." She nodded. "What a godsend."

As she passed me the leash I got a quick look at her wrist. There was a brownish-yellow bruise that wrapped around it. She pulled her sleeves down and went inside.

# 12

AH, SATURDAY NIGHT. Or in certain parts of Arlington: the Night When High School Couples Pick a Parentally Approved Activity as an Excuse to Go Somewhere Safe and Make Out. Or at the very least, attend a party at Vanessa's. (Of course she was having a party, and of course Dora and Boots were in; they'd already bugged me to come.) But I didn't even have a full night to myself, so for me the choice was simple. Amir. Just Amir.

The clock was ticking. Two hours from now I would be with Titi, babysitting my sisters. Mom and Dad had their own Ramadan "date"—their word (lame). Then again, they absolutely deserved it. They needed a kid-free break. I even told them as much. Though if I were like Mrs. DLP, if the window to my soul were wide open, they would see that I craved a break from them, too. Honestly, I was relieved. There was still so much they didn't know, and so much I didn't want to share. Anyway, I was lucky even to get *this* time. Since Mariam had moved away, I'd almost forgotten how permissive my parents were.

Amir and I had to make the best of Saturday afternoon. As I approached his house, I vowed to make the best of it. I owed him. For a lot. For waiting for me in the Franklin parking lot after I'd been saved from scaring the shit out of those two little morons. For giving me a ride back home. For not calling me out for being a jerk when a lesser person would have. For letting me help Mrs. Turner with Drexler.

For being able to see through the curtains, just a little.

After ten seconds of incessant doorbell ringing, I finally heard approaching footsteps—at a sprint. I grinned. Definitely not Mr. Ammouri.

"Surprise!" yelled a familiar voice as the door swung open. It was Mona. Child number four.

"Oh my God!" I screeched back. "What are you doing here?"

"I drove down for the weekend," she said. "You know, to make sure in Mom's absence that Baba and Amir don't starve to death."

"Oh," I said, not realizing that Mrs. Ammouri had already left town for baby duty. "Did Marwa have the twins?"

She laughed. "Marwa definitely did not have the twins. Actually, it's Maya that's having the babies. But whatever, at least it's not me." She pulled me inside. "Come on in and have a seat."

I could hear the faint strains of a drumbeat in the basement. Ah, so Amir was listening to music. That explained why Mona had answered the door. But I was happy to have a little time with her. She's the older sister I've always wanted—loyal, witty, hella badass.

In the living room, she pushed aside her graduate school

books and patted the couch. "So, how are you and Amir doing?" she asked, raising her eyebrows.

"We're good," I said, eying the coffee as I waited for it to cool. "Actually, he's the good one. I'm the head case. Loud, emotional, angry. Not at him, I mean. But at the world—or our world. Franklin really. Specifically our White Power Principal."

"Oh, don't get me started on Philip," she groaned. "He was only an assistant principal and the lacrosse coach when *I* went to Franklin, but . . ." She left the sentence hanging.

"What?"

Mona swept her curly brown hair over her shoulder and looked at me. She had the same dark eyes as Amir; all the Ammouri kids shared them. "He escorted me out of a game for cheering when my boyfriend—well, my boyfriend at the time—hit a shot at the end of the second quarter."

My eyes narrowed. "He kicked you out for cheering?"

"It was *what* I cheered. And I guess it was the timing of it. It wasn't that long after President Obama caught Osama bin Laden."

I shook my head, not following anymore.

She smiled sadly. "You can't guess? *'Allahu akbar.'*"

"Oh." I felt myself crumple a little bit. Of course. It would make sense that Principal Philip found that frightening and offensive. But the saying is completely nonthreatening, and not always religious. Sometimes it's just the equivalent of yelling "Awesome!" If only Philip could attend the World Cup and hear the Arabic broadcasters rooting for Middle Eastern teams. *Allahu akbar* or just *Allah* is shouted constantly. He would have entirely missed the context: how over the centuries the language of devotion has woven itself into every-day expressions far removed from the mosque.

Before I could grill Mona more about what happened, Amir came bounding up the stairs.

"Hey!" he said breathlessly, appearing in the living room. He glanced between us, then sat down beside his sister. "Uh-oh. Did I interrupt something?"

Mona winked at me. "She's *your* girlfriend. I'm the one who's interrupting." With that, she pulled her laptop across her legs, elbowing him in the ribs. "So scrawny. Why don't you order some Chinese? I'll be upstairs if you need me, which I'm sure you won't."


Several minutes later Amir and I were standing over a collection of DVDs, trying our best to narrow down the options. "How about this?" he asked, holding up *Kingdom of Heaven*.

"Really? That one?"

"Uh-oh. I thought you'd be psyched."

I skirted past Amir and headed straight for the shelf, where I plucked out *The Italian Job*. Then I whirled around with a smile, wriggling my eyebrows.

"Huh? Huh?" I was kidding, sort of. But I was on my parents' page. I needed a break. Something escapist. Dumb, even. Norton as a greedy one-note villain. Norton-lite. And we could skip the boring parts.

Amir got it, because he smiled back. "Salma, we've seen it like a hundred times." He did a little eyebrow wriggling of his own and held up his DVD. "Besides, this has a better soundtrack. Huh? Huh?"

I laughed. "Point taken. But in yours, you don't even see your favorite actor's face."

Amir couldn't argue there; Edward Norton played King Baldwin IV, a leper. He wore an expressionless metal mask throughout the entire film. But Amir just nodded. "Exactly right," he deadpanned. "I'm trying to keep *your* Edward Norton crush in check."

I blushed, still laughing as *The Italian Job* fell to my side. "Okay, how about this? No movie. Instead you practice right here, right now, for me. So you can get ready for your . . . your . . ."

"Show?" he finished.

"Thank you. I can't bring myself to say—"

"Gig?"

"How about *performance*?"

He laughed. "Deal."

I flopped down on the couch. His oud bounced on the cushion beside me. *Yikes*. Without looking first, I'd nearly crushed it under my butt. Amir always kept it in its case . . . so he must have been practicing when I arrived. It was perfect. There was no way he could turn me down now.

"Epstein's thing is tomorrow night, right?" I asked.

"Yeah," he said. He stared at the oud. "But I don't know if I'm actually going to play. Officially, I'm going to help with the setup. The playing is a big if."

I frowned. "Is that coming from him or from you?"

He shrugged but didn't respond. With a sigh, he approached and lifted the instrument, settling into the couch beside me and cradling it in his lap.

"Why the cold feet?" I prodded. "You've been practicing, haven't you?"

Amir tucked his hair back. "Yeah," he murmured. He placed his left hand over the fretboard, silently forming a chord without plucking or strumming the strings with his right. "I've even streamed a few more videos."

I knew, of course. I subscribed to his YouTube channel under a username he wouldn't recognize.

When we first started going out, he made me promise that I wouldn't stalk him online—he wanted to limit my access only to music he felt confident in sharing, not works-in-progress he ran by fellow musicians. I didn't want to make him self-conscious. But he probably knew or suspected I'd ignored him and stalked him anyway. A smile curled on my lips. Of course he did. The last video he'd posted was a flawless rendition of "No Woman, No Cry," the Bob Marley song I'd seen in Epstein's papers. Amir told his subscribers he'd requested the sheet music "because my girlfriend loves this one."

"What?" he asked.

"Nothing," I said. "It's just . . . it's not the same: playing live and recording yourself. You have nothing to be afraid of, Amir."

His smile faded. "I don't?" He adjusted his posture and shifted in the cushions to face me, his eyes on the instrument.

After a moment he plucked a measure of the song he'd composed for Yasmin, at a much slower tempo than he'd recorded for her project. I opened my mouth to argue. No words came. He was right. His talent spoke for itself—as it spoke to Mr. Epstein, and me, and the people he was "in touch with overseas" (*His friends, Detective Tim; do you have any friends, here or abroad?*)—but beyond that I couldn't bullshit or soothe him about what people might think or do. There was plenty to fear. With my lips still parted, I leaned forward and kissed him on the cheek.

His face flushed. "What was that for?" he asked, still playing.

"For writing that song for my sister. For everything else."

"How about something for you?" Without pausing, he tapped out a different tempo on the body of the oud—*tap, tap, tap, tap*—and began strumming loudly. In a heartbeat I recognized that unmistakable syncopated reggae feel. "No Woman, No Cry." I had to laugh.

"What?"

"I understand your girlfriend loves this song," I explained.

He laughed, too, not missing a beat. "Oh yeah?" His eyes flicked up to mine. "Where'd you hear that? I told you that if you cyberstalked me you'd end up getting jealous of all my other Bob Marley–loving girlfriends."

I smirked but didn't say anything more. I wanted to hear him play. He did more than that; to my astonishment, he started to sing. He looked at me again, eyebrows arched, message clear: *Sing with me. You owe me.* So I joined. Of note: I, Salma Bakkioui, have a horrible voice. Not just pitchy— putrid. Proverbial nails-on-a-chalkboard awful.

Amir's smile widened. Using his picking hand, he made the universal *Cut* sign with a slash across his throat, and—a true testament to his musicianship—*still* didn't fumble or interrupt the song. I grinned back and raised my hands in surrender; it was all him.

When he finally opened up his throat, unshackled by my sour off-key contribution, I saw it. Pure joy. He closed his eyes, blissed out—wailing like Marley himself, but adding his own Middle Eastern touch: a couple of *"aiwas"* and a *"ya salaam."*

Sheikh Epstein would be ecstatic.

So would everyone else, if they had any sense.


Later, I told Amir to stop at the mouth of the Mason Terrace cul-de-sac instead of giving me the usual door-to-door service. He slowed to a crawl.

"Why? Isn't your house on lockdown mode?"

"Only at night," I said. Which was true. It was six forty-five. The sun was still out, a hazy orange ball skirting the tree line. Yasmin and Hala were in plain sight, huddled together and giggling on the front steps. If Mom and Dad and Titi were comfortable enough to let them hang around outside after what had happened—alone and unchaperoned—then Amir *had* to feel comfortable enough to let me walk the short distance to them from his car. He parked the car curbside and unlocked the doors. I hugged him tight and climbed out.

He rolled down the window. "Sure you can make it all the way?"

I laughed. "Yes, Amir. Oh, that reminds me, you better be sure to film tomorrow night. Mom still refuses to let me go. Or to ever change my curfew." A thought occurred to me. "But hey, now that you're wise to my little cyberstalking secret, you can just get someone to stream it live. Okay?"

He nodded.

"Promise?"

"I promise," he said. "Cross my heart and hope to die."

"No dying, please. But I guess I *should* tell you to break a leg . . . ?"

162

"Oh, yeah! Then I could finally get to meet the famous Mrs. DLP." He winked. "Who, by the way, takes up way more of your time than Sheikh Epstein takes up of mine—not that I'm jealous or anything." He blew me a kiss, pulling away slowly and leaving me there laughing like an idiot.

As his Jetta roared off into the evening, my sisters giggled again. I groaned and turned toward them, quickening my pace.

It turned out they weren't giggling at me. They weren't even looking at me. They were preoccupied with . . . *Whoa.* Were they watching something? Yes. They were. On a phone.

"Mom let you use her iPhone?" I asked, baffled. Maybe she didn't want to be distracted.

Neither sister even bothered to look up. I cleared my throat. I positioned myself so that my long evening shadow fell right across Yasmin.

"It's not Mom's," she said after a minute.

"Then whose is it? What's going on?"

"It was his," said Hala. She waved her hand, distracted, toward the street. I put up a hand to shield my eyes from the glare of the setting sun, turning around. Mason Terrace was deserted . . . no, not quite. Kyle was watering Mariam's (*his*) shrubs. Had he been there the whole time? I hadn't noticed. I dropped my hand and faced my sisters again.

"It's Kyle's?" I asked.

"Mm-hmm," said Yasmin. "He gave it to us."

"Wait . . . what?" I asked.

"Kyle gave us the phone," Hala said, sounding exasperated.

I stared at them. "Kyle gave you that phone," I repeated, just to be sure.

Hala looked up, annoyed. "Yeah, so?"

"To borrow? Did he want to show you something? It doesn't make sense—"

"He *gave* it to us," Hala groaned. "Like, forever gave it. We came out here, and he just walked over, okay?" Her eyes went back to the screen. "It has YouTube."

"Does Mom know?" I asked. They must have misunderstood Kyle's intention. Or maybe I did. Maybe I just needed to find out exactly what Kyle's intention was. If he "forever gave" an iPhone to two little girls he barely knew, it was more than generous. It was creepy.

Instead of answering my question, my sisters exchanged a sneer, clearly disgusted with my disapproval. So Mom didn't know. I doubted if Dad or Titi knew, either. I leaned forward and grabbed the phone, prompting an outraged gasp from the two of them.

Yasmin lunged at me in a desperate attempt to snatch it back. I was too quick for her.

"Go inside," I snapped. "Or I'm telling Mom that you stole another pair of my headphones."

"I—I . . . ," she stammered.

"And you," I said, pointing at Hala. "I know about those candies you stash under your bed."

Her jaw dropped. "Worst. Sister. Ever." She stood.

Yasmin shot up next to her, matching her ridiculous indignant scowl.

They stomped inside and slammed the door behind them.

Too bad they had no clue that I was probably more upset than they were. Not that they'd care.

I whirled and marched across the street. Kyle was turning the spigot to shut off the hose. With his hoodie sleeves rolled up, I caught a glimpse of another tattoo—under his left bicep and close to his elbow. I couldn't tell what it was. Maybe mountain peaks or a crown that looked like it had barbed wire or thorns in it. I guess I'd been right about "the family that tattoos together" . . . more weirdness. Was that even a thing? I'd have to look it up.

I shifted my glare back up to his face.

"Hey, Salma," he said cautiously. "Everything okay?"

*He calls me by my first name to my face and my last name behind my back. Isn't that weird?*

"Did you give this to my sisters?" I shoved the iPhone toward him.

He nodded vigorously. "Yeah. Is that all right? You sound pissed—"

"I'm not pissed," I lied. I tried to keep my voice calm. I tried to remind myself of the fact that this was the kid who'd saved me from an ass-kicking, for which I still hadn't thanked him. "I just want to know why you'd give two little girls an iPhone out of the blue."

"It was a p-p-present," he stammered. He dropped the hose. "I thought they'd like it. And I thought it could . . . I don't know, be useful. You know, in case they ever go missing again."

"They won't."

"Okay, okay." Kyle flashed an anxious smile. I wondered when he'd last seen a dentist. I wondered if he was on medication. Or if he was so fidgety because he had zero social skills. Because he'd been homeschooled . . . or if it was the other way around: he'd been homeschooled *because* he had zero social skills. *Astaghfirullah*, I sounded like such a bitch. "But, Salma, please keep it anyway," he added. "My dad gets phones dirt cheap. I'm more of a Samsung guy. I wiped it clean, reset the personal data, removed the GPS—"

"No," I interrupted gently. I stepped forward, arm out-stretched. I wanted to remain as kind and neighborly as I possibly could. "We're touched. Really. But it's too much. Please take it back."

"For real?"

I nodded. "Yes. Thank you."

All at once, something shifted. It was almost as if his face had gone from plum to prune in the bright sun—he looked suddenly overripe, his features hard and shriveled.

"Fine," he spat. He took the phone and pocketed it. "This is what I get for trying to be a Good Samaritan." He sounded as if he were talking more to himself than me. Before I could reply, he hurried inside, slamming the door behind him.

I winced at the sharp crack.

Nice. Another door, slammed in my face. Two in under a minute. What a way to kick off the weekend. I was spreading animus like wildfire. Hala and Yasmin had a right to be upset, though. I would be, too, in their shoes. Maybe Kyle did as well? Had I acted like a self-righteous jerk? No. It *was* weird. He should have asked my parents' permission first. That's what I would have done if I wanted to give *him* a device worth hundreds of dollars. I glanced at my watch. Six fifty-five. Mom and Dad would be leaving in five minutes. For a second I hesitated on the street, debating if I should tell them about all this—then decided it was best to let it go. They were anxious enough. Why add to their stress? Plus, honestly, I didn't want to give my sisters an excuse to hate me even more than they did right now. I wasn't sure if I could handle a third door slammed in my face tonight.

I was still standing on the street alone when Mom and Dad emerged in their evening finery. They waved at me, blissfully unaware. I waved back.

They climbed into the family minivan and sped off without a word.

Over the next few hours, I indulged Yasmin and Hala to the point that they had to forgive me. I plied them with pizza for dinner, followed by Salma's salon time. I actually let them touch my curls. They brushed and braided, pulled and tugged. It was torture, but by the end of the night I was no longer "the world's worst sister" but the "world's best." Even Titi joined the fun, giving us all traditional Amazigh face tattoos with leftover Halloween face paint.

Even better, Mom and Dad came home glowing. "*Chérie, who knew you could be so funny?*" Dad kept saying to Mom. He giggled the way Hala and Yasmin had on the stoop, lost in some memory.

Best of all, Dad slipped me two twenty-dollar bills for my babysitting services, and Mom saw, and she didn't protest.

I took this to mean that Mom was feeling a little better about the world and that maybe *chez* Bakkioui won't be on such intense lockdown mode. I took it to mean that next weekend maybe I could have a normal night out—all mine, all Amir's. Maybe I could actually be home by, dare I say, eleven? I glanced at Mom, eager to make a deal, then realized that it was better to wait.

I would make sure she was well rested and finished with the annoying paper she had to write and the hundred papers she had to grade, and *then* I would ask.

167

# 13

AT ELEVEN-THIRTY, WITH everyone in the Bakkioui household sound asleep, I found myself still wide awake. A second wind. EDS tends to do that, to make me tired or wired at equally annoying times. In my basement cave, I binged on *Law & Order: Special Victims Unit.* I was just starting another episode when I heard the telltale sound of the Turners' truck pulling up. The engine stopped; doors closed quietly.

Seconds later I heard a massive thud out front—massive enough to *feel:* a subtle split-second quake.

I sat upright and blinked, then paused the screen.

The night was silent except for our dehumidifier. I set aside my laptop and went to the window to stand on my tip-toes. (A hassle even without EDS.) Across the street, Kyle Jr. and Mr. Turner were struggling to unload a massive bur-lap sack from the back of the truck. I could see them winc-ing, glistening with sweat in the dim streetlights. No lights were on inside their house, or out. I caught a glimpse of Mrs. Turner at the garage door, her finger poised above the manual opener—

*Thud.*

It was the same sound; Kyle and his father had dropped the sack on the driveway, right next to a silhouette I'd missed in the shadows—an identical sack.

The garage door opened. All three Turners hustled as best they could to drag the bags inside. Once the second one had been swallowed up in the black abyss, and the family with it, the garage door closed. The street was quiet again. And it stayed quiet. No lights came on inside the Turners' house, either. Finally my tiptoes could no longer handle the strain.

I nearly collapsed. I was breathing heavily. What the hell was that?

Best to be rational. Detached. Granted, this was the *second* weird thing I'd seen go down in their driveway. . . . Or was it? I tiptoed back to my laptop, determined to focus only on what I knew. The Turners had just moved in. Which took time. It was a gradual process, a work in progress. Maybe the sacks were full of long-awaited electrician's tools or lead piping or barbells. What I knew to be truest of all: I'd wanted to dislike the Turners from the moment they arrived. I didn't need Amir or my parents or Mrs. DLP to tell me that. These were the strangers who'd taken over my best friend's home. My mind was predisposed to play tricks on me.

On the other hand, Kyle was a weirdo. (Terrible of me to think this way, but it was true.) He probably thought I was, too. From *my* perspective, it was weird that he and his dad had matching tattoos and matching first names. It was weird that they had talked about me using my last name. It was weird that Mr. Turner had so many "dirt cheap" phones, one of which they gave to my little sisters. Maybe it was a case of Loving Thy Neighbor. Amir would say that if he were here right now. Maybe my problem with this little late-night delivery was that it wasn't so much weird as creepy. And yes, I fully realize this all happened while I was watching *SVU,* but still. There were real *shayateen*—evil spirits—out there.

Maybe I was paranoid. Fine. I'd be happy to prove myself paranoid—in a rational and detached way, now, on my own. There was nothing wrong with learning more about my neighbors. Nothing unethical. Plenty of information was out there for the taking. Once I found out what I needed to know, I'd be able to sleep.

I opened my laptop and dove in.

Within two minutes, I'd strategically narrowed my search. Kyle Turner and Katherine Turner were common names, obviously. But I knew my way around keywords and metadata (eye color, truck model, address, profession; the list goes on) enough to zero in on my neighbors—even on the clunky national, state, and municipal databases, which almost never get updated. Over and over, I came up empty. Apparently I was paranoid. The Turners had left almost no digital footprint. Well, nothing bad, anyway. No police records. No lawsuits or restraining orders. Not even a speeding ticket. Aside from Mr. Turner's profile on the electric company's website (full of rave reviews about his friendliness and skill), the biggest hits came from a 2012 article via Portland, Oregon. The Turners were living there at the time. Mrs. Turner had won a charity bake-off.

Now *I* felt creepy. They were model citizens.

So why was the voice in my head still whispering? Why was I so convinced that something was off with these people? I was probably insane. But to prove I was insane—if I wanted to be absolutely, 100 percent sure—I knew what I could do. I could break my promise to myself. I could hijack their router, just as I'd hijacked the Muhammad family's router. It would be simple. Fast. Definitive. A peek at their search histories and personal data.

If wrong, I'd wipe all their information clean from my mind. I prayed I *was* wrong. But this one quick shady act would allow me to wear a white hat from here on out. . . .

Or so I told myself.

My fingers had already moved to the keyboard, one step ahead of my ethics.

Unfortunately, Mr. Turner's security appeared to be more sophisticated than Dr. Muhammad Muhammad's. After three different kinds of attempts, I still couldn't gain access. I'd been wearing the black hat for over twenty minutes now, much longer than I'd wanted. And I was grumpy, which wasn't exactly optimal for getting into the hacking zone. I was losing focus. Getting sloppy. I was probably forgetting one simple crucial step. . . .

Pulaski88 would know. I'd been fishing for an excuse to catch up with him anyway. I also knew better than to leave my own digital footprint by taking the same path more than twice—so I switched to a different overlay network, 12P, and logged on to his forum anonymously.

**Me: It's Jack's cold sweat. Jack's smirking revenge. Looking for Pulaski88.**

No response.

I waited and waited, the cursor blinking in empty space. A minute passed, then two . . .

**Pulaski88:** Thought you were Jack's colon.

**Me:** Ha ha. Good one. Need advice.

**Pulaski88:** Sorry. About to shut this baby down. Too much heat. Gotta go.

For a second, I wondered if he was joking. Or drunk. He sounded as if he were trying to imitate an old cop show from the 1970s. I typed "???" but as soon as I hit the return, the screen turned gray.

A message flashed:

**Can't open the page www.goldenrulehackers.onion because the server can't find www.goldenrulehackers.onion.**

*No shit.* Fine, so be it. Pulaski88 had disappeared into the black hole of the Dark Web. Par for the course. It wasn't as if we were friends. He wasn't "my boy." I still felt hurt, though. This was the part of internet-only relationships Amir was much better at navigating. I knew from cyberstalking him that he could just let people come and go. Then again, many of his friends came from war zones. Their reasons for disappearing had nothing to do with anything illegal, other than to form a community. . . .

So what now?

Time for Plan B: legal, but pricey. I'd go to BeenVerified, the nosy citizen's public records aggregator of choice. I was already sneaking upstairs to the kitchen. There, I slipped into

Mom's purse and snagged her credit card. Was it worse than hacking? Yes. It was stealing from my mother. Nothing ethical about it. But I couldn't let it go at this point. I wanted results and I wanted them now.

Back downstairs—twenty-six dollars and eighty-nine cents later—profiles of Kyle Turner Sr. and Katherine Turner emerged. Again, most of the data was benign. They had two mortgages, one in Virginia and another in Oregon. Boring. *Too* boring. I already knew they had zero social media presence. Even Grandma Thiede had signed up for a Facebook account. Their only subscriptions consisted of three magazines: *Taste of Home, Canine Companion,* and *Occident Rise.*

The last one didn't even have a website. Print only. Okay, *that* was weird. Subjectively.

I vaguely remembered the term *Occident* from my Western Civ class, so I Googled it.

The countries of the West, especially America and Europe.

My pulse picked up a beat. I quickly found a PDF of the most recent issue.

There, in barely legible type, I found a link to a blog: occidentrisewife@wordpress. It belonged to "Debbie," a nurse turned stay-at-home Army wife. Bare bones. No frills. I couldn't decipher a lot of it (too many acronyms), but from what I could gather she'd started the blog to celebrate. A superior officer in her husband's unit was recently discharged OTH. I looked that up, too.

Other Than Honorable.

I didn't need to read any more.

The superior officer's name was Kyle Turner. Only then did I realize that I *had* been sloppy. Not in my coding, but in my searching. I hadn't noticed a glaring absence. There wasn't a single record online of Mr. Turner's having ever served in the United States military.

# 14

"AMIR?" I SHOUTED into the phone. "Can you hear me?"

"Yeah, are you okay?"

His voice was barely audible over the music pumping in the background. It would have been funny if I weren't so frightened. Here I was, alone in my room in the middle of the night, and my boyfriend was . . . out. Having fun. I suppose I should be relieved that one of us was enjoying life? At least he'd answered my call.

"Not really," I told him. "Where are you? I need—"

"Wait one second!" he shouted. I could tell by the jostling in my ear he'd started running. The crowd noise faded. "Hey, you still there, Salma?" His voice got clearer. "Sorry," he gasped, out of breath. "I'm at the Black Box with Mr. Epstein."

"Oh." The word stuck in my throat. My room suddenly felt very quiet and lonely. The computer screen had gone dark; the desk lamp was the only source of light. I wondered if Amir's parents were aware he'd gone out. Probably. Mr. Epstein was a favorite and trusted teacher, after all, and Amir would never sneak around behind his parents' backs anyway. My parents? They would have insisted on chaperoning—if they would agree to let me go in the first place, which they wouldn't.

"But isn't your show tomorrow evening?" I asked.

"He just wanted me to get a feel for the room before we play. You know, the acoustics. It's really cool . . . I'll tell you later." He was speaking faster than usual. "What's up? It's late. Are you okay?"

"Not really, because I found out that Kyle Turner's dad was discharged dishonorably from the Army, and that he's managed to scrub this information from the internet." My words also tumbled out in a breathless rush. "And believe me, that's hard to pull off. Takes considerable skill and/or a whole lot of money."

Amir was quiet. My mind flashed back to Mr. Fancy and that briefcase. "Amir?"

All I could hear was the muffled sound of drums and a fuzzy, indistinct bass line. "How did you find out?" he asked.

"Do you really want to know?"

"Salma, you need to be careful, please—"

"I'm always careful."

"Listen, let's talk about this tomorrow, okay? Mr. Turner could have been discharged for all kinds of reasons. Maybe he was a conscientious objector. Maybe he got a DUI."

"He has no record of *anything,*" I protested.

"Maybe the power company wouldn't hire him if he did!" Amir exclaimed. "Maybe that's why he scrubbed it."

I tried to think of a smart response. I heard a toilet flush. "Gross. Are you—?"

"No, that's someone else." He lowered his voice. "The bathroom is the quietest place here."

I managed a tired laugh. "You think I'm crazy, don't you? Go back and have fun."

Amir sighed. "I don't think you're crazy, Salma. But right now, considering where I am, I have to say . . . it's *a very strange time in my life.*"

Ugh. If Amir was referencing *Fight Club* right now, he was obviously trying to rein me in.

"Time for some new material there, Tyler Durden," I muttered, but I was softening a bit. Maybe I *was* crazy. I was just about to ask him something else when the connection suddenly failed. I tried him again; the call went straight to VM.

Probably for the best. I'd ranted plenty for one night.

Debbie from *OCCIDENT RISE* had zero interest in being contacted, as she'd made that abundantly clear in her most recent blog post.

Dear friends: We are moving to an undisclosed location so I can be closer to the hospice. Rick's condition has worsened. He remains a medical mystery. I can't help but wonder if it is all related. Mr. Twelfth Star is capable of anything. This 7J business he was preaching was over the top. He had no business proselytizing to his unit. And even though he may be a seditious bastard, he isn't stupid. Either way, I have neither time nor energy to keep track of him. I just can't. The kids and Rick need me. I need me. Please respect our privacy. Don't try to reach out. Uphold the Oath. It's all that matters. We pray you take no part in what's to come, for God and Country.

Army Strong,

Debbie

I felt sorry for her. And even though I had no idea what she was referring to, I empathized. Her life was unraveling at the seams; one more tug and it could fall apart. I was starting to imagine how that felt. I raised my hands and closed my eyes: *Protect her, strengthen her, hear her prayers—Ameen.* Then I clicked on the word "Oath," highlighted in gold. It was hyperlinked to an external website, an official site of the U.S. military, featuring an American flag blowing in the header: *The call of duty is a call to support and defend the Constitution of the United States against all enemies, foreign and domestic.*

I wondered how someone like her could get mixed up with someone like Mr. Turner. Yes, she was a patriot. Yes, her husband deserved thanks for his service. Still, there were hints—some subtle, some not—that Debbie also had some views in common with the Confederate flag promoters at the Daughters of the American Revolution.

Above all, the source: *Occident Rising.*

*Occident* is code for "the West." Code, like the word *heritage* . . . another dog whistle, a noble euphemism for what motivated bigots like Barbie and the Bot.

I back-clicked to Debbie's blog.

Several terms leapt out: *undisclosed location, all related, 7J, seditious bastard, Twelfth Star,* and most ominous of all, *what's to come.*

I reached for a sticky pad and jotted down anything that seemed pertinent. I circled the word *seditious* and drew a line to Mr. Turner's name. Of all the tenuous possible connections, it seemed to be the only one that might make sense, at least directly. An act of sedition—"incitement of discontent or rebellion against a government"—would certainly get someone an Other Than Honorable discharge from the U.S. military. Sedition might have even prompted his higher-ups to disavow him completely, which could mean *they* were the ones who'd scrubbed his service from the web.

So was "Mr. Twelfth Star" an alias of his? It had to be, right? He was Rick's superior officer.

I entered *12th star* into SurfWax, a hacker's search engine. My stomach squeezed as the screen spat back the results. Maybe I should have been more surprised. But the sickening picture had already begun to form. A dark chasm of online hatred opened up before me, and down I tumbled.

As a Muslim living in Virginia, as the oldest sister of three, I'd kept an eye out for hate groups. So I'd been here before, seen how the rabbit hole veers off in a million directions—a grotesquely diverse underworld whose only unifying principle is a hatred of diversity. There are religious fundamentalists, Western triumphalist renegades, gun aficionados, hardcore KKK, softcore robe-free Klan "realists" . . . and the just-plain-freakish, like the manosphere of Nordic-style pagans. Oh, and the Doomers. I bugged out a little on them, especially their stockpiling recommendations. What if the proverbial shit *did* hit the fan, and World War III decimated civilization? The Bakkioui family would be screwed. We had nothing from their DIY prep lists in our basement: no gold bars, or spirulina, or gas masks, or camping gear, or high-powered weapons. We might as well prepare our white flag of surrender now. White would certainly go over better than any other color. . . .

*Focus. Focus.*

I resisted the urge to slap my own face, even though I needed to. My EDS-related caffeine-like midnight boost had already receded. My body was exhausted.

But my mind—

I couldn't let go of the fact that I still needed to figure out elements of Debbie's last post, those key words that told me what I wanted to know about the Turners but still meant nothing to me. What was this Twelver stuff? And 7J? I was puzzled.

And intrigued. Obsessed. I couldn't let it go. No way was I falling asleep.


Nearing one o'clock, I stumbled into a chatroom called "Domain of the Twelve Generals."

The page was encrypted in a way I'd never encountered before. Once again I cursed Pulaski88. Couldn't he have waited one more night to "shut this baby down"? He would have known a backdoor. But now I was at a dead end. It mocked me; the box in the middle was a royal F-you. *Username and password? Go ahead and try,* it seemed to snicker. Bound to be a futile endeavor. Types like this are too clever and obsessive. They change passwords with OCD frequency. But they're also arrogant. And frustration aside, that was something I could usually bank on. I grabbed my pen and studied the page with a naked eye, hoping to discern a pattern.

A few sequences grabbed my attention. I jotted them down:

*G 1:28, I 2:2, 48764, 1493*

I froze on the last one, tracing the sequence with my ballpoint pen. I felt sick. 1493: the number Mr. Turner and Kyle had etched into their forearms. I kept scrolling. Several visitors had left messages in the open comment section. Some were annoyed, complaining that they lacked access. Others bemoaned that their passwords were no longer valid. At the bottom, I stumbled on the lone conversation thread, where: *bingo.* The number-letter combo *7J* immediately jumped out.

FallenSheClimber * 9 days ago
7J Survivors: Get out while you can. Inside 43ers, heed my warning: The 12 Apostles are false, the doctrines warped. GET OUT.

PatriotAmerican * 8 days ago
Fuck you, snowflake.

Evola14 * 5 days ago
Stop distracting us from the real enemies: weak whites, Muslims, BLM

Odin'sAXE * 3 days go
Jump off a cliff, bitch.

FallenSheClimber * 3 days ago
I'm a masterless, fearless, Christian Ronin and I won't take orders. You're a Nazi.

Odin'sAXE * 3 days ago
As much as I need to be. And proud of it. *Sieg Heil!*

The thread continued like that, on and on . . . *ad nauseam* to *ad nazium*.

I sipped my water and rubbed my eyes. FallenSheClimber's last post was only five minute ago. I glanced at the clock on my menu bar: 1:13 a.m. Not *that* late. Maybe she was still online.

I left a comment for her: *On your side, Christian Ronin,* with a plea to DM me on one of my anonymous Twitter accounts. *Urgent and want to talk.* I switched screens and waited. A minute later, I got a new follower: @fallensheclimber. I followed her. Ten seconds after that, the DM appeared.

thx for reaching out. r u free to skype?

Whoa. Hadn't expected that. It was sort of a crazy move. Most wouldn't Skype with a total stranger. I took another sip of water. I was definitely curious. Besides, what could she do? Reach through the screen and ring my neck? Track me through my triple VPN? Yeah, right. I agreed and gave her the info, my heart beating a little faster as I waited.

It froze when FallenSheClimber appeared on my laptop screen.

She was lighting a cigarette, focused on the flame. Her hair had been dyed black, cut short, spiky and messy. Though stripped of her makeup, without a doubt it was Kate Turner.

My neighbor. The woman who'd brought my sisters home. The woman who'd devoted herself to bringing her husband lunch, to the point where she'd allowed her semi-disabled teenage Muslim neighbor to walk her dog. . . .

In a panic I slapped a sticky note over my camera. The

little square in the corner of my screen went black. This was bad. She knew exactly where I lived.

I held my breath as she inhaled and exhaled a cloud of smoke, then blinked. "Check your connection," she whispered. "I can't see you."

"Yeah, I'm trying to fix it," I lied. "Sorry. The video cuts out sometimes. . . ." I knew I couldn't stall forever or else she'd get suspicious. She seemed even more frightened than I was. Her hands were shaking; her big, dark eyes kept darting over her shoulders. From the little I could see, waist up, she was wearing a white nightgown. Or evening wear? It was sleeveless, billowy. A far cry from her usual mom-look. Instead of being a dove perched in a nest, she looked like an exotic bird trapped in a cage, the kind that plucks all its feathers out. A lit cigarette dangled from the corner of her mouth. She even had a tattoo. Also not mom-ish. It was bizarre, almost reminded me of a QR code. The skin around it was still pink and puffy from the ink. . . .

"Are you there?" she asked urgently. "What's going on?"

I was about to hang up when I took another hard look at her. She looked emotionally battered. Something inside told me I should go on, hear her out. I yanked off the sticky note.

She gasped, her eyes widening.

"Oh my God . . . Salma! Sweetie, what are you doing here?"

"You didn't know it was me?" I shot back, trying to keep my voice even.

"No!" She shook her head and abruptly stubbed out her cigarette. "I'm just as surprised as you. I swear it, on all that is holy, or all that's left." Her voice cracked. Tears welled in her eyes, and her mascara started to run. *My God,* she wasn't just broken. She was desperate.

"Tell me what's going on," I whispered. "Maybe I can help?"

She sniffed. "You're a sweetheart, darling. But no. I'm about to get dressed and get out of town. Tonight. Finally leaving him. But not before I stop them. Not before I convince my—"

Getting out of town? They just moved here. "Wait, stop who? Mr. Turner?"

After wiping her eyes, she reached for her cigarette and tried to take a drag before remembering she'd put it out. Her eyes flicked away from the camera. They narrowed, as if she were reading something—no doubt a second window open on her screen. She blinked and drew a shaky breath.

"I want to help you, Salma," she hissed. "I do. But you need to get offline. Now—"

"Just wait. Mrs. Turner, Kate, please. What does *fourteen ninety-three* mean?"

With another glance over her shoulder, she leaned close to the camera. "The Ninety-Three-ers, the Twelve Generals, Twelfth Star, and now Seven Jewels. All code for the same thing." She spoke in a rapid whisper. "*Inter Caetera* . . . *limpieza de sangre.* It's their motto, their holy writ. To unite church and state, as intended. Look it up. *Inter Caetera.* C-A-E-T. But do it from a secure location. Not your house. You understand?"

I nodded, even though I couldn't comprehend a single word. It sounded like gibberish.

"They say we've been at war for five hundred years," she went on. "They *say* . . . for America. It's for the land. For the white patriarchy, as handed to them by God. They've sworn to destroy anything or anyone who keeps them from it. All in the 'name of Christ.'" Her lips twisted in anger. "Liars. All lies. They're blasphemers. But they believe it, and that makes it real enough. And they're smart. They keep rebranding themselves. They brainwashed a lot of us who believed in the Seven Jewels, including me. Until they wanted me to . . ." Her voice caught. She shook her head and leaned back from the lens, reaching for her cigarette. "But I won't. They're wrong. People who aren't like us aren't evil; they aren't even all that diff—" She coughed, then sucked in a deep breath. "I'm tired, Salma. Done. The spell is broken."

She was rambling, but I didn't want her to stop. The more she spoke, the closer I would get to the truth. *The spell?*

Mrs. Turner was crying now, her body shaking with silent sobs. I didn't press her as she relit her cigarette. I wanted her as calm as possible. But before I could say another word—to console her, encourage her, to question her about "Seven Jewels"—there was a loud rattle on her end, like she was sitting in a locked room and someone was trying to get in. She spun around in a puff of smoke.

"Shit," she hissed, her back to the camera. "Get offline, Salma. Now!"

She dropped her cigarette into the ashtray and leapt from her chair without bothering to close her laptop. The session was still live. All I could see was her empty chair. I should have heeded her advice, but I couldn't. I was frozen in horror. I stared at the chair, straining to listen as she opened the door and began arguing with someone.

"No," she was saying. "Enough is enough."

Footsteps cut her off. The audio suddenly dropped. The

connection popped and started to fail, noise rushing in and out . . . nothing discernible beyond a distant scream and a thud. The screen flickered; blackness filled the empty chair.

It took me a split second to recognize that the blackness was fabric. Matching jeans and a T-shirt. Without hesitation I slapped the sticky note over my camera once again and held it there with damp fingers.

A man in a ski mask now sat at Mrs. Turner's laptop.

He stared back at me. Staring, but not seeing. He had blue eyes, arms the color of chalk. Neither of us spoke. As abruptly as he appeared, he vanished, the screen blank and connection lost.

# 15

IF AMIR HADN'T texted me first, I could have stayed in the basement until dawn. My knee had healed, but I was immobilized. Both knees had turned to liquid. I'd been sitting in silence like this . . . for how long? Poised to jump, my right hand on the cold metal of the closed laptop, my left on the plastic switch that shut off my lamp. In the inky darkness, time stopped. I could only see that ski mask—those eyes—until a sudden glow from my desk shattered the vision. Who was he? I doubt it was Mr. Turner. Who wears a ski mask in their own home?

I jerked. My phone vibrated beside my laptop. 1:23 a.m. There was Amir's face.

> Just leaving Black Box! Fun night but worried about u.
> R u awake?

I snatched it up and, hands shaking, I replied:

> Don't go home. Meet me at PC Galaxy in 30 min.
> Real life 911.

He texted back immediately:

On my way.

I took several deep breaths and forced myself to stand. Okay. This was happening. *This is happening.* Should I call the police first? Should I tell them to meet Amir and me at PC Galaxy? I'd been on autopilot, with only the vague notion to show Amir what I'd discovered about the Turners—in a safe place, away from my home and family.

Then it occurred to me: What *could* I tell the police, anyway?

*"Good morning, Arlington Law Enforcement. So, after I met with some of your ruder employees, I overheard Kyle Turner, my new neighbor, call me by my last name. Then I saw him unloading some heavy sacks into his home with his dad. Also named Kyle Turner, who fixed my boyfriend's power outage. Then I ended up discovering that the mom of the household is also a rogue defector and is clearly very scared of her family and was possibly just kidnapped in her own home by a man in a ski mask."*

I could picture how well that would go over with those "ruder employees," Detective Tim and the Silent One. It also left the question of how safe I was at the moment. Or how safe the police would make me. Those cold blue eyes behind the ski mask didn't belong to some school bully or grown-up idiot bigot. They weren't the eyes of an amateur.

I needed to get the hell out of here. Now. Not just for me, for Amir. I grabbed a hoodie from my laundry bin and tiptoed upstairs, and out the back kitchen door, grabbing Dad's keys on my way out.

Outside, the night was warm and breezy . . . just right.

Normally, I loved this time of year. It felt like summer, like fun times with Mariam. Glancing up, I could see there were only a few stars sprinkled across the hazy sky, grains of sand shaken off after a day at the beach. I tore my eyes away and opened the door to the garage. A part of me felt awful about taking Dad's new Chevy Bolt. Then again, the minivan was old, and I didn't want its clunky engine waking up my family.

I got in the driver's seat, shifted it closer to the wheel, and started the engine, grateful that I had injured my left knee and not my right. It was weird, though, sitting behind the wheel of a car when I've barely driven one. Oh well, now was not the time for self-doubt. Now was the time for answers. I pressed the garage door opener and closed my eyes. The part-squeaking, part-rumbling sound was something I had never paid attention to. Would it wake up my family? Door open, I pulled forward just enough to see if any lights had been turned on inside my home.

Nope. The house was pitch black.

Onward.


Ten minutes later I was pulling up to Arlington's one and only twenty-four-hour internet café—actually more of a home for insomniac gamers than a true café. I locked the car and flipped my hoodie over my head as I dashed under the security camera at the front entrance. I also checked my phone.

One forty-nine in the morning.

No word from Amir. He was driving, though, so he wouldn't text.

I pushed open the glass door smudged with a thousand grubby hands, remembering why I hated this place. It was a dark, smelly hole-in-the-wall. I slapped two dollars on the front desk. The clerk waved me in. He didn't even ask to see my ID; he was too busy gaming (I assumed). My head down, I made my way past a rowdy gang of drunken college students and settled down at a desktop in a shadowy corner. I could barely see the keyboard—probably for the best. I doubt it had been sanitized since this place had opened.

My first fear was quickly confirmed.

When I logged onto Skype, Mrs. Turner, aka FallenShe-Climber, was no longer active. I returned to the encrypted page where we first met. It, too, had vanished. I knew there was no point dwelling on the loss. Our conversation was gone forever unless I was magically given the time or the wallet to track down digital crumbs. I glanced around, my eyes adjusting. There was a bigger late-night crowd than I'd first realized. That was good; Amir and I would be safe here. Not so good: all were middle-aged white dudes, some balding, some skinny, most with beer guts bulging over their waists.

One of them winked at me. Gross. I texted Amir:

> Meet outside.

Pulling my hoodie tight over my head, I hurried back into the Bolt and locked the doors. I waited and waited, checking my phone and the street a gazillion times for Amir's arrival even though I wasn't sure what we'd do after that. I just knew I had to do something. Talk to someone I trusted. Maybe even go to his house and use his computer. Maybe Mona, the big sister I always wanted, would have ideas, advice, something.

I glanced at my cell. It was 2:03.

Where the hell was Amir?

The boulevard was deserted. There couldn't be bad traffic coming from DC. Weirder, he hadn't even read any of my messages. He always checked his phone at red lights; he knew it was an emergency. I punched his number and pressed the phone to my ear, scouring the night for the Jetta. The call went straight to voicemail. I chewed my lip. My injured knee and head throbbed with EDS, the symptoms fueled by exhaustion and anxiety. *All work is easy work,* I reminded myself, and hating myself for it. *Everything I want is on the other side of that pain.* I sent him another text:

> New plan. Meet at ur house.

Something was very wrong.

I had a sense of it about a half mile from Amir's house, beginning with the faraway sirens. They grew louder as I drew closer—and then: silence. A minute later, two unmarked black sedans sped past me, headlights off. They roared back-to-back through a stop sign, headed toward Amir's neighborhood. I drove faster, following just behind. A block away I caught the first glimpses of flashing lights through the trees. But nothing could prepare me for what I saw when I rounded the corner.

The street had been blocked off with police cars. An armored truck was parked in front of Amir's house. Spotlights were trained on the windows; the sidewalk and yard were crawling with men. Definitely *men.* There were no Olivia Bensons or Wonder Women. Only men . . . in cop uniforms, in business suits, in bulletproof vests, in tactical gear complete with assault rifles.

My brain seemed to shut down. I was no longer in control. I hit the brakes, pulling off to the side of the road, wondering if I should leave the car running. It was quiet, barely audible. Even so, I felt nervous. Like I should hide. My chest felt as if it were locked in an iron vise. My fingers and toes tingled. My head spun. I was hyperventilating. Not good. *Get it together, Salma.* I reclined the seat and opened the sunroof. I needed air. I gazed at the faint stars, gasping for breath. Strange how earlier they'd reminded me of a day at the beach. Now the whole of the night sky was quicksand, suffocating me.

*What happened, Amir? What is this? If—*

A blinding glare silenced the voice in my head.

The light was so bright it hurt. Physically. I covered my face with my hands, fighting back terror. When I peeked through my fingers, I held my breath. Silhouettes were approaching. I could hear their boots on the pavement. My stomach plummeted.

A loudspeaker crackled and whistled with feedback, followed by the sharp command: *"Do not move. Hands on the wheel!"*

I did as I was told. My eyes remained closed. My entire body was trembling.

All of a sudden there was a knock on the driver's-side window. *Shit,* I thought. *They said hands on the wheel. What now? Am I allowed to take a hand off to push the window button?*

Tap. Tap.

I slowly lifted my left hand and pressed the button. The window slid down. Even though my eyes were closed, I could sense the presence of a light. A flashlight. A familiar voice filled the air. "Well, hello, Salma. Just the girl I was hoping to see."

I allowed my eyelids to flutter open. *Detective Tim.* Of

course: I'd thought of him earlier, and my sudden shitshow reality had conjured him up, as if by magic. I thought of the star. *Be my strength, be my strength.* Then I forced myself to return his smarmy smile. Better to focus on his face than the armed men forming a semicircle around the car. He was dressed in the same rumpled suit he'd worn to Franklin, his tie loosened. If he had a gun, I couldn't see it. He hunched down, draping one arm over the door.

"Where's Amir Ammouri?" he asked me.

The question was like a slap.

"He's not here?" I whispered, honestly shocked.

"No, he isn't," Detective Tim said. "Were you planning to meet him?"

My eyes flitted to Amir's house. Every light appeared to be on. "No. I mean yes. As a surprise. I was going to surprise him."

"Really." Detective Tim tilted his head. "At two-thirty a.m.?"

I glared at him. "I'm not the first girl who's ever wanted to surprise a boyfriend late at night, am I?"

He smirked but ignored the question. "Whose car is this?" He reached into his jacket pocket and glanced at his phone.

"My dad's."

"Does he know that you're out with it?"

"Yes," I lied, without hesitating. I glanced back at the Ammouris'. Dark shapes moved behind drawn curtains: people who weren't members of the Ammouri family. Intruders. Bringing chaos to a place of calm.

"So, your parents, they approve of your late-night surprise?" Detective Tim prodded. His tone was friendly now. Casual.

Sweat pooled on my lip. With outrage and fear came a flicker of hope. Maybe it was a blessing, *insh'Allah,* that Amir wasn't home. He might have sensed trouble, as I had. Maybe he'd been wise enough to turn around and find somewhere safe to lay low.

"Miss Bakkioui?"

I began to jabber, without thinking, lies building upon lies. "They do, and so does my grandma Titi. She's a romantic. She didn't approve of how you thought she didn't exist, though. She's convinced my parents to file a lawsuit against your department—"

"That's enough," Detective Tim interrupted. He leaned through the driver's-side window, peering into the darkness of the car. My smile widened. *Go ahead and search, asshole,* I thought, even as I caught a whiff of that aftershave, just as I had at Franklin. It made me want to vomit. . . .

A radio crackled. Detective Tim suddenly withdrew.

There was commotion over at the Ammouris'. The spotlights spun to the front door. Mona stepped out first, and turned. Mr. Ammouri stepped out next, flanked by two blue-uniformed cops. Each wore a bulletproof vest. My stomach twisted. Mr. Ammouri's face was drawn, his shoulders stooped. As I watched him, I felt a pang of recognition. I'd seen that same grim resignation before. I'd seen it on Mrs. Turner's face. Like her, he looked broken.

I wanted to howl at these assholes. *What are you doing? He's a sweet old man! He's practically deaf! His son is missing! Don't you have any humanity?*

Detective Tim leaned over the car.

"Some of these detectives are going to talk to his parents down at the station. . . ."

Amazing. He thought Mona was Amir's mom. Amazing and gross.

"In the meantime, maybe you can help me out," Detective

Tim continued, slipping back into that same off-putting easygoing persona, as if this scenario weren't some surreal horror, but just two people chatting. He began scrolling through his phone with his thumb. "You mentioned that Amir's friends overseas were musicians. . . ." He squinted into the screen. "But I have here in my notes that some—"

"No," I croaked.

He paused and glanced down. "No, what? No, some aren't musicians?"

"No, I'm not going to wait here with you." I gripped the wheel with both hands, my gaze flickering between Detective Tim and Mr. Ammouri as he was hustled into a van. I glanced toward the front door. Mona's path was blocked; she couldn't accompany her own dad.

Detective Tim slapped the hood of the car. "Okay, then. That's fine, Salma. I'd advise you to get some rest. I'll be following up with you and your parents first thing in the morning." Then he slipped me his business card. "In case you hear from Amir," he said.


I knew I'd have to contact my parents at some point. But instead of heading home, I drove back to PC Galaxy. Right now Amir was my only priority. None of my WhatsApp messages were showing up as read. Delivered, yes, but not yet read. And if he wasn't there . . . what next? He might be hiding out with Mr. Epstein. If his night had turned out remotely like mine, then anything was possible.

The parking lot was empty. Fear rose up inside, so I fought the only way I knew how: by focusing on the task at hand. Pining for the Jetta wouldn't help him or me. I took solace in action: parking the Bolt, flipping my hoodie over my head, hurrying inside. The pudgy clerk at the front was still there. Still gaming. I pulled my phone out of my pocket, opened photos, and waved Amir's face in front of him.

"Hey? Have you seen him tonight?"

"Huh?"

"Look at the screen," I snapped.

He shot me a dirty look, his cheeks sagging, but obliged. "No, I haven't," he groaned, annoyed. "Feel free to take a look around."

I tossed another few bucks on the stool. My phone told me it was 2:57 a.m., but my mind was hyperalert and my body seemed unaware of being depleted, as if it had simply abandoned the normal cycle of day and night. I paced the café. No sign of Amir, or anyone else. Deserted, it seemed darker and smellier than before. The stale air reeked of sweat and beer and leftover cigarettes. Smoking was prohibited, of course. I scowled at a beer can. It sat beside the mouse at a desktop, discarded after being used as an ashtray. It made me think of Mrs. Turner, the frantic way she'd put her cigarette aside and picked it back up again. I hadn't even known she was a smoker.

Slumping down at the computer, I couldn't fight the fear or the pining any longer. I willed Amir to reach out. I took a different sort of action: I typed three words into my phone, words I should have said out loud a thousand times.

> I love you.

Delivered, but not read. Would it be enough? Would it carry some unseen weight or magic or *barakah* that could tip the scale? Provide the response I craved, *insha'Allah*?

Seconds later, the two little WhatsApp checks shifted from unread to read—from depressing gray to Morpho blue. My heart leapt. I texted again:

> U there?

Text bubbles loaded and loaded and disappeared. . . . Nothing was delivered.

I gripped the phone. My palms were damp; my hands shook. I typed his name.

> Amir?

The message was stuck in the ether; only half of the process had been completed. One gray tick instead of two. The server had uploaded the data but couldn't download it onto Amir's phone. Which meant, he was . . . offline. Somewhere. With me, but not with me. Gone, just like that. I closed my eyes, trying to breathe again. I was no longer in physical pain, but my spirit was bound in barbed wire. And I'd been here before. Not in this awful place, but *here*. At a computer, fueled by anger, and with tools at my disposal.

Hang on, I typed.

I didn't know when he would receive it, or if it would ever get to him. But I wouldn't worry about it. Tucking my phone away, I sat down, powering on to start with what I knew—which wasn't much. But the most crucial bit of knowledge: Mrs. Turner had warned me I was in danger just before Amir went missing. Clearly we were both in danger. But why and from whom? What did I, Salma B., have to do with Mr. Turner's weird alias, or the stuff about the Seven Jewels and the Twelve Generals and the five-hundred-year war and blasphemy?

*Focus, focus . . .*

Google was the homepage, of course. Perfect place to start. I'd keep my searches simple at first, preferring not to access the Dark Web here. Yes, I was (basically) alone; besides, I'd keep my searches untraceable. Although who knew what surveillance the gamer had rigged up under his not-so-watchful eye? For a moment I closed my eyes, envisioning the Morpho in the garden, focusing on its beauty as I breathed in and out. I reminded myself who I was. I was a hacker. I was methodical. I'd go one step at a time. Maybe I should start with the totally incomprehensible and work backward. There was that Latin word she harped on; what did it mean? Inter-set . . . something. And Columbus.

As I typed, it popped right up on Google: *Inter Caetera.*

Reading the Wikipedia entry on Inter Caetera, a song from kindergarten popped into my head. *Oh, Columbus . . . with the* Nina *and the* Pinta *and the* Santa Maria, *too.* My mind and body might be succumbing to exhaustion after all. Delirium was kicking in. It was relevant, of course; Columbus sailed to America in 1492, and Inter Caetera was a legal document written by Pope Alexander VI right afterward. There was a link to the full document. I read that, too. I had to, if I were to remain rational, detached, methodical. I thought of Olivia Benson, how no clue, no matter how trivial or random, was ever ignored. I was open to any possibility, anything that would lead me to Amir, even a modern-day needle in a medieval haystack.

The language was archaic. The gist was simple enough to understand, though. God and the Church and Europe's royal families—the document put them all on equal footing, above the rest of humanity—were happily bequeathing (the document's word, not mine) all the lands to the "west," aka "the Americas," to Spain's "beloved son": the one and only Columbus. It was their divine right to do so because the nations of the new world were "barbarian" and therefore in need of such a "holy blessing."

I thought of Titi. I knew from her that Berbers loathed being called Berber. It literally means the same exact thing: *barbarian*. The term isn't theirs. It was thrust on them by the same sorts of people. I never took it that seriously or that personally. But sitting here at the computer, reading this grossly arrogant document, I felt the same disgust, the same anger she did. It suddenly and viscerally dawned on me how a single word or label can yield so much power. *Berber. Barbarian. Infidel.* All were weaponized. Connected. And so were these histories.

What else? Mrs. Turner had mentioned the "Ninety-Three-ers." The papal document was written in 1493, the number inked on the Turners' bodies. So it was an identity thing, a little subtler than a swastika, but basically the same message. I knew from tenth-grade AP History that 1493 was the height of the Spanish Inquisition, when Jews and Muslims were given the impossible choice of death, expulsion, or forced conversion. Right around the same time, the Crusades officially came to an end. Or so I remembered from my boring old textbook . . . although a thought dawned on me.

Maybe that book was more outdated than it looked. Maybe it was wrong, period. The Crusades didn't end with the Reconquista. They simply turned in the opposite direction. To the West. Across the ocean to the New World. Home sweet home. Of course: the "five-hundred-year war" for America. The Turners were fighting it. . . . *"They believe it, and that makes it real enough,"* Mrs. Turner had said. Did they want to convert me because I was white and Muslim? Was that it? I ignored the sting in my chest. Just yesterday (*was it only yesterday?*) Amir had tried to convince me to watch *Kingdom of Heaven* . . . had he been trying to tell me something, too? No, of course he hadn't.

I needed to get a grip. My mind was spinning out of control and that damn Columbus song was still playing. A continuous eerie loop, in the back of my head. I couldn't get it out. I felt ashamed that it was still there. Ashamed and pissed. Was it lodged in the brains of Yasmin and Hala? Were we all equally conditioned, state-educated sponges? Singing about one of the worst genocides in history as if it were all rainbows and butterflies?

*Um . . . hello? Salma B.? You have no idea where your missing boyfriend is.*

Onward.

I held my breath, and suddenly realized my phone was buzzing. I yanked it out of my pocket.

It was just after five and Mom was texting me.

# 16

_____

BY THE TIME I made it back to Mason Terrace, the sun had cracked the horizon, scattering the cover of darkness. The curtains in the bay window were wide open. Mom was pacing back and forth in front of the sofa like she, too, was in need of a savior. There was zero point in trying to sneak in. Mom knew I was out. Her sparse text said as much.

> Come home this instant.

As I pulled into the garage, I noticed that the minivan was gone. I was out for so long Dad was probably out there, losing his mind, looking for me. I parked the car and walked over to the house. A sparrow chirped. The sky brightened. It was tranquil, just another late-spring Sunday morning in Arlington. If only.

Steeling myself for a lecture, I pushed the front door open. I would take it.

Mom stood still. Hala and Yasmin were sprawled on the sofa, half-asleep and half-intertwined. It was Sunday. Why did she pull them out of bed? To make an example of me: Salma, the miscreant? The wild teen who stole the car, probably to liaise with her boyfriend? Salma the haram? Fine. There was nothing to do at this point but tell the truth.

"Thank goodness!" Mom screamed, running to my side. "You're home! Safe and sound."

I stared at her. *Safe and sound? Thank goodness?*

"Mom, I—"

"Girls!" she interrupted, clapping her hands at Hala and Yasmin. "Wake up! We need to get going." She turned around and clasped my arms, looking deeply into my uncomprehending eyes. "I don't care where you were. You can explain it to me later. Right now, Titi is all that matters."

I felt as if I were in some parallel universe. "Why? What's going on?

"Titi had a stroke. Sometime after two in the morning."

At that point, sleep deprivation finally won. My knees buckled. I collapsed—luckily into Titi's favorite chair, the one Grandma Thiede had given her as a welcoming present several years ago. A stroke, a few minutes after I left. Titi must have discovered I'd snuck out.

"But she's okay, right, Mom?"

"It was a minor stroke, according to the doctors," she said, nudging my sisters. "So that's good? She's weak. Very, very weak."

"And Dad?" I asked.

"He's there with her now—"

Just then there was a loud knock. A second, a third, and then dead silence.

Detective Tim, no doubt. I shut my eyes and nervously twisted my ring as Mom hurried to answer. Was he here to continue that conversation? Had Amir been found? Arrested? A thousand questions swirled in my head.

"Oh! Hi." Her voice was high and welcoming. It was someone she knew; not the cops. My eyes popped open. Someone she . . . *Amir?* I rushed to her side—

Mr. Turner stood on our stoop. Hope evaporated. Not only did Mr. Turner look freakishly calm, but he had Drexler, on leash, like he was doing the morning walk. Mr. Turner never walked the dog. Mrs. Turner had made that abundantly clear.

Mr. Turner pulled his attention away from Mom, looked me in the eye, and tightened his smile.

"I saw an ambulance at your house last night. Is everything all right?"

I stared back. The subtext was clear to me, as clear as day. *He did something to Mrs. Turner. He was up and watching my house in the middle of the night. His wife was missing. Amir was missing. He was the missing link.*

"My mother-in-law, she . . ." Mom stopped, almost breaking down in tears. "She had a stroke."

"Oh dear. That is awful," he said, as if he even cared. "I'm so sorry to hear that. Can I do anything?"

"No, thank you," Mom answered. "We are about to go to the hospital."

"All of you?"

Mom nodded.

Mr. Turner's crinkly eyes remained on me. "I've been through these ordeals before, waiting for my fellow vets to recover. I know what a strain it can be. I'm off this morning. Mrs. Turner is at home resting. Why don't you leave the girls with me?"

"No!" I cried.

Mom shot me a disapproving scowl.

I tried to smile. "I mean . . . no thanks. We have two cars.

We're fine. Um, I can watch my sisters, and we're just fine." I reached for the doorknob.

"I think what Salma meant to say is that we thank you for your kindness," Mom grumbled.

Kyle Sr. nodded, a bundle of fake concern. "Of course, I understand. But the offer stands—"

I closed the door on him before he could finish. Ignoring Mom's aghast expression, I bolted the lock and stood on my tiptoes to peek through the six small windows at the top of the door—watching him as he trekked back to his own home. There were lights on in the dining room. Several people were gathered there, engrossed in a conversation. An odd hour to have guests. Someone stood and drew the shades. Someone who was *not* Mrs. Turner. I slumped at the door.

Fortunately, Mom seemed to have given up on me and had started gathering my sisters.

"Let's get to the hospital, girls."


With my sisters resting in the back of the Bolt and Mom intent on getting to the hospital as fast as possible, I reclined my seat and turned toward the window, cupping my phone to continue with my research. Even if Mom knew that I was on it, she would probably assume that I was sending Amir love notes. Let her think that. Let her punish me. None of it mattered now. Only the truth mattered.

After a few more dead ends, I stumbled upon something promising—not to mention ironic, considering I was now under my mother's thumb. She, more than anyone, would appreciate it: a graduate thesis from Academia.edu entitled "The Dangers of Theocratic Politics and the Seven Jewel

Mandate," by Mary Whitaker. Academic jargon aside, the preamble hooked me. Members of the movement had embarked on a modern-day "crusade"—their code for domestic terrorism—against Satan, nonbelievers, and the army of -isms: multiculturalism, liberalism, feminism, secularism. According to Whitaker, they'd been at this for decades, by slowly infiltrating the seven jewels: religion, family, education, media, the arts, business, and government.

Right, thanks, Mary. Now I understood what 7J stood for. Apparently the seventh jewel—that of government, was the most precious. One jewel to rule them all.

Even crazier, they had so-called Prophets who gave orders to a standing army, orders that came from God Almighty.

How convenient. Maybe they could ask God where Amir was.

Unfortunately, I couldn't dig deeper; the site wouldn't allow it. Not one more word. Unless I paid. Mom's credit card wasn't handy. Her hands gripped the wheel, her lips in a tight line.

If Mr. Turner was a general in some wacked-out underground movement, then this was . . . bad. As in dangerous. Maybe the Turners were on the same "Punish a Muslim" vibe as Michelle and Chris. Maybe Michelle and Chris were part of their movement. Or maybe I was paranoid and none of this was real. I mean, so what if the Turners might be a little nutty on the religious side? Crazy people aren't always violent. Sometimes they're just good old crazy. America is a free society. People can believe whatever they want to—that God speaks to them, that God has given them orders, whatever.

I slouched into the seat. This was pathetic. I was pathetic. Nowhere. Nowhere near finding Amir, who was still MIA.

Nowhere near figuring out how the Turners and their mission were related to Amir's disappearance. Besides, my discoveries were so wild and esoteric I had trouble believing them myself. I could see Dora and Boots spoofing my paranoia in one of their video parodies. Maybe even uploading it to—

YouTube.

Why didn't it dawn on me before? Why didn't I check the world's second-largest search engine, also known as the world-wide pulpit, where everything from the sacred to the profane to the middle-of-the-road harmless animal video reached the masses?

Minutes later I stumbled upon a promising channel: "RealGenerals93."

I patted my pocket. Good. Earbuds. I slipped them on and clicked play so Mom couldn't hear. The top link featured a flabby man in a ski mask, no shirt, holding an assault rifle. Charming. He had a ghoul-white chest. Could he be the same guy I'd seen? I clicked Play, mostly to see if he had blue eyes. The video began with a close-up of a woman; she was pretty and fair, almost like a younger Kate Turner. She sat on a grassy lawn, like those real estate sites. As the camera zoomed out, ominous music kicked in: "There are truths we'd rather ignore, choices we'd rather avoid," a deep voice intoned. "Neither is an option. We, the white tribes of the West, have seen our countries wounded by ghettos, migrating hordes, and internal parasites. By breeding communities that fail or refuse to integrate."

I blinked. For a second the screen was dark. Then a string of light appeared, highlighting Europe and North America. The lights flickered. Some faded. Others burned. The Earth cracked. The special effects were cheesy. But the low production value aside, they were no less chilling.

"Evil thrives if we do nothing."

Another fade to darkness, and the pretty lady reappeared: anxious, stricken. In need of a savior?


I was the last family member to enter the partitioned little area in the ICU: section 43C. The reports I'd heard from my family were consistent, at least: Titi was sound asleep and needed her rest. The nurse who'd escorted us from the waiting room confirmed them. She was competent, a professional—she wore scrubs and carried a clipboard. Not to mention that she was the one who'd advised us to go in slowly and quietly in case Titi was still sleeping. Mom went in first with Hala and Yasmin. I waited in the hallway for a second, bracing myself. I desperately wanted to hug Titi but was still gripped by the all-consuming fear that her being here was 100 percent my fault. I twisted my ring.

"Don't worry, darling," the nurse whispered. "Your granny is strong. I saw it in her eyes. She's going to be home in a few more days, you'll see." She slipped her pen over her plastic ID card, dangling from a chain. Lower-self Salma found her annoyingly chatty. But then I chastised myself. She was only trying to comfort me.

"Thanks," I said.

Mom and the girls returned to the hallway. Their eyes glistened with tears. "It looks worse than it is, Salma," Mom said. "We're going to get some cocoa in the cafeteria." She glanced at her wrist. "It should be open by now."

I nodded. My throat had clogged, making speech impossible.

"Go on," she said, patting my back. "Your turn."

I entered slowly, pausing before the curtain. I've been on the other side of that curtain many times over, but not like this. Not as a visitor. I was afraid, too. Afraid of what I'd see. Afraid of losing Titi. Because if that happened, I'd—

"Salma, is that you?"

Dad's voice.

"It's okay, pumpkin. Come on in."

I pushed aside the curtain. Dad sat beside the bed, clutching her hand. His face lit up when he saw me, though his cheeks were damp, too. Titi was motionless. A wide ventilator covered her mouth; several more slim tubes and wires connected her tiny, frail body to an assortment of fancy machines, all beeping and pulsing with different rhythms. Her eyes were closed, eyes that could brighten the room with a single wink. Would they ever open again?

Before I knew it, Dad had swept me up in a great big hug.

"Shhhh . . . *Habibti,* it's fine. She's going to be just fine."

I wanted to ban that word—*fine*—from existence. I sniffed, willing myself not to cry (failing), and stepped away from him. "It's all my fault, Dad."

"What?" he said. He wiped a stray tear from my cheek. "Nonsense. This is no one's fault—"

"But it isn't," I interrupted. "You know how Titi wakes up sometimes for *tahajjud* and prays over our beds?"

"I know, yes," said Dad, his puzzled eyes searching my face.

"I—wasn't there," I stammered. "I snuck out, Dad, to meet Amir," I finally blurted, avoiding Dad's eyes. "So what if instead of finding me in my bed, she found me missing? After Hala and Yasmin and everything else, it must have given her a shock. . . . But, Dad, Amir never showed."

I finally looked up. I stared into Dad's eyes, expecting him to lose it, to come down hard on me for breaking a gazillion rules. I was about to tell him about the cops, how Mr. Ammouri had been arrested, about everything and anything else when Dad put up his hand, telling me to quiet down.

"Honey, Titi is old. And she's always struggled with high blood pressure. This is not your fault. And about the rest, we'll talk later," he said, kneeling by Titi's side.

She began to stir. She winced, then tossed her head from side to side. She wasn't conscious, though. After a moment, her body relaxed and her breathing became even under the ventilator. Even so, something wasn't right.

"We will talk about this later," he repeated, his voice grave. "The only thing that matters right now is this family. *Your* family," he stressed. He left the room to find the nurse. She immediately came back into the room and checked all the various machines Titi was hooked up to. She turned to my father and smiled. "Don't worry, sir, she's doing just fine. I've adjusted her meds to keep her a little more comfortable."

Just then Mom and the girls entered the room.

"The cafeteria isn't open yet," said Mom.

Still in their pajamas, my sisters looked befuddled, exhausted. So did Mom. A sudden faint light appeared on her face, like she had just remembered something. She reached into her purse and handed a small bag over to Dad. It had gold writing on it, in Arabic.

"You remembered?" he said.

She nodded. "Of course."

I didn't recognize the bag until Dad opened it up, revealing a small jug. It contained Zamzam water, holy water from the well in Mecca. Mom and Dad had saved it from their long-ago hajj trip. "Good," he said. "Let's say a prayer, shall we?"

"But . . ." My voice petered out. Dad motioned us to step closer.

My sisters huddled around me. We stood over Titi. I felt as if I'd suddenly split in half, as if two entities were now watching each other—Salma Detached and Salma Dihya—wary and at odds. Present and absent. Part of me missing, alongside Amir.

My father recited a Shadhiliyya prayer. The rest of us followed his lead through the Quranic verses. He ended by passing around the sacred water from Mecca, sprinkling some over Titi.

Only then did I feel present. And even though Titi was totally out, something was different. It was too subtle to touch, but too real to miss. And it wasn't my head voice or my delusions or my weariness. To this day, I'll swear it: She looked more peaceful. Our love and the *barakah*-fied water had brought her joy.


It soon became apparent that neither of my sisters was going to last another minute. Everyone needed sleep. Mom and Dad switched car keys so Dad could have his Bolt back, then we said goodbye and headed home. Dad stayed behind, by Titi's side.

Mom was quiet the entire ride. She only spoke once, at the entrance to Mason Terrace. "Someday soon we'll discuss what you were doing last night. But now is not the time. I need to sleep. Your sisters need to sleep." She pulled the car into our driveway and glanced back at my sisters. "Can you get Hala while I get Yasmin?"

I nodded and did as told. Once the girls were in bed, Mom collapsed onto hers, leaving me to myself. I grabbed Thomas and headed to my basement cave.

After lying in my bed for a while, I realized I had entered that hinterland where exhaustion and restlessness are one and the same. My heart squeezed for Titi. It ached for Amir. And every time I closed my eyes, the man in the ski mask glared back at me, reminding me of that YouTube video and Earth imploding and Kate Turner's tears and Debbie's scary-ass warning about "what's to come." It was too much. Sleep was unreachable.

And then came Dad's photo texts, three in a row, all Titi in bed. Awake. Giving a thumbs-up. Waving. By the fourth text, the doctors had successfully removed her breathing tube. She was up and smiling, her entire arm wrapped around Dad. I quickly snapped a selfie in return—with Thom, using his big ears to hide my face. I didn't want her to see me . . . like this. For the first time in a long while, I truly wanted to bring her joy.

The exchange did the trick, at least. I was able to close my eyes and finally conk out.

# 17

SOMETHING WAS BUZZING in my bed. It took several bleary-eyed seconds to understand that it was my phone, lost between the sheets. I was groggy, in a stupor. My eyelids started to close. The melatonin Mom forced me to take last night because I was so anxious was doing a number on me.

Again. My phone buzzed.

Its soft glare was too bright in the darkness of my room, so I snatched it up and squinted at the screen: 5:02 a.m. All I wanted was to throw the soul-sucker against the wall, smash the thing into a gazillion pieces. That and to wake up to a different world—one in which everything that had transpired over the last twenty-four hours was nothing but a bad dream, like my sisters' favorite movie, *Freaky Friday*. What day was it, anyway? I remembered coming home and crashing. I remembered Mom waking me up and forcing me to have dinner, then taking a hard look at my gaunt face and forcing me to return to bed. Hence the melatonin. "I can't have you getting run-down, too," she said, tucking me in.

So what day was it now? And where the hell was my sweet Amir?

Phone check: it was Monday, May 19.

I sat up. I had several missed calls from an unknown number and now a text from a second unknown caller. I read the text. It came from a number that made no sense—it was too long to fit on my phone and began with 001971 and ended with eight or so more digits. What was this? I read the cryptic text:

nedruDrelyTmorf.

Now I was wide awake. And I was scared shitless. Who had called me? Who'd texted me? Was it a message from the Mr. Gun-Toting Ski Mask? Was it from one of the Kyles? I kept studying it. It didn't look like encryption. It looked like nonsense. Which might mean that someone who didn't know a thing about coding could have sent it . . . someone, say, like Amir. I squashed the flicker of hope. I forced Salma Detached to take charge. I turned on my bedside lamp and grabbed a pen. Since the message made zero sense at face value, I would try various permutations.

First: backward letter by letter. f-r-o-m-T-y-l-e-r . . . *Holy Sherlock.*

Well, that was easy. In an instant the grouchiness turned to elation. Who else would contact me as Tyler Durden? I wasn't that crazy. Not yet. I pressed the number to call him back, but couldn't. It went straight to a recording, something about how I couldn't dial internationally on my current plan.

*Where are you, my prince?*

I probably shouldn't call Amir back from my cellphone anyway. I copied down the number on my sticky pad and then deleted all traces of it from my phone. After that, I threw the covers aside. Mom and the girls were sound asleep, so I left a note. It was the least I could do for stealing one of their cars again. There was a 7-Eleven just two blocks away. I pulled away in the clunky minivan intent on calling Amir. All consequences on the table.

"A FIGO Orbit, please?"

The clerk looked at me for a long time. He said nothing. I repeated my request, wondering if he had a hearing issue. Or if I had simply spoken too fast. "That one," I said, pointing to the nearest phone. Guess he wasn't used to teenage girls rushing into his store at five a.m. and asking for a burner. I handed over the bulk of the cash Mom and Dad had paid me for babysitting Yasmin and Hala.

A few minutes later I was standing outside. My fingers shook as I punched the digits scrawled on my crumpled Post-it. At long last, I heard a *bzzzt-bzzzt*, then a crackle.

"Hello? Salma?"

A tsunami of joy coursed through my body. "Amir . . . Amir. What's going on? Are you okay? Where are you?"

"I'm in—" I lost the rest. He was barely audible.

"Amir!" I shouted. "Mouth to receiver. I can't hear." I cranked the volume as far as it would go.

"Dubai. I'm in Dubai."

"What?"

"DUBAI."

I'd heard him the first time, actually. Unbelievable. Dubai had stolen my soul sister; now it had stolen my boyfriend. I felt myself sinking—literally: I slid down against 7-Eleven's storefront window and plopped on the dirty sidewalk. Right next to the trash can. Whatever. There was so much I wanted to say, to ask. Instead I started bawling.

"Hey, look . . . I'm okay, really. Please, shhhh," Amir begged. "Don't."

I couldn't help myself. The two people closest to me outside my family had ended up in the same place, halfway around the world. And here I was alone, at the butt crack of dawn, sitting beside a stinking heap of trash. Waiting for the Crusaders to finish their five-hundred-year war for this very land. It was tragic and fitting and symbolic and just plain gross—on all sorts of levels.

"Salma, just look at the sky, please? We can see the same sky, remember?"

*Fine.* I sniffed and looked up. The sun was up now.

He started to hum "No Woman, No Cry." His voice, naturally low and earthy, cracked when he tried to hit the higher notes. Unlike his previous rendition, this was downright awful. I laughed and wiped my eyes. "Okay, okay. I'm here. But I don't get it, Amir. Why didn't you reach out? My world is upside down and Titi's in the hospital and—"

"What? When? Why? What happened?"

"She had a stroke." As I blurted out the words, more tears came streaming down.

"Shh . . . love, it's all right. She'll be all right. Titi's crazy strong. And I did, Salma. I tried to reach out." He stopped, drew in a sharp breath. Like he was about cry.

"Through Epstein," Amir continued. "His house is on the way to the airport. I left him instructions in his mailbox. I tried. Salma, I really did. It was brutal. Leaving without you. But I had to—to keep you safe."

I exhaled. "Okay, go on," I said. "Tell me what happened. I need to hear this."

Amir spoke in a rush. "So I was with Mr. Epstein at the Black Box, right? And literally right after I got off the phone, I practically bumped into Kyle Jr. He was coming into the bathroom as I was leaving. I asked him what he was doing there. He told me he loved the band Mr. Epstein loved, that Mr. Epstein told him to check them out, too . . . and he was heading home soon, but he acted all surprised that I was there . . . said he didn't see my Jetta. I didn't think much of any of it—not even him sort of following me out of the club after I left, I just thought it was a nervous-white-boy-walking-late-in-DC sort of thing. Anyway, I was on my way to meet you but I needed gas. That's when I realized that Kyle wasn't heading home at all. He was following me. I knew it was him because of the bumper stickers. He parked at the 7-Eleven on Washington Boulevard, next to the Shell station."

My chest tightened. The 7-Eleven on Washington Boulevard was exactly where I happened to be standing at this exact moment. I glanced to my right at the Shell station, envisioning the story as it unfolded on the other end of my burner.

"He was sitting in his truck, window down, talking on the phone," Amir went on. "I decided to go and listen. Your paranoia was starting to rub off on me. So I left my car at the pump and pretended to go inside to the Mini-Mart, then I went out the back and snuck up on him from behind. He was on the phone with his dad. . . . Hang on a minute, it's—here. I wrote it down. Uh, let's see. He was arguing with his dad, reassuring him that he had his eye on me. Asshole. Serves him right that I was hiding behind his truck with my eye on *him*. Anyway, he mentioned you, that you weren't there, something about Podrasky Eight-Eight and a clown. No. A clone. I think. I'm not sure, his truck was insanely loud . . . but Kyle Jr. made it very clear to his father that he had his eyes on the both of us."

Amir kept talking, but I no longer heard him. Podrasky Eight-Eight? That must have been Pulaski88. Suddenly I'd been plunged into a new abyss, another whirlwind of unanswerable questions. How did Kyle know about my Dark Web friend? Not even Amir knew about him. Was Kyle "the heat" that Pulaski88 had mentioned?

"Salma?" Amir asked. "Can you hear me? The line is fuzzy."

"Yeah, sorry—go on. I'm listening."

"Anyway, he said he'd call his dad when I was close to home. But what he said after that, that's when things got really creepy." Amir paused as though he was remembering Kyle's face. I could hear his breathing; it was labored. "He said our last names."

*Our last names.* I stared across the street at the empty gas station. Part of me didn't want to hear any more. My own definition of strange had changed so much these last few weeks that change itself was the only constant. Everything fit into a catchall phrase: *strange and getting stranger.*

"Kyle was straight-up bragging to his dad. 'See how easy it is to pin it on Bakkioui and Ammouri? The third, and this? But first that Ammouri boy. First him. We'll deal with her during phase two.' Then he told his dad not to worry, that he had his sights on me and would leave the package in my car as soon as I got home. He said that last part a few times." Amir paused, catching his breath.

I pulled my knees close to my chest. My head ached with confusion. The third? The bombings? The Turners did that?

217

Amir drew in another long breath. "It was that last part that scared me. So I ran to the Jetta. That's when I finally read all of your WhatsApp messages. I was in the middle of responding to you when my father called. He told me that the cops were there. He was really panicking. And it wasn't just a knee-jerk reaction because he grew up in Syria where everyone fears the cops, especially the *mukhabarat*. . . . No. It was *Ummi*'s work with PANDA."

Amir paused.

I stared at the red and yellow neon lights that lit up the word Shell. I had totally forgotten that Mrs. Ammouri volunteered for PANDA, a nonprofit. When Amir and I first started dating, I thought the organization had something to do with the adorable Asian cuddle bear; turns out it's a civil rights watchdog. The first time my parents met his parents, they had a long discussion about politics, the Japanese American internment camps, and the post-9/11 War on Terror. Apparently our government can label people enemy belligerents and detain them indefinitely, so they could disappear overnight and their families would have no idea where they were. And there were recent laws, based on older precedents, that made this all legal.

A legal hell.

For a second it seemed like the Shell sign was agreeing. The lights behind the *S* were dim and dull. But the last four letters burned bright.

"Oh my God, Amir. Holy shit."

"Yeah, I know. That's when I realized how real this all was and how it was coming to a head that night, that there was more and that I had to get the fuck out. Salma, I had to."

"Yeah, okay, I get that. But . . . you left. Without me.

I've been losing my shit, Amir. Why didn't you do more? You couldn't have done—" My voice started trembling. "I mean, seriously, a letter to Epstein?" My heart flipped with fear and rage and a swell of pain. "A letter, Amir? A *letter*?"

"No . . . Salma, please. I didn't have any options. Yes, I left a letter for Epstein, but I also left instructions for my sister; she was supposed to leave the house and find you. Tell you what was going on in person." His voice stopped. He broke into a full cry. "But then the cops showed up at my house before she could do that. And we both knew that I was phase one. You are phase two. Whatever that means. So she had herself arrested. To buy us both time."

"Yeah, I know. I saw them leading her out. But still. I just—"

"Salma, I had to leave like that. There aren't that many direct flights out of Dulles. I had to GTFO while the window was still open. Besides, I had already gotten lucky once that night—with Kyle not finding my Jetta before the show. The fact that I parked at the farthest lot, the one that costs fifteen bucks instead of twenty-five. It saved me . . . saved me from whatever it was he was going to put in the Jetta, probably something to connect me to the bombings. So he had to follow me. And I got lucky, lucky that I was paranoid, lucky that your paranoia rubbed off on me. But I wasn't going to push my luck. Salma . . . I love you. I had to go like that."

He took in another breath, then kept talking.

"But once I was safe, once I was here in the UAE, texting you was the first thing I did."

The cryptic text: *nedruDrelyTmorf.* He did. And it worked. I guess, in a way, he was right.

I started shaking. My mind was finally putting together all the pieces. The third. The Turners. Pin it on Amir and Salma. Triple fuck shit. My mind shifted gears.

"How did you get out?" I asked Amir. "What were the logistics?"

"Baba. His GTFO paranoia. It finally paid off. He walked me through the plan over the phone, with the cops right there. It was brilliant, Salma. My old man is actually a genius." My heart ticked upward, just a little, thinking of Mr. Ammouri tricking the cops. "He spoke to me in code. He told me that he didn't have time like usual to stop by the ATM—'like usual,' his words—so that I would have to stop by instead. He said that I could pay back Ahmed in person that way."

"What?" I asked, not following.

"He doesn't know how to *use* an ATM, remember? He was telling me to get money!"

"I . . . But who's Ahmed?"

"My boy in Dubai, the one I've been doing oud sessions with for over a year, via Skype," Amir said. "Remember? It was Dad's way of telling me to go to Dubai and stay with Ahmed."

"Oh my God," I gasped. I finally got it. I nodded as if Amir could see me. He was right: it *was* pretty brilliant. I wanted to hug Mr. Ammouri. . . . Sometimes it was so easy to mistake loss of hearing for cluelessness. He wasn't broken at all. He was sharp enough to get his son the "f" out without incriminating himself. Amir was safe. And finally I had someone who believed me. Someone who saw the Turners for who they were. I looked back up to the sky, knowing it was evening to my morning where he was.

"Salma," he continued. "I know you. I know what you're thinking. Stop. This is possible. You can do this."

His words echoed in my ear. Literally. And something cracked. The line was breaking up.

"Salma?"

"Yes?"

"You're in serious danger. Tell your family everything you know and come here. Get to the airport before it's too—"

*Click.*

The morning sun beat down on me.

It was a new day. How would I survive it? Every passing second was more painful than the next. Each brought more unknowns, more uncertainties. I wanted to scream. I didn't want to end the conversation, either. I wanted to tell Amir that I loved him, but that I also loved my home and my country and that love wasn't love unless you went into the ring swinging for it. That this wasn't over. That there was one last move I could try. I pressed redial, but all I got was a pre-recorded message.

Blah, blah, blah, *mughlaq*. The line was dead.

# 18

AMIR WAS RIGHT about one thing: it was time to come clean with my family. I guess it was time to embrace his GTFO plan. Either way, I needed all the help I could get, including theirs.

I scrolled down and called Dad as I finally left the store and walked toward the minivan. Compared to Mom, he was the calm one. When Hala and Yasmin went missing and then returned, she totally flipped on them. He's the opposite in emergency situations—focused. I dialed his cell. He answered on the first ring. "Hello?"

"Hey, Dad . . . it's—"

"Good morning, dear. How are you?" he answered brightly.

I stopped walking, standing in the middle of the nearly empty parking lot.

*How was I?* It was nearly six in the morning and I was calling him from a burner phone—so no caller ID—having snuck out for the second night in a row with his car, and Dad was asking me how I was? I wasn't expecting comatose calm.

"Did you get my text?" he asked, his voice still blasé. Alarm bells rang in my head. Was he speaking in code like Amir's dad? Was someone listening? Was he even still at the hospital? Unsure how to respond, my answer spilled out more like a question. "Um, no . . . hang on a minute." I took out my other phone, the real one, and turned it on.

> Still at hospital. Mr. Ammouri called a few minutes ago. He was just released from the police station. Go home. Mom is waiting. PANDA.

*Go home? Mom is waiting? PANDA?* Did this mean that Dad was on the same page as Amir? That they all wanted me to GTFO before GTFOing wasn't possible? But still, had my life really come to this? Fearing my own government? And my crazy-ass neighbors?

"Dad, um, wait. Are you saying what I think you're saying." My stomach tightened. I wasn't good at this kind of subterfuge.

Dad drew in a sharp breath. What he did next was brilliant. I doubt Northern Virginia cops, even if they were working with the feds and a team of translators, could quickly unjumble the polyglot message he imparted. Hell, even other native Arabic speakers don't understand the languages and dialects of Morocco. Using a mix of Spanish, French, colloquial Arabic, and rarest of all, Riffian, he confirmed my question. YES. GTFOing was a go. A short-term fix for a possible long-term clusterfuck. It was something. The best he could do. "My hands are tied with Titi," he said, basically in tears.

I put one foot in front of another and walked closer to the car. A breeze rustled my hair, carrying with it the sweet scent of pine needles. It was beautiful, surreal. And yet it hurt. I'd never realized that beauty could be so painful to behold. I swallowed the lump in my throat. "Mom's . . . okay with—" I stopped talking, opened the car door, sat down, and locked it. I wanted to ask if Mom was on board with this plan, but I didn't know how to ask that without giving the plan away. I think Dad got me, though. There was a long pause. And a sniffle.

"Yes, Salma. Yes. Please. Listen to your parents. Go home."

His tone stressed the word *go,* but stopped after *home.* That last word barely eked out of him. Home, like the beauty surrounding me, was painful to hear. Stinging my heart like a pine needle. "Okay," I said, finally relenting. "I will."

I got Dad's message. And I didn't want him to spell it out any more. I put the key in the ignition and stirred the minivan to life. Washington Boulevard was also stirring to life. The early go-getters of the world starting their day—a lone jogger, a dog walker, a few commuters waiting for the bus. If my own life had any normalcy, I'd be fighting with my dad about waking for another typical day of high school instead of deciphering coded speech and realizing that my parents wanted me to GTFO of Arlington. I shook my head.

"I'll go home, Dad."

I could hear my father full-on crying. Something I've rarely heard.

"I love you."

"I love you, too, Salma. With all my heart," he said slowly, gravely, and hung up.


As soon as Mason Terrace was within view, I slowed down to five miles per hour and checked the surrounding streets for suspicious vehicles. Nothing. Good. Kept creeping.

But the moment I saw Chez Bakkioui, down at the far end

of the cul-de-sac, I hit the brakes. Tapped them. There's no hitting when you're moving at five miles per hour. But there it was—a cop car, sitting in our driveway. Dad said nothing about the cops being at home. Home was supposed to be safe. I pulled out my phone. No messages. I texted both of my parents. Nothing. What the hell do I do now?

I drove the minivan slowly past the entrance of Mason Terrace and did a U-turn so I could face the house, watch it. I sat there for what felt like an eternity, waiting for instructions. My head was pounding and my stomach flipped like a dying fish. The car suddenly felt claustrophobic. Like everything that was happening outside was putting pressure on it, on me. Like all my fears and paranoia and exhaustion were pressing down on it. I felt like I was going to implode.

Seriously? Had I gotten this far to only get *this far*? Completely and uttered cornered? And why was my hand stinging? I glanced down. My hands were swollen from gripping the wheel so hard that my pinkie ring had cut into my finger. I licked the skin around the ring and gently wound it off. I switched it to my right, glancing at the quote that was engraved on the inside from Mom's favorite poet, Rumi: *Never lose hope, my heart.*

Mom always said it meant more coming from Rumi—someone who lived through multiple wars, the Mongolian invasion, the Crusades, a decade of wandering as a refugee from country to country until he finally settled in the West, or what was west at the time—in Turkey. He knew the worst of pain and loss, and he never gave up. Hence the later part of the quote . . . the part that didn't fit on the ring: *Miracles dwell in the invisible.*

But do they, really? I mean, what was Rumi smoking? Miracles dwell in action. In life saving . . .

Fuck it.

I unbuckled my seatbelt. I wasn't going to sit around waiting. Doing absolutely nothing while my entire world imploded. It was 6:55. Any minute now Kyle would be going to school. If he left with his dad, *ya rab,* let it be, let it be, then that would mean they'd both be gone. Junior for the entire school day, senior off to work. Even if Kyle Sr. did come home, the trip there and back would at the very least buy me a good thirty minutes to snoop around. I'd have the opening I needed. And the woods that wrapped around Mason Terrace, the same woods where my sisters hid, where Mariam and I encountered our make-believe monster, were right there. Right outside my door.

Leaving the minivan with the keys in the ignition and the car off but unlocked in case I needed a quick getaway, I snuck inside the tree line and walked around the back of the cul-de-sac so I could see both the Turner house and my own. As I made my way over, my eyes flashed to my favorite bay window. Detective Tim—Detective McManus, whatever he felt like calling himself—was sitting right there, in my spot, behind the glass. I glanced at my phone. Still no messages from Mom or Dad.

At 7:03, both Kyles exited their house and hopped into their truck. It was parked not too far from where Kyle Jr. rescued me from Michelle and Chris. And he had. He really had. Strange and getting stranger . . .

I waited a few more minutes, set a thirty-minute in-and-out timer, and whispered, *"Bismillah."* I stepped out from the forest and into the suburban backdrop of birdsong and distant traffic and a cop only forty yards across the street, and snuck up to the side of the Turners' house, my peripheral vision wide open. But no one was around.

*Thank you, God. I promise you, after all of this is over, I'll definitely give up committing crimes. I'm really sorry about that. Please hang in there with me.*

Within seconds I was kneeling down in front of the tiny basement window that Mariam and I had snuck in and out of a thousand times before. If only she could see me now. I held my breath. If the Turners kept the same alarm system the Muhammads had, then this window was safe. Mr. Muhammad saw no point in wiring it, considering its size. Only a small child or a person with dislocatable limbs could pass through it. Hopefully it was still the same.

I pulled the lever on three . . . two . . . the window opened. Silence. Good, great, perfect.

*Alhamdulillah.*

I crammed my skinny body through the opening, head first. It wasn't pretty. It was also when I encountered my first problem: Mariam's basement wasn't hers anymore. The couch that had once cushioned our falls was gone. A stupid oversight on my part; here I was dangling from my feet. I had no choice but to drop to my hands, somersault onto my back, and hope for the best. It was more of a collapse than a drop, more of a flop than a roll, but I'd conquered the first hurdle.

I stood up, closed the window, and left my shoes behind. Better to snoop in quiet clean socks than in filthy shoes. I checked my phone for updates, but there was nothing. Back to my mission.

Sparse basement. There were a few unpacked boxes in a corner, but other than that, nothing. No furniture, no decorations. No signs that read "Secret society meets here" or Crusader flags or Klan robes or any other weird regalia. What was I expecting? Whatever, I was on the clock. I sped toward the stairs, then came to an abrupt stop. There was Drexler, tied to the bottom railing. He glanced up at me with the saddest doggy eyes. I bent down for a moment and patted him on the head. "I know you're one of the good ones," I whispered.

That's when I smelled the bleach. Being frustratingly sensitive to manufactured chemicals, I was immediately overwhelmed by a sharp headache. Shit. What had happened here? I patted the doormat. Damp. I lifted it up, then immediately let go of the rug. Bloodstains.

I was sure of it.

Drexler whimpered.

I wanted to untie him. Let him go. But I couldn't. With a hole in my chest, I left him alone and hurried up two flights to Mariam's old room, now Kyle's. It could have belonged to any teen. A few posters on the wall of bands I had never heard of, and dirty clothes on the floor. I wasn't about to go rummaging through anything, seeing how dirty it was and how his laptop was sitting right there—calling my name.

On a whim, I opened it. Locked. I typed Pulaski88, not really expecting—

*Jackpot.* Access: granted. I felt a surge of vengeful joy. *Now you know what it feels like, asshole,* I gloated silently. Hunching over his desk, I quickly scanned his home screen. There were several folders . . . mp3s, Odin'sAxE . . . Of course. *Kyle* was the one who'd argued with Debbie in the now-defunct Twelve Generals chatroom. The Odin'sAxE folder was stuffed with Nazi memes. I passed over the *Sieg Heil* nonsense and clicked on a picture of Christopher Columbus with an out-sized thought bubble.

Dear Conquered Peoples,

The history of humanity is one of constant conflict and competition. We fight for resources: land, food, water, and childbearing women. You whine about how the Godly White Man has always triumphed. You losers want me to regret my superiority at conquest? You want apologies and reparations from someone who is stronger and smarter than you? News flash: my fellowship and I won the conflict. We won the competition. We aren't sorry. We owe you nothing.

I closed the folder. It was what it was: idiocy reframed as sacred wisdom. (Seriously: "childbearing women"?) I quickly scanned a few more memes—several that questioned the Holocaust, a couple of memes about black-on-black and black-on-white crime, and something that resembled a family tree but more ancient. It had a quote: "God shall enlarge Japeth." Okay, weird. Who was Japeth? I checked the time . . . 7:20. Whatever, there wasn't time to explore that. His meme folder was crass and childish.

My eyes roved the screen, desperate to find anything that would redeem my prince, myself, my family. I zeroed in on a lone PowerPoint. OPERATION AQY. I double-clicked on it. The file was huge, encrypted with block cipher just like the blog that first led me to FallenSheClimber, Kyle's presumably dead mom.

And that's all I really had at that point: dead ends. Yes, I had something. Kyle really *was* Pulaski88. Which meant he'd been stalking me before Mariam and her family had moved out. How? Actually, I knew the short answer: he was light-years ahead of me, tech-wise. (Which pissed me off.) So no doubt he'd also stirred up the hate that had ruined Dr. Muhammad's practice. That seemed to be the gist . . . we were the perfect "operations base." He'd lured me right to him, setting me up to ask him for incriminating advice in that stupid "ethical hacking" forum. And he'd kept records of our incriminating exchanges. I'd been such a sucker.

But there was no point in dwelling on the mistakes of the past. Knowing that Kyle was Pulaski88 wasn't enough. I needed to get my hands on the encrypted files. I took out my thumb drive and copied the file. Or tried. The jerk had disabled his USB port. I couldn't even email myself the file because that would require logging into my email account, compressing the file, and erasing the browsing history so he couldn't see that someone had been active on his computer. The erasure itself would be proof of my presence, and I had no time for more intricate track covering.

*Think, think, think . . .*

*Bzzzt. Bzzzt. Bzzzt.*

My cellphone suddenly vibrated. I stiffened in terror. It wasn't the alarm I had set. I fought to stay calm. But the incoming text or whatever it was sounded weird, amplified. I removed my phone, placing the burner and my real phone on Kyle's desk. On my real phone was Mariam's face. My best friend was calling me, here, in her old bedroom. It buzzed a second time. In stereo. No, there was a third phone somewhere in the room, also buzzing. It was close, muffled, coming from inside Kyle's desk. I opened the top drawer and found an iPhone, facedown. Hmm. Kyle was a "Samsung guy," wasn't he? This whole ordeal was threatening to turn me into a lunatic. When I flopped the third phone over and saw Mariam's face, my lunacy seemed to be confirmed.

Here, in Kyle's desk, was my phone. And somehow I still had my phone.

*Salma, you dumbass . . . look at it. Closely.*

I reached into the desk and flipped the phone over. The trim was black. My actual phone—the one I came with—was silver. I compared the two even more closely, flipping the phone in the desk back over so I could analyze the fronts. The screen savers were identical. The one in Kyle's desk was exactly the same as the one on my phone: an old photo of me, Vanessa, and Mariam. An iconic image of the three of us as tweens.

What was going on? Was I seeing double? I put my phone down and grabbed the one from the desk. I tapped the screen. I punched in my passcode. Access denied.

And then it dawned on me. This was the "clone." The one Amir had heard Kyle mention to his father. He thought Kyle had said "clown." But he'd said "clone." Kyle had cloned my phone.

I held the clone in my hand, staring in disbelief. How far back did this go? How many private moments was Kyle privy to? Had he been watching as I frantically texted Amir this weekend, searching for him, imploring him to hang on, confiding my deepest love?

I dropped the phone.

It felt dirty. My soul felt dirty. Ruined. Hacked to bits . . . one private moment at a time.

The phone landed on the floor, unbroken. Pulaski88 had taken advantage of my do-gooder impulse to save Dr. Muhammad's practice and to keep my best friend in Mason Terrace. He wormed his way into my life under an alter ego, somehow cloned my phone, then straight up chased my boyfriend out of the country. My body burned. I wanted to violate him right back. Destroy his house, their lives—do to them what they wanted to do to my family and Amir's family and Mariam's family. At this point, what did I have to lose?

*Nothing. Go for it, Salma. Remember what Amir said the day you were a jerk to him: "Screw them all."*

*Bzzzt* . . . Mariam's face appeared on the clone. "What up, girl? You're mega ignoring me."

My eyes flashed between the two screens, to Mariam's disappearing face. But there was my answer. I had Mariam to lose. Amir. Vanessa. My family. Everyone I've ever cared about. Even Mrs. DLP. And Dora and Boots.

The alarm went off. My real alarm. I nearly fell out of Kyle's chair.

It was 7:38. No Kyle Sr. But a few seconds later a text came in—on my real phone and its clone. A message from Dad:

> Apologize for the blackout. Titi's had a spike in her vitals. May need a minor surgery soon. Was stuck w/ doc. Detective McManus at the house. Meet us at hospital. Same, same. We'll make it work.

*Make it work? Okay, Dad.*

> ON. MY. WAY.

What I didn't text was that I'd be on my way after I snooped around Kyle Sr.'s office. I snatched all three phones,

232

making sure they were on mute, then ran to the study. Unlike his son, Senior was a neat freak. Immaculate. There was a custom-made bookshelf and accent lighting. It was fancy. But the message was clear: Be smart, Salma. Kyle Sr. will notice.

I opened drawers and closets, then closed them; scanned the bookshelf, wincing at titles like *The Submissive Wife;* and then stopped, like a deer in headlights, at a painting. It was inside the bookshelf, a nook, like where one might put a TV, but Kyle Sr. had hung a painting. A painting of our nation's capitol.

The dome of the U.S. Capitol was prominently displayed. Except now it had a flag protruding triumphantly from the top. With a cross on it. Church and state no longer separated.

I thought about Grandma Thiede. How she said that the cross symbolized the *nafs* transformed—a soul made free by sacrifice and humility and boundless love. But this was something else entirely. This wasn't about spirituality. This was about control. Dominion. Empire. This entire room was making me mental.

Just then, Drexler barked.

I peeked through the window. It was the Turners' truck. It slowed as the wheels hit the driveway. My heart pounded against my ribs. I scanned the room one last time. Wait . . . on the top of the bookshelf was a small box. A very pretty box. It looked important, given the metallic black lock.

On instinct, I swiped it. Shoved it into my now-bulging cargo pockets. I flew down the stairs, past the front door. Outside, Kyle Sr. cast a brief shadow across the morning sun. I nearly tumbled down the basement stairs once I reached them. Drexler stopped barking when he saw me, tail wagging.

*I'm so sorry, buddy.*

Down in the basement, I forced myself to breathe. My arms and legs sang with the sour alarm of EDS. I was not made for rushing or playing spy. I stopped and took a deep breath. I needed to slow things down. I needed to be quiet. The front door slammed, and I froze. Kyle Sr. was inside the house.

I squeezed my eyes shut, waiting for the barking that never came. Was Drexler being quiet for me? Did he somehow sense that I needed help? Or maybe he just knew me now, since I'd walked him and brought him into my home. But there was no time to think or dissect. I forced my eyes open and tiptoed across the basement and reached for the tiny window. There was no way I could hoist myself up and through it without Mariam's old couch for leverage. I wasn't Spider-Man; I wasn't a comic book hero on a poster in Mrs. DLP's office. I needed a lift.

*The boxes.*

Right.

I grabbed my shoes and tossed them through the window. Next, me. I needed a box. I grabbed the nearest one, but it was too heavy. What was in them? Was it safe to touch them? A second box was lighter. Next I had to fit through the small window at an awkward angle. It would hurt. But at this point, what wouldn't? Summoning my resolve, I sucked in a breath and shoved my right shoulder out of joint—using every ounce of strength in my left side to pull myself through the window and out of the basement. . . .

A cold sweat broke on my face. As I scrambled to my feet, I bit my lip to keep from screaming in pain as I shoved my shoulder back in place. After that, I saw stars. I closed my eyes. I couldn't afford to pass out. I pressed my back against their house, cradling my arm. I had two options: run to the car and get to the hospital, or run to the house, find something to open the lockbox, and then get to the hospital. I chose the latter. But my body was still pressed to the Turner house.

I could hear Kyle Sr. shouting in the kitchen. The kitchen windows looked out to the woods. Now was my chance. I counted to three, then sprinted across the street, praying I wouldn't be seen.

I ran to our side door to grab the spare key, but Mom had left in such a hurry, she didn't lock anything. Did she take a cab? Did McManus force her to leave? Was that even legal? Stupid question . . . cops can do whatever the hell they want.

Shuddering at the thought of my sisters riding in the back of a paddy wagon, clueless and afraid, I stepped inside the kitchen. I had to open this damn lockbox. The cereal in the girls' breakfast bowls was bloated and soggy; dirty dishes were stacked beside the sink, and coffee was still dripping. I poured myself a glass of water and rummaged through the medicine cabinet. I needed prescription-strength ibuprofen. Leftovers from my last injury. My shoulder pulsated with a twitchy pain. I grabbed Mom's nearby scarf, assembling a makeshift sling.

My master of calm, Thomas, came padding into the kitchen, begging to be fed. I opened the fridge and dropped last night's can on the tiled floor. He gobbled it up, then brushed against my legs. Happy. I wanted to trade places with him. Scratch that . . . I wanted to *be* him. For now I had to be content with shoving a piece of Mom's burnt toast into my mouth, then rummaging around for some sort of large destructive tool. An ax, preferably. Anything, really, to crack open the lockbox . . . a hammer. Perfect. I wedged the lockbox between the metal edge of the sink and the cutting board

and began smashing the box again and again until pieces of
metal flew upward and finally—

*Pop.*

The lock gave.

With a sigh, I set down the hammer and flipped open
the lid. The cold sweat returned, a deluge now with the pain
and stress, dripping from my forehead onto my wrist, into the
box . . . and onto its only contents: a wooden signet ring. Gar-
ish. Bulky. Crappy-looking. Nothing particularly distinctive
about it but the dots stamped on the top. There were several,
maybe a dozen. Even so, it looked like a cheap souvenir. Not
something worth protecting. Despair crept in.

*Don't you see, Salma Dihya? You're deluded. You're suffer-
ing from the same white-savior complex as everyone else. Can you
stop already? Have you learned nothing in the last few weeks?
Give up and give in. You're not in control. They are. Better get
your sorry ass to the hospital. Better hope your dad's plan will
work, that you can GTFO before it's too late. Otherwise, it's your
25th Hour. Remember that Norton film? Would love to see you
surviving jail. Or Gitmo. Hello, orange jumpsuit.*

Just then, Thom jumped onto the counter. I wanted to
sweep him up into a death hug, but couldn't. Couldn't even
pick up my own damn cat because of these Turners.

"Hang on, Thom."

I unzipped my pants pocket and grabbed what I hoped
was the right phone. Bingo. The clone. With my one good
arm and a wrath-infused blow, I smashed that fucker to pieces.

Thom let out an innocent meow.

"Guess it's time to say goodbye, buddy. I'll miss you."

I placed my forehead against his. He sniffed my nose and
licked my cheek.

Teary and numb, I got to packing: my still-intact phones, more ibuprofen, my laptop, a few basic toiletries, and valuable photos of family, friends, Amir, Thom. I swung my jean jacket over my aching shoulder and headed out the front door, trying to look as casual as possible as I made a beeline toward the next street, walking toward the minivan.

# 19

THE HOSPITAL WAS a quick drive from the house. I had ten minutes. Ten minutes of illusory freedom, ten minutes in which I was the master of my destiny.

*Master of your destiny? Okay, Miss Cray-Cray, are you sure it was ibuprofen you ingested?*

I shook my head. Time was precious and I wasn't going to waste it arguing with Salma Durden. I had two important phone calls to make. Goodbye calls. Only I couldn't actually say goodbye.

First, Vanessa.

Her phone went straight to voicemail. Of course it did. Vanessa was at school. Like every normal teen. My bottom lip quivered as I managed to spit out the sappiest message I'd ever left her. I told her that she wasn't just my second bestie, but a first, really—tied with Mariam. I told her that I couldn't wait to go putt-putting, but that she might have to embrace the heat. I asked her to give Dora and Boots some love. I told her that if I survived any of this, I'd really like to have one of her homemade brownies. A whole big batch of them. Actually, I could just go for a vial of pure CBD oil. Like right about now . . . my shoulder.

I hung up. All at once I start sobbing hardcore, gulping for air and shaking—which made my arm hurt even more. I shook my head and sniffed, willing myself to stop. There was no time for a nervous breakdown.

At the light I popped another ibuprofen, wondering how many my stomach could handle.

The light turned green and I dialed Mrs. DLP to leave her a message.

I was startled to hear her voice. Her office didn't open till ten. She immediately recognized mine. "Hey there, Missy Miss. To what do I owe this honor?"

I wiped my nose on my arm, smearing grossness all over my jean jacket. She was like my auntie. She had me at Missy Miss.

My voice started to crack. "Hey, Mrs. DLP. I just wanted to thank you. You know, because it's International Auntie Day." I totally pulled that one out of my ass.

"It is?"

"Yeah, it is. It's a thing, you know. Like Cupcake Day and spring cleaning."

She paused. "You all right, Salma? You sound really strange."

I tried my best to keep my eyes glued to the road. There was something about her voice that was undoing me. "Um . . . I need some advice. I kind of fell out of a window and did something to my shoulder. I think I tore my rotator cuff, or dislocated my arm." I said those last words fast and low. Knowing she'd flip.

"Girl!" Yup. Here came the flipping. If I hadn't been talking to her through the car's Bluetooth, I would've had to pull the phone away from my ear. "You know you can't self-diagnose or self-treat," she growled. "Listen. I have walk-ins and they start in just a few minutes. Put your mom on the phone. Better yet, put your mom on the phone and get yourself to the hospital. You hear me, young lady? And what in the world were you doing falling out of a window?!"

I turned the volume down. She mumbled something imperceptible, about my stubbornness and how I needed to be more careful.

"Don't worry, Mrs. DLP. I'm on my way to the hospital." It was true. Mostly. But not for my own medical treatment.

"Oh," she said, her voice relieved. "Good. Then—"

"Wait." I cut her off. "But hypothetically speaking, if this was just a tear, and not a dislocation, could it go untreated for a while and, you know, not do any permanent damage—"

"Good Lord. If it were a full dislocation your arm would be dangling from your side, totally useless. And the pain would be increasing, every minute. You probably have a tear. But you are on your way to the ER? Aren't you?"

"Yeah, absolutely. Mom's here in the car with me." I fake-voiced an adult "Hi."

Mrs. DLP was quiet. She had a finely tuned bullshit detector.

"Salma, cookie, is there something you're not telling me? I can feel it in my bones."

Another red light. I sighed.

"I promise on everything that's holy that I will answer you one day. Which is a lot because in a sense all things and all people are holy. But I can't right now. You wouldn't believe it. I hardly believe it. It's *that* complicated."

There was a beep. Mrs. DLP sounded flustered. "Damn it," she said. "I don't know how to switch the lines. Hang on, I'm going to put the other line on hold."

The call suddenly ended as I approached my exit and turned off George Mason Driveway and onto the hospital complex. Guess Mrs. DLP hit the wrong button.

Dead teen walking. That's what I felt like as I parked the car and nervously walked into the hospital, riding the elevator up to the ICU.

My phone buzzed. Another text from Dad. Actually, a voice memo. I hit play. Three attempts later I finally deciphered his polyglot jumble of international languages and Moroccan dialects. The result? McManus was here. At the hospital. Waiting in Titi's room. I had five to ten minutes max.

My stomach dropped. I pictured Mom and my sisters, watching the detective's every move. None of this would work. I was certain of it—certain that Dad was in way over his head, that McManus would call Dad's bluff, that Mom wouldn't be able to keep a poker face. I probably would have missed my floor had two staff members not joined me in the elevator, talking among themselves about their busy night and what they were going to do once their shifts had ended.

"Remind me," said the older one, "to finally put those tread rugs on my old hardwood stairs."

"My thoughts exactly," said the younger nurse, flicking some crumbs off her scrubs. "It's a miracle I've never tripped, flying up and down the stairs doing laundry for four. My goodness, that poor woman. Such a nasty head injury."

"Damn shame," the older one said. "And did you see that tattoo she had? At her age? What was that? A barcode?"

The elevator dinged, and the door to the ICU slowly opened. I considered exiting, but my ten minutes weren't yet up . . . and I had to hear more. Had to eavesdrop on this conversation of theirs. I mean . . . could they be talking about Mrs. Turner?

"It's the latest fad," said the younger nurse. "Talking tattoos. My nephew has one."

"Stop pulling my leg, Darcy," said the older nurse. "There's no such thing as talking tattoos."

We rose to the next floor, and when the door opened, the two nurses stepped out, the older one babbling on about this crazy world and how she was born in the wrong age. I jabbed the button to return to the ICU floor, where I guessed this woman, possibly Mrs. Turner, must be. My heart rate soared.

*Chill out, Salma. The ICU floor is the same as Titi's. The cops are somewhere nearby, waiting for you. Better to exit slowly, go in stealth.*

As the door pulled open I popped my head out and scanned the hall. Coast was clear.

I started with the nearest door and worked my way down the hall toward Titi's room, ducking in and out of rooms, trying my best to avoid an awkward conversation.

"Excuse me, miss. You can't be in here."

By my seventh or so room, I found her. At least, I hoped I had.

I approached this person who was hooked up to a gazillion machines, a breathing tube cut into her throat, skull wrapped up like a mummy . . . covering everything except the face. I moved closer to the bedside and studied it. Though swollen and bruised, her face was still dove-like and sweet, except for her eyes. They were wide open and lifeless. She was alive. But barely so. I heard voices outside the room. Feeling like a total asshole, like I was violating her space, her body, her privacy, I lifted up the hospital sheet that covered her body. Her lower arm was exposed. I snapped a single picture and left the room, offering a pathetic "Sorry, I'm lost. I thought this was my grandmother's room" to the incoming doctor.

He was busy enough not to care.

Whatever it was, the clock was ticking. I left the room and hurried down the hall to finally face Detective McManus.

A minute later . . .

"Salma Dihya Bakkioui."

My head jerked up at the familiar voice.

Detective Tim stood outside Titi's room, smug in his rumpled suit. I wondered if he'd changed since I'd last seen him.

"And I was just beginning to believe that you weren't here," he said. "That was one long trip to the cafeteria."

*Think quickly, Salma Gitmo. Speak.*

"Yeah, no. I was there. It's just that the vending machine for the drink I wanted was broken."

He reached forward and touched my shoulder. The injured one. I winced. He lifted his hand up.

"I'm not here to hurt you. I only want to take you down to the station to talk."

I nodded, forcing myself to approach and peer inside the door. Mom, Dad, my sisters: all stood in the back of Titi's room, frozen. Titi was sound asleep. At Mom's feet was a suitcase. Not exactly small enough to quietly slip my way, or Dad's way or whatever. My eyes darted back to Detective Tim. The circles under his eyes seemed to betray that he wanted this over as much as I did. When I glanced back into the room, I saw Mom slip Dad a small ziplock bag. He tucked it into his shirt and walked out into the hall.

"Detective McManus," he said deferentially.

Detective Tim turned. "Yes?"

"Thank you again for waiting. I'm ready now to join you and Salma down at the station."

Detective Tim sighed. "Well, all right. Shall we?"

Inside the room, Mom was fighting back tears. So was I. Either Dad would successfully create a diversion and hand me the ziplock bag, presumably stuffed with a passport and other GTFO basics, or he wouldn't and we were off to the station. No matter what the outcome was, this was goodbye. I lifted my hand subtly and waved. It was all I could do . . . without bringing attention to myself. My sisters stared back, eyes wide. I didn't know what they knew or had been told. I could only pray they'd been spared the very worst.

Detective Tim used his phone to wave us down the hall. "Let's move it. I'd like to get to the station before ten."

We entered an already full elevator. Detective Tim squeezed in last, turning his back on us for just a second to check to press the elevator button. That's when Dad slipped me the bag. Thankfully, he was standing on my good side. I shoved the baggie into my back pocket seconds before the elevator doors dinged and opened. We all stepped out.

Dad slipped his right pinkie around my own, squeezed, then pulled away. He stepped out in front of Detective McManus. The move was abrupt, noticeable. Threatening, in fact.

"This liar claims to be a police officer!" Dad shouted, stopping in his tracks.

I gaped at him. *What the hell—?*

He looked crazed, hysterical. Out of character. He never yelled or screamed.

And almost instantaneously I realized: *This is it.*

Dad thrust a trembling finger toward Detective Tim.

"This man produced no identification! He is armed! He is forcing me to leave these premises against my will! False arrest! False arrest!"

All at once he and Detective Tim were standing nose to nose. Detective Tim reached for his handcuffs. Patients scattered, a nurse dropped her clipboard, a doctor called for security over the intercom. My view was blocked, but the next thing I knew, my dad was in a headlock, getting slammed to the ground. Detective Tim was zip-tying him. For a brief second, Dad turned and craned his neck so I could see his face. His eyes pierced mine. *Go, Salma, go!* he mouthed.

I turned around and sprinted out the door.

Everything in my peripheral vision faded into the shadows. Even my *nafs* abandoned me. I was *of* my body but not *in* it. There were curious stares as I ran out into the parking lot—where an ambulance was meeting an ER team. In the midst of serendipitous chaos, I ducked in and around cars and people and darted away from both the hospital and the parking lot. I couldn't take the minivan: the cops would be looking for it. I flagged the nearest taxi instead.

"You all right, miss?" asked the taxi driver as I toppled into the back seat.

"Yeah, thanks, just a second. Um . . . I'm going to the Falls Church Metro."

That seemed to satisfy him. I avoided his gaze in the rearview and reviewed the few supplies I had with me: my burner, my true cellphone, my laptop, and a toothbrush. Um, right, so brush up and flash my pearly whites at all the bad people? Smile my way out of jail?

I moved on to the ziplock baggie, evaluating the supplies that Mom had packed. There were four items: a wad of cash, my American passport, my Moroccan passport, and a note, scribbled quickly.

> Writing in the bathroom. McManus escorted us here. I told him you went to see Titi.
> If you are reading this, then you are on your way to the airport. Use the Moroccan passport. For once it's advantageous.
> Love you more than words can say.
> Get rid of this note. We will get thru this. Somehow. Some way. —Mom

Below her name she scribbled in Arabic the very words that the Prophet Ibrahim uttered when his own people threw him into a burning pit: *Hasbunallahu wa ni'ma'l wakil.*

Whoa. Heavy analogy. I rubbed my temples and took out the Moroccan passport. *Advantageous?* What did she mean. I opened it and scanned the first page.

Right. I'd conveniently forgotten that Mom had recently renewed our Moroccan passports. Why *would* I remember? I didn't care; I'd never intended to use mine. But now it all came flooding back: how pissed she was at the Moroccan embassy for butchering the English transliteration of my name. Instead of Salma Dihya Bakkioui, I was Selmeh Daha Bakewei. She'd calmed down quickly, of course—it was just a hassle to go through the passport renewal process again due to a clerical error by a non-native English speaker . . . an innocent error. Not deliberate. Not like with certain native English speakers at home . . .

No, here it was suddenly serendipitous. Or could be, *Inshallah.*

# 20

———

I OVERPAID THE cabdriver with a fat twenty. Slamming the car door, I walked-ran to the Metro station, then down the escalator and straight to the public restroom, where I flushed Mom's note down the toilet, splashed water on my face without looking in the mirror, and whispered, "I can do this."

While standing near the ticket machines, I scanned the commuters for a friendly face, an unsuspecting helper. And a victim. A young man in a business suit smiled at me. Pretending to be a tourist, I smiled back, asking that he explain the Metro lines to me.

As he pointed to the map and the differences between the Orange and Blue lines, I slipped my personal cell into the outer pocket of his computer case. Poor, poor soul. A real shit storm was headed his way, but if he was a good guy to begin with, he could talk his way out of it. I thanked him profusely.

After he left, I flagged another taxi and headed for the airport.

Several hours later, I was in a foreign land: the international wing at Dulles. It really was the best place to lie low, teeming with people. As I glanced at the masses, especially at the men in sunglasses, the girls and women in bright hijabs, I wondered if any of them were also running. Truth be told, you can't tell anything from how a person looks.

And I probably looked fairly normal, especially now that I had passed the first test. I had made my way past security and the probing eyes of TSA and into the main terminal. I'm not sure if the cops or feds or whoever had cast their net this wide, but even if they had, they were probably searching for an American citizen, not a Moroccan. At least that's what I told myself to keep my feral nerves somewhat in check. My heart was pounding and a permanent lump had lodged in my throat. Still, for now I could catch my breath.

Time check: 4:22. Flight EK232 was several hours away, a double-edged sword. It wouldn't be boarding until the butt crack of dawn.

I had ample time to figure out not only whether Kate's tattoo contained useful information, but how to scan and listen to it, or upload and listen to it, or however that worked. But more time for me meant more time for the authorities to find me.

The thought put all my senses on high alert. So I purchased a hat I'd never otherwise wear—super hokey and patriotic, with an American flag on the front—and sat down at Starbucks. In the cab on the way to the airport, I had emailed the photo of Mrs. Turner's tattoo to one of my anonymous email accounts, the one I used in my early days of naïveté, when I thought I could stop Mariam from leaving and save the day. Back when I thought Nazis and Crusaders were a thing of the past.

Since my 7-Eleven burner was so pathetically basic (what

the hell is a FIGO Orbit, anyway?), I had to figure out how to access Mrs. Turner's tattoo using my laptop. After a quick search, I found a company called Skin Story. *Bingo.* Not only were there custom tats, but there was a technical description about sound wave technology: how any surface with the right sort of texture—as in human flesh coated with a certain kind of ink—could be used as a recording mechanism. I uploaded a photo of Mrs. Turner's tattoo and pressed search. Seconds later, a clip popped up with her name right beside it.

I plugged in my earbuds.

The clip was two minutes long. As I brought the cursor over to Play, I thought about my interactions with Mrs. Turner. First she was the sweet mom, appreciative of our welcoming gesture of Ramadan sweets. She was also the obedient wife. Kyle Sr. had asked for his beer "five minutes ago." I thought about the night she brought my sisters home and the cookies she sent over the following day. I thought about the bruises and her fragility, how bugged out she was the night we Skyped, and then how she looked just this morning—her body lifeless, her eyes empty. Her spirit shadowed by the presence of death. I clicked Play, then immediately paused it.

I glanced around me at my fellow travelers. Eating, smiling, chatting away without a care in the world. I wasn't sure what felt more illusory—them or the thoughts inside my head. What if there was nothing useful to her Skin Story? What if this was one ugly-ass dead end? Stress on *dead*.

I swallowed.

Eyes forced open, I took a deep breath and clicked Play . . .

My maiden name is Katherine Rose Gordon. I'm forty-two years old and this is my story, the story of my life—a life I am only now beginning to understand and to live . . . on my terms. I was raised in the Seven Jewels movement. Listen and obey. That was our holy writ. A writ we were never to question, especially us girls, for questioning was the work of the Devil. And I didn't. Not in the beginning. It was all I knew. We lived in a parallel world. . . . And it wasn't so bad . . . not as a kid, surrounded by all those big families, that endless love. I went to college in Portland, where I met Kyle Sr. He swept me off my feet. Seemed to have all the answers my soul craved, steady resolve in an ever-changing world. We married quickly, but that's youth. As the years went by, as his career waxed and then waned, another side appeared. But I thought that if I loved him, fed him, had his child, things would change.

But they didn't. . . . And those late-night meetings at our house . . . I was never privy to them, but I heard bits and pieces. I guess you could say I should have known better. But it was all so dark then. I was lost and alone. Scared of Kyle Sr. and what Kyle Jr. was fast becoming. And then an unexpected sort of happenstance came my way. I had never known their kind, not personally, but that family . . . so happy and loving. Living in the Lord's grace.

The sovereigns say it's God's will. That we're securing our own future. *"Let the dogs out,"* they joke. *"Let them turn on each other, then they'll know their master."*

Well, I've seen that master. I've felt his terror, suffered his blows. I can't let this go on. Find the ring and you'll know their plans.

You don't want what's coming next.

The message ended. I lingered in the silence, absorbing her last words. *You don't want what's coming next. Find the ring. You'll know their plans.*

*Find the ring.*

The ring! I had completely forgotten about its existence.

Feverishly I patted my pocket. *Alhamdulillah.* It was still there. I pulled it out and looked at it closely. There were a couple of things I hadn't noticed before: like the little dots etched on the top. They weren't dots. They were stars. Twelve of them. And then a line . . . a seam where the top of the ring joined the body. I placed the ring in my bad hand and with my good one gave it a hard twist.

A USB port disguised as jewelry. Of course. I had to admire the whole hiding-in-plain-sight approach. I jammed the stick into my laptop and clicked away. Bingo. No encryptions.

Not surprisingly, Kyle Sr. was organized. I started with the biggest files: maps of the entire DC grid. I didn't know what it meant yet, so I kept digging, searching for anything related to Operation AQY. Taking a few digressions when files appeared intriguing, which was admittedly quite often. (Okay, fine, it was Human Behavior Porn—I was in the mind of crazy and it was utterly fascinating.) I double-clicked on "CO's log." Kyle Sr. kept files on all his "subordinates," including his son. It was a "proficiency and conduct" report in which Kyle Sr. noted by date the pros and cons of Kyle Jr.'s behavior. A few entries stood out, all from last year:

September 17: *Discuss K's Adderall dosage with Dr. Z*

November 11: *Discipline K for backtalk*

December 3: *Report to the Generals and humbly submit that K idiotically used founding city of the KKK (Pulaski) with numerical code (88) for Heil Hitler. Apologize for the both of us.*

I was tempted to laugh.

What had I first believed? What had I assumed *Pulaski* signified? A Podunk town in Virginia where someone had helped us? And *88:* the year a kindly hacker was born, or a nod to his math skills? Kyle Sr. had been way off in thinking his kid had aroused suspicion. Yet the entry ended with three punishments: *food denial, confinement, labor.* Followed by a big question mark. For a second I almost pitied Kyle Jr. Growing up in this household, in this . . . cult.

The next entry was dated more recently, from late April: *Proved wrong. Junior understands guerrilla tactics better than I realized. Excellent use of video simulation. Final draft almost ready. Use of immigrant boyfriend and RWM ploys will help expand operation theater, tactical efficiency.*

I read the entry several times over trying to decipher it. Immigrant boyfriend? That had to be Amir. But what was an RWM, and where was this video?

I kept scanning files, but the more I searched, the more unfocused my mind became. A headache was lurking, and my eyes were parched. I glanced outside. The sun was a ball of fire, full of rage. I thought of my dad, how he exploded with bravery. How Detective McManus exploded with anger. What had become of him? And what will become of any of us?

I glanced around, checking my surroundings, half expecting to see a SWAT team closing in. Nearby sat a family. Three daughters. Doting parents. They seemed happy, excited to be leaving on their own terms. Together . . .

No. Wake up, Salma B. Wake up. I slapped my face for real this time, garnering the attention of the nearby family. They seemed to laugh it off. To them, I was just another traveler, perhaps jet-lagged. I smiled wearily and pulled my cheesy-ass hat over my face.

Click. Click. Scan. Scan.

I resumed my prowl, speed-reading Kyle Sr.'s files, fighting to stay focused. There were files that I desperately wanted to open, like this whacked-out doctrine called "Initiates One."

It was an introductory letter to newcomers, explaining the history of the 43ers and the symbolism of their emblem. Eleven of the stars represented the eleven states of the Confederacy: the first attempt by the pure white Christians to break off from the Union, which they saw as perversion, to forge their Utopia. The twelfth represented their true and enlightened aspirations. But this wasn't about the South. Not exclusively. This was bigger. The 1493ers had allies nationwide. The document said as much. The Twelfth Star would be born in a sea of glorious "ashes," literally. That was clear from Kyle Sr.'s archive of news items about the aftereffects of major disasters—tsunamis and earthquakes and hurricanes—the looting, the crimes, the panic.

*What happened to your focus, Salma B.? If you don't find something big to stop these lunatics, then panic will definitely follow. And it won't be illusory. Everything you love—your family, the South, your country—will erupt in bloody chaos.*

Right . . . okay . . . so—

And there it was. An MP4 video file labeled "final draft."

I clicked it open. Staring back at me was a thumbnail of my own face. In this video, I was sitting at my desk, in my own room, staring at my laptop. Almost like a Skype session frozen.

I pressed Play. The voice was mine. The words were mine. And yet I had never uttered them, at least not like that and not in that order. As I watched the video, two new discoveries became frightfully clear. *RWM* was an acronym: *Radical White Muslim.* The second discovery was just as deadly. I, Salma B., had been digitally cloned.

# 21

I HAD SEEN deep fakes before. But I'd never seen a video as professionally doctored as this. I didn't think it was possible outside of Hollywood movie studios. Kyle Jr. had even encoded the subtle presence of blood flow—the color of my skin slightly changing from light red to barely present green—simulations of life flowing through my long digital face. Her face. My face swapped onto a digital version of me.

At first I was so mesmerized by the realness of the video that I didn't comprehend all the words. I hit replay. Salma the clone was ranting—about the West, the treatment of Muslims, the politics of disbelievers, and then she was pledging allegiance to Al-Qaeda North Africa and ISIS.

And then she was boasting. Salma the clone was confessing not only to the attacks of May 3 but to the "great blackout" of May 19.

I paused the video and stared at the clock. May 19 was tomorrow.

I glanced over my computer for the umpteenth time. No SWAT. The family who sat across from me earlier had long ago left, and another family had replaced them. A nearby worker was emptying the trash can. When he reached for his belt, my heart froze. Was this it? He was undercover; he had to be. My eyes flitted across the room: every small movement, a random person checking their phone, another their purse, suddenly felt circumspect.

The worker . . . he's . . . bumming a cigarette from a co-worker?

My shoulders dropped.

I returned to the video. My confession was ending. "Good luck trying to fix the Arlington IXP. Or finding me. By the time you get this, I'll be gone. Or gloriously blown to bits and living in *Jannah*. Doesn't matter. Our mission will continue."

A cascade of apocalyptic shivers coursed through my body. Maybe I should have purchased the Doomer kit. Because if they succeeded in blowing up the Arlington IXP— the one Dad always stupidly joked about—then the DC area could suffer a massive blackout. I thought of Puerto Rico, the months it took to rebuild after Hurricane Maria, work that remains unfinished, on a land forever scarred. It would be a lot like that. No internet, no phone, likely no backup electricity for weeks. And the hospitals: the danger to Titi and Mrs. Turner and anyone else dependent on power and technology to keep them alive.

Even with backup generators, there would be dire consequences, for them and others. Kyle Sr. and his group were right: All the jewels of our society would be at risk. People would flip. They'd probably be willing to accept just about anything to regain some semblance of normalcy. Which explained why Kyle Sr. had all those files on natural disasters. He wanted to turn Arlington into Aleppo, to create chaos, to divide, to blame, and ultimately to conquer. Next step: take over DC and institute their plans for a white fundamentalist Christian theocracy. Hence the painting.

I stood up in my little corner of the airport. Raw energy coursed through my veins like hot lava. My mind was on fire. My soul was alert. I had to figure the rest of this out. The doctored fake confession said that the mission would continue. *What else were the Sovereigns planning on? A full coup d'état? Destroy or alter the Constitution?*

I paced.

The photos . . . those aerial images I'd stumbled upon just a few hours ago. Or was it minutes? Whatever, it didn't matter. It had to be the IXP joint.

I sat back down, searching. . . .

Bingo. I studied the images. Typed in small font in the bottom right-hand corner was a message—something I hadn't noticed earlier. Something that seemed insignificant. "0000 19 05 2020." It was a time and date. It all fit.

I pulled my hand away from the keyboard. *Holy shit.* Tonight . . . I glanced at the clock: seven p.m. Checked my surroundings: nothing. In just five hours, the "great blackout" would commence. I returned to my screen, dripping in sweat.

I had to go to the internet hub, catch them in the act. No, before the act. Stop them. Get proof that Salma the clone wasn't behind this. Because if I didn't, that was it. The confession alone would be enough proof for the world to make up its mind. People see what they want to see. Salma the RWM, Amir the immigrant—we were a twofer. The perfect couple to convince the world that no Muslim can be trusted—heritage or convert, practicing or not. Hippie or cripple. It didn't matter. If Islam was inherently evil, then all Muslims were potentially terrorists. Plus Kyle Jr. had evidence on me—joking about dosing Franklin, texts admitting anger, yearning for revenge. Real but not real. Joking, actually. But out of context?

*You are so screwed, Salma B.*

"Miss?"

Part of me didn't want to respond. Was this it? No, no, no, no, no—

"Miss!"

Standing in front of my table was an annoyed barista. "Sorry, but you've been sitting here for hours. We're getting busy and other customers would like to sit."

I swallowed. *Thank God. Bitchy baristas are way better than SWAT teams.* "Of course, sorry. On my way."

Smiling big, I gathered my stuff and headed down the terminal looking for an empty gate where I could finish my work uninterrupted. Along the way, I scanned TVs, fearful that at any moment I'd see my face plastered on the news: RWM WANTED.

But nothing happened. Maybe Mom's last words were having an effect. Maybe God really was my *wakeel*. His protection right now would be awesome. But what I really needed was the location of the IXP center. All I had was the time-stamped photograph.

Once I found a quiet gate, with only a janitor sweeping the floors, I sat down and opened my laptop. How was I going to narrow down a location based on a generic photo? Tired of staring at my laptop, my eyes roamed the gate, burning with rage and jealousy over Pulaski88's evil genius. He'd know the answer to my question. He was one clever son of a—

Wait. That janitor. His name tag. The company's name

was stitched in white letters over the breast pocket: Geo-Services. "Oh my God, that's it." *Wait, did I say that out loud?* He shot me a perplexed look but moved on to the next aisle.

I quickly returned to the aerial photos. Most people have never heard of EXIF data, unless they're photography nerds looking to understand what kind of camera took a certain picture and what the settings were. But even most aperture nerds don't realize that EXIF data can also be mined for where a picture was shot. If I was lucky—*God, please let it be so*—then I could tap into the geotags of that building Kyle Sr. had so many pictures of. I just had to . . . a little bit of . . . There!

He forgot to remove the embedded coordinates.

*Bingo. I know your plan.*

I feverishly typed up a summary of everything I knew or thought I knew and composed an email to Detective Tim. He did hand me his card, after all. And ironically it was also the only email address I had, as there aren't exactly public directories for security agencies. And even though it was a deluded leap of faith, I compressed all of Kyle Sr.'s files and attached them—geotags included—to a hastily written email, said *"Bismillah,"* and hit Send. It was nearly eight p.m.

For the next few minutes, I sat there staring at my inbox, hitting refresh. Then, curious about what was developing outside the airport, I opened a new window and Googled my name.

Holy motherfucking shit. There was a BOLO ("be on the lookout") on me. I, Salma Dihya Bakkioui, was wanted for questioning. My photo, age, race, weight, and height were plastered all over the internet. Every atom of my body trembled in panic. I had to get out. I had to get in front of this colossal train wreck.

I closed my laptop, tucked my hair into my cheesy patriotic hat, and ran to the exit, where I flagged a taxi. I handed the driver one of the $100 bills and told him I needed his cell, explaining that I was on my way to my best friend's party (puke) and that I couldn't be late but that my phone was dead. It was all lies, pathetic ones, too, but my cheap-ass FIGO didn't have Google Maps on it and my real phone was still with victim X, the man from the Metro. Yeah, *Astaghfirullah,* I still felt bad about that one. But no time for regrets. The clock was ticking. Besides, my life as I knew it was already over.

The cabbie looked at me dubiously.

He glanced at the $100 bill and shrugged, handing me his phone.

I typed the IXP coordinates; he was connected by Bluetooth to his dashboard. The screen on his dashboard mirrored the phone's. According to Google, the site was twenty-three minutes away, zero traffic.

"Hey, Yusuf, is it?" I said, leaning forward.

He nodded.

"Mind if I hold on to this for the ride? I see you have Abdul Basit 'Abd us-Samad on your playlist."

Our eyes met in the mirror. I saw a tentative smile cross his face. "So you're Muslim?" he asked.

Usually it annoyed me just as much when my co-religionists were surprised by my religion as when non-Muslims were, but whatever. The poor guy was aiding and abetting a fugitive.

"Moroccan dad," I said.

He nodded, eyes back on the road. "Sure, sis. Play what you'd like."

I thanked him, then blasted Quran for the rest of the ride, to earn his trust and distract him. I needed his phone. It had everything I wanted—anonymity, the internet, Facebook, no screen lock. I embraced the luck and formed a plan.

When we finally made our last turn down a dark road, my pulse picked up a notch. The map indicated a three-minute ETA. It was nearly nine p.m. Would they be here? Was I early? Whatever, I'd wait. This was it. I asked Yusuf to drop the headlights.

"No, sis. I can't," he said. "It's against the law."

I handed him another $100 bill from my stack; the money didn't seem real, anyway.

*"Fi sabillilah?"* I asked, which basically means "Do it for God?" but sometimes also means "Do it for me?"

He shut off his lights and took the bill. In the mirror, I could see that he was no longer smiling.

"This is for a party?" he asked.

I swallowed. I needed to sound convincing. "Um, it's really a rave. We need to keep it quiet, if you know what I mean."

A quarter mile later, we approached a lot surrounded by a chain-link fence. At the center was a dilapidated concrete building. It looked as if it had been abandoned years ago. Unbelievable. The butt of my father's jokes—Arlington's IXP, one of the nation's most critical internet hubs.

Yusuf jerked to a stop. "Where is the party?" he demanded.

As I squinted across the deserted landscape, I felt a shudder of relief and dread when I found what I was looking for: the Turner truck behind a dumpster. I leaned forward again. "That's the deejay!" I said in a voice that sounded like a complete stranger's. "Well, thanks for the ride, *ekhi*. Time to get this rave started."

He glanced at the building and back at me.

Desperate, I pointed to a bumper sticker on the Turner truck. Odin's Axe. "Yup," I said. "See? That's the company logo. The axe—for breaking in and breaking out. In fact, the rave should be over soon. I'm kind of late as it is. I don't expect to be that long. Mind waiting?" I said, dangling another bill.

He shrugged and grabbed the bill. "I'm already here, aren't I?"

"Cool. Thanks, brother." I opened the car door. "Just keep your lights off, okay?"

I was about to step out and hurry my way toward doom and death when Salma the rational paused. *Cool?* Did I just say the word *cool?* Out loud? Nothing about this was cool. Who the hell was I kidding? Nothing felt real, including my own existence. Had I become Durden? Had Durden become me? *Doesn't matter Salma B. Your fate is sealed either way. Put one foot in front of the other, etc., etc. This plan of yours might be batshit crazy, but at least it's yours. End this. NOW.*

I thanked the cabbie, grabbed my jean jacket, and slipped into the dark of the night, leaving all of my worldly possessions—photos, passport, computer—in the back seat of his taxi.

I approached the fence.

*Right, so what exactly is the plan of yours, Miss Crazy?*

My inner Durden voice was right. But calling me *majnoon* wasn't exactly an insult. We're a nation of crazies.

*You didn't answer my question. What's your plan, hurl rainbows and butterflies at them? Ask them to stop with a pretty please? Get a videotaped confession? You're more of lunatic than I thought. Might as well dig yourself two graves—one for your plan and one for theirs. You know they will probably kill you. On sight.*

I told the voice in my head to shut the hell up. It was time to implement my plan. Step one: gear up. Step two: call the cops. Step three: catch the Turners—in the act.

Step one was a pain in the ass, or shoulder, but I had no choice. I needed the sling to keep my jacket close to my body, to stabilize the phone. I was also hoping that of the two Turners I might encounter, it would be Kyle Jr. Maybe my sling would trigger that tiny part of him that wasn't fully indoctrinated. The part of him that was more his mother's son than his father's clone. Step two: done (anonymous call). Now for step three.

The fence around the grim warehouse had been tampered with. A thick length of chain that kept the door locked had been cut off. The door hung open like my arm had when I first climbed out that basement window, its lock still bolted shut and attached.

I slipped through and tiptoed over to the dumpster, snapping incriminating photos of the Turner truck—with a clear view of the building behind it, and time stamps added. I uploaded the photos to the local police Facebook page. It wouldn't allow me to create a new post, so I left the photos under their most recent post: SUSPECT WANTED: SALMA DIHYA BAKKIOUI.

My story was already trending. Why not make use of it?

I also made use of the cabbie's own Facebook page, tagging the Arlington Police Department while I said, *"Bismillah,"* and hit Facebook Live. I slipped the phone into my breast pocket, camera facing outward, and walked toward the entrance of the dilapidated IXP building, channeling the fear that coursed through my cells. I climbed the front steps and reached for the door, whispering a *"Hasbuna'llahu wa ni'ma'l wakil"* in case the Turners did indeed "shoot on sight," when all of a sudden the door swung open. I tumbled backward, down the stairs, hitting my head hard on the pavement.

I scrambled to my feet.

There was Kyle Sr., pointing a pistol at me. I'd envisioned this scenario, of course. I'd seen him in his combat fatigues and boots and headband and whatever else he believed made him a warrior like Balian from *Kingdom of Heaven*. No, not Balian. Balian was actually pretty cool. Someone nasty, like that greedy king. What I hadn't envisioned was that warm smile. As if he weren't surprised. As if he'd been expecting me—

"Apprehend enemy combatant," he barked.

All at once, Kyle Jr. appeared, brandishing a rifle.

"Hands up and behind your head, neighbor," he commanded.

I did as I was told. I clasped my hands together behind my head, which was wet with blood. I felt dizzy, spots popping up in my vision. I teetered a bit, stepping backward slowly, away from the building. Something beeped, a timer.

"We're on a tight schedule. Son, I need you to go back inside and finish with the wires," Kyle Sr. said. "Leave her. I can handle it. She's about to pass out anyway—an advantage, really."

Kyle Jr. stepped away from me, smirking. His dark stare penetrated my insides, waking a fear so deep and so overwhelming it jolted me to action. *That's it, girl! There's no time like the present, and the present is saying set the damn bait or go down in history as the most hated RWM.* I glanced down at my jean jacket. The camera was still in place. My breathing slowed down. Irony of ironies, in this moment of maximum danger I felt nothing but calm and fearlessness.

This. Was. It.

I opened my mouth and uttered three words: "Don't do this."

Kyle Sr. stared at me. His hazel eyes flashed with unbridled certainty. "The existence of my people depends upon this."

"No, it doesn't. You've got it all wrong. Please—"

"Enough," he interrupted. "The devices have been set. A new day is on the rise."

I took a deep breath. They actually fell for it, like Adam and Eve. Equally blinded with hubris, equally complicit. It felt so good to be the serpent in this scenario.

Kyle Sr. removed his finger from the trigger, letting his arms fall to his sides. He slid his pistol into a leg holster and turned away from me, confident that I was about to pass out. I thought he might be right.

I looked down at the ground, thinking maybe I should just curl up now and sleep. My head was throbbing. I'd gotten what I needed at that point—a confession from the Turners about their plan and about their framing me—all live. And then all of a sudden a massive, powerful light shot out from behind me. From everywhere, in fact. I stumbled some more. *What the—*

"*Police!* Drop your weapon at your feet! Hands over your head! Remain where you are!"

I kept my hands pressed firmly against my head, trying not to make any quick moves, trying to stay steady . . . even though the tiny black spots had returned to my peripheral vision. They were merging into one big hole.

I forced my eyes to remain open.

Kyle Sr. slowly complied with the police orders. A shadow moved inside the IXP building, in and out of the windows. That's when Kyle Sr. ducked down and pressed a band on his wrist.

In the blink of an eye, a wave of energy, light, and heat blasted through the air, smashing windows. Smoke billowed. It felt like someone had rammed an ice pick into my eardrums. The world seemed to be moving rapidly away. It dawned on me that it wasn't the world that was moving, it was me. The blast had lifted me up into the air and I was free-falling back to the ground.

*So this is where it ends. Get ready to reunite with Grandma Thiede in three . . . two . . .*

"I've got you, Salma."

I'd fallen into someone's arms. A man's arms, judging from the sound of his voice. Mystery Man X hoisted me over his back and sprinted away from the blast. I watched the ground shift from gravel to grass to pavement, then the world turn upside right again as I was placed gently on top of a gurney. For a brief second, I caught a glimpse of his arm. He wore a glow-in-the-dark watch with a bright blue face. The next thing I knew, two EMTs were strapping me in, their mouths moving with speech, but I couldn't make out the words, as my hearing was totally shot. An oxygen mask was slipped over my mouth and after that there was a heavy metal click and a beam of light.

Inside the ambulance, the ringing in my ears started to subside and I could hear muffled voices.

"Check the patient for secondary blast injury." That's when multiple hands inspected my body, lifting up my clothes. Once I heard words like "shrapnel" and "blunt trauma," I passed out.

# 22

I SLOWLY CAME to, feeling as though I were lying on one of those pool floaties, weightless over a body of water. There were muffled, whooshing sounds in my head like the radio was on but the reception was horrendous. I also heard the faint click of a keyboard. Was I in a hospital?

How could that be? The Turners had succeeded. Was this the realm of *barzakh*? Had I crossed the great divide? Why would there be clicking sounds? I thought the hereafter was a completely different plane of existence, spiritual. Computers are anything but.

"Well, look at that. Our hero is finally stirring."

I opened my eyes. A round-faced lady with rosy cheeks and curly hair was beaming at me. I glanced down at her nametag: NICKI. She pushed aside her mobile workstation. "You're at the hospital. Arlington Inova. *In-o-va*." She spoke deliberately, like English wasn't my first language or she knew I was high on painkillers. "Do you remember what happened last night?"

I nodded. "Sort of." *Enough to know that I failed, miserably.* I reached to scratch my leg, but couldn't. My arm was in a full cast. She scratched it for me.

"Your burns are relatively minor. So is your head wound. The arm, however, will take several months to heal. But all things considered, you came out miraculously unscathed."

My throat was parched, but I creaked out an answer. "That's really great. But . . . mentally, I, um, I'm hearing sounds. Whooshy. Like there's a radio playing."

She smiled sympathetically. "What you're experiencing is MES, a very common side effect of proximal exposure to a loud explosion. It's usually temporary. A form of tinnitus."

"MES?"

She launched into a textbook explanation.

"Musical ear syndrome. It refers to a nonpsychiatric condition in which those with hearing loss experience a range of musical auditory hallucinations from ringing, hissing, and buzzing to more complex tunes like Christmas carols or patriotic music." She leaned forward, her brown eyes sparkling with excitement. "I bet you're hearing patriotic music. I know I am."

*What the hell is this lady jabbering about?*

I lifted my arm to scratch my head, because that was bandaged, too, and itching, but I couldn't manage it thanks to the cast on the one arm, the IV in the other. I rested my head against the headboard and sighed.

"Another itch?" she said. "Let me. It would be an honor."

*To scratch my head?*

"Bet you're hungry, too. Just say the word. Nurse Nicki will get you whatever you want. You deserve it, sweetheart."

*Why is she saying that? And how is it possible that this hospital is still wired?* I was seriously tripping.

My stomach grumbled. "Uh, buttermilk scones? Maybe some coffee?"

"There's a Starbucks across the street. I'm certain one of our staff members will be more than happy to do a run. Let me inquire." She walked toward the door. "Dear me, I almost forgot. There's a gentleman here who is eager to speak with you."

She shuffled out of the room, smiling and whistling and exuding all sorts of happiness. The door swung back open and in came the cop I'd only known as the Silent One. He looked more disheveled than the last time, but he was smiling, his eyes full of warmth.

"Hey! It's Salma Dihya Bakkioui!"

Uh, okay. Did this mean I was no longer a suspect? I forced a smile. "Hey . . . you." I frankly didn't know what else to say.

He pulled up a chair next to my hospital bed. "Apologies, never properly introduced myself." He offered his hand. "Detective Hynds." I shook it wearily. But then I noticed his watch. Nautical and blue.

"That was you last night, wasn't it?" I whispered. "Oh my God. I am so sorry. Thank you—"

"Please." He brushed my apology aside as if rescuing people were a daily occurrence. Maybe it was. "I came here to thank *you*, Salma Bakkioui. You're a real patriot. Because of you, we succeeded in stopping what could have been a major catastrophe."

"Excuse my language, but what the hell is going on?"

Detective Hynds hardly flinched.

"The blast . . . this hospital . . . I'm so confused. I thought they blew everything up?"

"No," he said, pacing the room. "The blast we encountered wasn't the real deal. It was a small IED, a theatrical

269

technique to distract and evade. As far as the main explosives go, the bomb squad successfully defused them."

"Wait," I croaked. "Evade?"

As he opened his mouth to answer, Nurse Nicki came back into the room, carrying a tray full of food. "I've got good news for the both of you. They had plenty of scones, Salma. I got you three kinds—blueberry, buttermilk, and chocolate. And you, Officer, you'll be pleased to know that your partner is out of surgery. They saved his lung. He's a real trooper." She batted an eyelash.

Detective Hynds blushed. "Thank you, ma'am. That's good news indeed." He patted me on the back. "We can discuss this tomorrow when we get your official statement. Family and celebrations first." He stood up to leave.

"Please, Officer, just tell me."

"Kyle Sr. is in custody," he said.

"And Kyle Jr.?"

Detective Hynds glanced at Nurse Nicki, who smiled uncomfortably. "I'll leave you two alone," she murmured, quickly ducking out the door.

My mind was littered with so many fears and traumas and awful memories that I kept spewing questions. One after the other. "What about the guy in the ski mask? And the other Forty-Three-ers? And Mr. Fancy? And, oh my God, Mrs. Turner? Is she even alive?"

"Shh," he said. "I promise that we'll continue this discussion soon enough. But I have some people here who have been waiting too long to see you." He opened the door. My whole family—Mom, Dad, the girls, Titi in a wheelchair with a nurse at her side—poured into the room.

I burst into a combination of tears and laughter. Detective Hynds slipped out the door. Yasmin, naturally in the lead, barreled straight into me, holding up this ridiculous teddy bear with a T-shirt that read HERO. The idea of being a hero was a strange thought indeed. A thought my *nafs* didn't need. Detective Hynds was right, though. My questions could wait. Right now, I was safe. So was everyone I loved. Maybe I could reassemble the shattered bits of my heart. Some had already begun to dance inside my chest.

The rest were waiting in Dubai.


Titi and I were discharged early the next morning. Before I left, Nurse Nicki came up to me and squeezed me so tight I thought I was going to pass out. She handed me a plastic bag. "Sorry, dear, we had to remove your jewelry and personal belongings. But they are all here. We don't normally do laundry, but we all chipped in. I insisted. It was the least we could do, all things considered." I looked down. My clothes were beautifully dry-cleaned, pressed, and folded. In the corner of the bag were two rings.

Later the following day, after a thorough debriefing with a cybersecurity team in which I finally handed over the Turner signet ring and they returned my recovered laptop, Mom's minivan keys, and miracle of all miracles, my phone (sorry, Mr. Metro Man!), Detective Hynds at long last dropped by.

After my family pampered him with all sorts of presents and food, when we finally had a moment alone I blurted out my remaining questions. He was wonderfully patient and surprisingly candid. Maybe, after all, I had earned his trust.

So here was the thing: Detective Hynds wasn't just a detective. He's a member of a joint task force for counterterrorism and a mentor of sorts for Detective McManus. He's also been privately researching the 43ers all along, even though he began his inquiry several months back with mere hunches and crumbs. Investigating far-right groups had almost become a side job, a hobby.

"Why?" I asked, failing to understand this limited approach to counterterrorism.

"Politics," he said. "Most of our resources have been transferred over to . . ." He shifted uncomfortably. "Well, um . . ."

"Muslim terrorists?" I said, finishing his sentence.

"Precisely," he said. "Or people who fit that category."

I twisted my ring. "Yeah, they are similar," I murmured. "But white supremacy, from the founding of this nation to this very moment, has always been our greatest threat."

He nodded in quiet agreement.

"I still don't get it, though. The timing of it all. How did you all arrive at the IXP joint so quickly? Instantly, come to think of it. But no one is that lucky. The Turners have been one step ahead of all of us."

Detective Hynds leaned forward. "Yes, but in the end it was Mrs. Turner who played the last card."

"What do you mean?"

"She mailed a letter to our local chapter, knowing it was the only safe way to communicate, knowing that her movements both online and on the phone were being watched."

I nodded in sympathy. This entire time Kyle Jr. had his eyes on me—cloning my phone, invading my privacy, setting me up. "And?"

With a sigh, Detective Hynds folded his hands. "What I

can tell you is this. She gave the FBI enough convincing details about her husband's role during the bombings on May third that the unit had to take her seriously. And to take me and my hunches seriously. It was a good thing her letter arrived when it did. By then her son had begun phase two. Remember the night you saw my partner in front of the Ammouris'?"

"Pretty unforgettable."

"We were there because our cyber unit had picked up on suspicious online activity. Kyle Jr. had hijacked Mr. Ammouri's router and was posting incriminating evidence online as if he were Amir."

I balled my hand into a tight fist. Hijacking routers was a trick I learned from Pulaski88. It was all coming full circle. Again and again. "Yeah, they're pretty—"

"Sophisticated?" said Detective Hynds, finishing my thought.

I nodded.

He broke off suddenly, biting his lip and looking me in the eye. "Like I said, it was a good thing Mrs. Turner flipped on them. Lord knows where we'd all be if she hadn't."

I swallowed, remembering her smile, her bruises. Her limp body lying in the hospital. "Is she going to make it?"

Detective Hynds cracked his knuckles. "I'm afraid that she passed away this morning."

After a long stretch of silence, in which I closed my eyes and rested the weight of my head in the palm of my *good* hand, Hynds finally admitted a second loss: Kyle Jr. had managed to escape. His father was in federal custody pleading the Fifth Amendment. Detective Hynds's gaunt face creased in disgust, or maybe disappointment—or both.

"Kyle Sr. was adamant. Said that we'd never locate his son

in 'Real America.' He claimed that his network had allies all over the country and overseas as well." He closed his mouth. It seemed that he wanted to say more but couldn't. Or wouldn't. Maybe he didn't want to frighten me.

I glanced out the window at the empty Turner house, roped off with police tape. A deep shiver cascaded down my back. Detective Hynds must have noticed my unease, as he laid his hand gently on my knee. "Don't worry, Salma. We have a unit posted to your house. I doubt that Kyle Turner Jr. will come back to this area. And believe me: we're doing everything we can to locate him."

"Yeah, but he's not the only one. Do you have any idea how vast their organization is?"

Detective Hynds didn't answer. He looked unsettled. Great, I'd returned him to Silent One mode.

"Seriously, how many of these crazies are there?" I demanded to know. I'd earned it. "I mean, what about my principal, and Michelle and Chris? Were they part of this?"

"No," he said resolutely. "As far as the rest of the organization goes, we're getting there. Us, the FBI, ATF." He shifted in his seat and straightened his back. "I know you have considerable skills—assets, really—that I'd like you to develop in a safe and professional manner. No more solo investigating." He lifted a brow.

I laughed, and so did he. It was a moment of camaraderie that was admittedly satisfying. He leaned forward.

"What I'm saying, Salma, is that I'd like you to consider joining us in some capacity once you're done with college. We need bright minds like yours, especially since you have your feet in—"

"Two worlds?" I interrupted. But I was smiling now, too.

He seemed hesitant to answer. "I don't want to put words in your mouth," he said.

"Well, I appreciate that." And I did, truly. It was another first between us: the first time I'd told him something true, without fear or suspicion. That wasn't to say that I was being *fully* transparent. As I walked him to the door, shook his hand, and waved goodbye, I still clung to a secret—as I'm certain he did, too.

Mine? I'd made a copy of all the files on that USB ring. Just in case.

# 23

A WEEK LATER, things were almost weirdly, freakishly normal. Normal in comparison to the roller coaster it had been. But still surreal. News had gotten out about the Turners, but no one knew about my involvement yet. I was forbidden from discussing it. Detective Hynds had explained the necessity of withholding my identity: Kyle Jr. was still on the run, and there was a broader conspiracy. I needed to remain anonymous for my own protection.

It was weird, though . . . keeping these secrets to myself, lying to Vanessa and Lisa and Kelly about why I'd left that sappy message: *"My new EDS meds screwed with my head."* (Detective Hynds had actually suggested that one. *"Blame it on a neurological side effect from a prescription."* I told him it was funny that so much law enforcement involved lying. He didn't laugh.) Of course, under the pretext of this phony EDS medication mishap and my real-life injured arm, I still hadn't returned to school. Communication had occurred almost entirely via text, except for one time.

Vanessa had been allowed to visit under parental supervision just once—to celebrate two straight-up miracles. The first: She had been accepted to Radford University, one of Virginia's finest party schools (resulting in a full-blown natural high, for once). The second: my decision to get a tattoo. Yes, that's right. Salma Bakkioui was getting inked.

After everything that had transpired—from our worlds nearly collapsing, to my supposed act of bravery, to Kate Turner's very real death—Mom and Dad relented. Fine, I milked them for it. Shamelessly. Telling them that even though tattoos were mostly considered haram, there were some religious scholars who disagreed, and that furthermore, it was heritage. Of the two of them, Mom was a little harder to crack, but once I brought up those unruly friends of hers (aka the Sufis) and how she couldn't have it both ways—encouraging broader thinking and yet enforcing archaic rules upon her own daughter—she smiled. "Fine, sweetheart. But make it discreet. And don't you dare tell anyone at the *masjid*."

In the end she even escorted us.

So did Titi. It was a true all-girls outing, me and nearly all my favorite ladies this side of the Atlantic. I even invited Mrs. DLP. She laughed and said I was twenty years too late.

And then she showed me the video of what she'd promised she'd do.


Sitting in the back of Mom's minivan, Vanessa and I swapped printouts. We had both agreed not to discuss our finalists until the day of. We wanted to heighten the excitement. I opened up her short list and immediately busted out laughing. "Oh my God, all weed tats? Seriously? You know this is a lifelong decision here . . . something you can't actually change unless you want to fork over some serious dough for laser removal." I pointed to several, my laughter steadily increasing. One was a purple bud, gnarly-looking and fresh, with a white ribbon that read *Forever free.* Another looked like an EKG strip, but in the middle of the black cardio lines there was a single cannabis leaf. The last—my favorite—was an anthropomorphized bud smoking a big-ass doobie. Underneath were the words *Devil's lettuce.*

"You should totally get this one," I said, trying my best to keep a straight face.

Vanessa snatched the printout away from my fingers. "Ha! I had you!" she said. "I mean, don't get me wrong, these are definitely me, but I was thinking about doing something a little more bougie. And a lot more meaningful, you know what I mean?" She handed me a new short list.

I unfolded the printout. There were a variety of Celtic knots—trees, hearts, endless circles—and a short description of their meanings. I smiled at Vanessa. "I love these, all of them. It's a lot like my short list," I said, handing her mine.

She uncrumpled the paper. "Amazigh tats," she said, smiling. "I knew it."

After a long study she asked me which one I had settled on. I paused, glanced up at the rearview mirror at Mom, who smiled back at me with her own growing excitement, then over to Titi. Titi looked peaceful, as if she was on the same wavelength as Mom. As me. We were two cultures, one family.

I leaned in close to Vanessa and whispered, "Actually I'm going to get them all, down the middle of my back like a hieroglyph."

Her jaw dropped. "Oh my God, your mom is much cooler than I thought."

I smiled as Mom made a hat-tipping motion, but with her scarf.

"Yeah, she is," I said, wanting to explain to Vanessa why exactly my mom was awesome, as in tried-to-help-me-escape-the-country awesome, but I kept my lips hermetically sealed. "Do you know what else she's done?"

Vanessa shook her head.

"She and the Ammouris and a whole bunch of other parents—not to mention Mrs. DLP and Mr. Epstein and Ms. Wallace and a whole bunch of teachers from PTSA—stormed Principal Philip's office and demanded his resignation. They got it on video, too, sent it to the board of trustees or something, and rumor has it there's an investigation."

Vanessa leaned in, closer to my seat. "What? That's awesome. You're dope, Mrs. B.! But back to the tats," she said, pointing to my printout. "What's the meaning?"

I pointed to each, explaining their significance to me. Not exactly what they meant originally. Tattooing among the Amazigh is a dying art, thanks to the haram police. But I was happy with my list and the personal meanings: a sun and moon for Amir and Mariam. A palm leaf for all the mother-goddesses, those who kept me stable, from Mom to Titi to Mrs. DLP. A lamp to remind me that even in the dark there is hope, and sometimes that hope, like Vanessa, comes from the most unexpected sources. A snake in honor of my dad and Dihya and Detective Hynds, those unsung heroes who surprise us all—ancient or contemporary. I had an Amazigh cross, too, though it didn't look like the standard cross. Either way, it was perfect—perfect for Grandma Thiede and Kate Turner. To paraphrase my main man Rumi, "In the religion of love there are no true believers. Everyone is welcome." True love, radical love, the kind that's worth dying for, embraces all.

Oh, and shame on me. How could I possibly forget?

The last tattoo—the one I wanted inked on the very top of my back—was the *yaz* symbol. Because even though it symbolizes "free man" among the Amazigh and kind of looks like a human being, it also resembles a butterfly.

*Of course, of course.*

# EPILOGUE

INITIALLY AMIR WAS going to return to DC as soon as possible, but when Mr. Ammouri discovered that one of Aleppo's living musical legends—whom he thought had perished in the war—was about to give a benefit concert at the Dubai Opera house, he insisted on a change of plan. He offered to fly us out, on his dime, to pick up Amir and sightsee. A generous thank-you gift for helping to clear his son of terrorism charges.

But Maya, who ended up being two weeks late on the baby front, delivered the twins right as Amir was GTFO-ing. As torn up as his mom was, Mrs. Ammouri stayed back. She said she'd kidnap Amir later for their own mother-son vacation. I had no doubt she meant it. I was also honestly (and selfishly) a little relieved that she wasn't coming. According to Amir, they were already spending at least two hours every day on Skype. The new babies reminded Mrs. Ammouri so much of her original prince that she felt the sudden urge to recount to Amir every moment of his golden childhood.

In the end, the only two people who could make it were Mr. Ammouri and me. A trip away for my parents was logistically impossible. Mason Terrace was a circus thanks to lingering gawkers, reporters, and the horde of investigators over at the Turners'. But the chaos outside paled in comparison to the chaos inside Chez Bakkioui. Mom and Dad were consumed with taking care of Titi and helping her adjust to being a bit slower, post-recovery, plus they had to deal with the addition of a two-hundred-pound slobber hound. With Kyle Sr. in custody, Kyle Jr. on the lam, and Mrs. Turner no longer of this world, Drexler was ours.

It somehow felt right taking care of the Turners' dog, like the scales of the universe had once again tipped, ever so slightly, toward a happier arc. And a hilarious one, too. Drexler chased Thom. My sisters chased Drexler. Titi was never too far behind, pushing her wheeled walker, complete with a sitting chair and a basket that she kept wet wipes in—to clean up after Drexler. As much as he slobbered, she cleaned, convinced it kept the angels more or less content.

As entertaining as it was, I couldn't wait to chase my own angel and GTFO my ass to the land of glitzy bling.

Two weeks after Amir GTFO-ed, it finally happened. Mr. Ammouri and I enjoyed fourteen hours in sky-high opulence. I shamelessly scarfed down half a dozen mini tiramisu cakes, hogged the onboard shower twice, watched four movies, and slept completely horizontal in my own little high-end cocoon. But despite all the luxury, I was eager to get off the plane the instant we landed.

Mr. Ammouri was palpably excited, too. We pressed past customs and headed toward arrivals. As soon we spotted Mariam and Amir, I let out a girlish squeal. Mariam was standing in the front row beside the professional drivers and VIP services, waving some homemade sign, while Amir—my sweet, sweet Amir—stood just beside her, his face nearly obscured by a bouquet of lilies.

That's when Mr. Ammouri reached forward and grabbed my suitcase. "Please, Salma. Don't let me slow you down. I'll get there soon enough."

"No worries, Mr. Ammouri, I can wait."

I was, of course, flat-out lying. Every collagen-deprived cell in my body wanted nothing more than to fling myself toward the exit, straight into the arms of Mr. Kareem.

Mr. Ammouri gave me that *I'm-your-baba* look, chin turned inward. *"Ya'llah,"* he said, a wide grin consuming his face.

I gave him a peck on the cheek, then bolted away, ducking in and around the crowds, my knee and my EDS in glorious submission, until I slammed, full force, into Amir's embrace. Moth to flame, soul to sun.

And now that Ramadan was long over and the two of us were finally united, I practically dove straight in for his lips.

"Whoa," he said, stepping playfully backward. "We can't exactly, not here." He lifted his chin, glancing over at an Emirati official. "It's kind of against their norms."

"Oh," I said. "Right."

And then he pinched me.

"What was that for?" I asked.

"I had to be sure I wasn't dreaming."

"Goes both ways," I said, pinching him back.

He was about pull me in for another hug when Mariam tore us apart, pushing away Amir and my beautiful flowers. "You can wait, Mr. Kareem. It's my turn. Salma and I haven't seen each other in over a month. That's like thirty-plus days and an eternity in bestie time," she repeated, as if I didn't know.

One long minute later . . .

"Okay," I said. "Death by asphyxiation."

She let me go.

I glanced down at her sign. She had taken my school photo—the same one the cops used when they put out that BOLO—and superimposed it on a ripped Jason Bourne body, fearlessly escaping a bomb blast. The caption read *RWM Gangster Crew.*

"Oh my God. That's priceless."

"Hells yeah," she said.

By then Mr. Ammouri had caught up with us. He was hugging his son and weeping. Amir lifted his head from his father's shoulder and smiled. *Thank you,* he silently mouthed to me.

Ten minutes later, while en route to drop Mr. Ammouri off at the hotel so he could rest, Mariam opened her purse and slipped me a card.

I read it. "No way! That is priceless," I said. "You got into BU. This is fantastic. And your parents? Are they game?"

Mariam's eyes lit up. "At first? No. But after some epic negotiations, yeah. They're actually going to parole me. I just have to check in with them every freaking day."

I reached across the seat and squeezed her hand. My universe was realigning.

"And MIT?" Mariam asked.

I glanced back over at her and flashed my pearly whites.

"Dang!" she said. "So you're gonna be the next Aaron . . . what was his name?"

"Aaron Swartz," I said. He was one of my favorite hacktivists, may his soul rest in peace. "Yeah . . . well, I think I've had enough excitement for a while. Plus his story didn't end so well, but yeah. . . ."

I glanced away for a moment, a pang of sadness filling my

chest, when the car suddenly jerked to the right. Amir's ride, some tiny European car he had borrowed from his buddy Ahmed—the same Ahmed he'd been Skyping with and studying oud with all these months and his dad used in code to help him escape—was nearly sideswiped by a local cabbie. Thankfully, it was just a "nearly." I hadn't yet met Ahmed, but I already loved him. Thinking about meeting Ahmed later that week helped me relax, until the cabbie cut in front of us again, and I nearly lost it.

I clutched my seatbelt as I strained to view the culprit: a *muhajiba* in a pink scarf. It perfectly matched the taxi, which was also pink. The idea of death by pink was almost amusing, but when she cut us off for a second time I raised my hand to show off my bendy fingers, or finger, when Mariam twisted around from shotgun. "Hand down, Agent Morpho. No vulgar gestures."

"What do you mean, hand down? That woman was seriously rude. She almost killed us!"

"True that. But all the drivers be *kaminays* here, so you just gotta get used to it. Hold in your road rage. Seriously, you can't flick people off. It's considered a jailable offense."

*What?* This was not Mariam. Girl was the most impressive curser and profanity hand gesturer I've ever known. And she was a polyglot about it, too. Polite Urdu for mild slights, English for pure crassness, and Punjabi for emotional flair. I leaned close to her seat.

"You're kidding, right? How can anyone even know? We're in a moving vehicle."

"This country is super high-tech. There are cameras everywhere. You don't get pulled over by cops—you get texted by cops."

"No way. What's the punishment for flicking someone off?"

Amir chimed in. "Truth be told, it probably doesn't matter if it's a non-Emirati, which is like eighty percent of the population. But if your target happens to be one, you could serve a month in jail or more. There's a bit of a pecking order here."

"A bit?" Mariam added.

I was fascinated. "How do I know if it's an Emirati?"

"You can't always tell," said Mariam. "But sometimes you definitely can."

"Look," said Amir. "Just don't do it. Period. We're all guests here anyway. But you can tell who's super important, and therefore untouchable, by the license plates."

"What do you mean? Is there, like, a symbol on the license plate?"

Mariam laughed. "It's all in the numbers. Zero-zero-one is the Sheikh. Zero-zero-eight is one of his children. It's all about prestige."

"So what are we?"

Mariam smirked. "Part of the low, insignificant masses."

I glanced out the window at the high-rise buildings and muted skies. *A month in jail for flipping someone the bird?* Whatever, it was just a vacation. Better to play it safe. I slipped my good hand under my bum to curb my reflexes. My other arm was curbed by the still-there sling.

"Wanna hear the day's agenda?" asked Mariam. I nodded as she rattled off a long list that commenced with the butterfly garden and ended with playing her favorite game: "Let's mispronounce the high-end European designer names as we window-shop at Dubai Mall."

"And after all that," added Amir, "dinner for two."

Mariam raised her fist with overly dramatic menace, then said, "Just kidding, bro. I'll keep to the deal. She'll be all yours by then."

Several hours later, since I was too spent to actually go out for dinner, Amir came to me. He brought Thai and a bottle of sparkling date juice to the comfort of my hotel room. He did, of course, invite his dad, but Mr. Ammouri, now fully rested, was ready to go out and explore. He followed Amir into the room but told us he wasn't staying. "Just don't do anything I wouldn't do," he joked, and then, with a truly serious voice, added, "Amir. I'm serious. Dinner and then you're back in my room. Got it?" Amir and I both nodded.

"Your dad is hilarious," I said, closing the door behind him.

"It's weird," said Amir. "Seeing him this alive. I think he's stoked to be back in the Arabic world, and to be here for the concert."

"He's stoked to have his son back," I said, about to ask if returning to the United States was really Amir's plan—the last time we spoke on the phone, just before I boarded the flight, he told me he had been accepted to the conservatory in Boston but was thinking about deferring a year. To stay and study oud here in Dubai for a little while longer.

Just then a heavy knock pounded at the door. It was so loud and aggressive that panic seized every fiber of my being. I started to have hot flashes, like a bomb was about to explode. Was it *Kyle Jr.*? Some other 43er? I started to shake. Amir dropped what he was doing and rushed over. "Hey, you're as pale as Edward Norton right now. I'm sure it's nothing. I'll be right back."

He left to answer the door. I closed my eyes. I didn't make it this far only to make it this far. . . . I couldn't hear what was being said.

The door slammed. "Salma, chill, it's a delivery guy." He returned a few seconds later with an enormous package.

"Are you sure?" I asked, relieved but still on edge. "What if the delivery guy is a spy for the Forty-Three-ers?"

"Who also happens to be South Asian and super friendly? Nah, we're good," he said absently.

He went to the kitchen to grab a pair of scissors, then came back to open the box.

"*Masha'Allah,* it's from your best friend, Sheikh Epstein. . . ."

I held my breath as Amir opened the box. Was it really from Sheikh Epstein? Yup. The Funk-a-delic Master had sent Amir a new oud. Amir read the note: " 'Dear Amir—I heard you got into the New England Conservatory. I heard you might delay for a year. Choose wisely. Choose to dream. The world will be better for it.' "

Amir took the oud from the box and started to tune it. As soon as he was done, he strummed a familiar tune: "No Woman, No Cry." But once Amir started to wail, the lyrics were totally different. He sang about his hero, about a girl named Salma, a girl he'd meet in Boston.

I closed my eyes, absorbing every note and chord, contemplating what life had taught me so far: that there's no true course, no real guarantees. The only certainties in this crazy *dunia* are God and death; the last few weeks had proved it.

Maybe that's the Morpho's secret. It knows instinctively

how sacred and fragile life is. It's a truth non-butterflies might as well embrace—to develop some courage, to grow our wings, to bask in the music of possibility.

Because if a former caterpillar can do it, so can we.

I had. And if Amir needed to stay here for a while to grow his wings, then so be it.

# AUTHOR'S NOTE

I'VE BEEN A Muslim for over twenty years. How and why I embraced Islam is a long story, but let's just say that Islam found me—a hippyish teen visiting Istanbul the summer before college. By spring break I took my *shahada*. By 9/11, I was a full-blown hijabi studying world religions at George Washington University. (Thank you, Dr. Eisen and Dr. Nasr, for your steady support.) Though I grew up in the melting pot of Northern Virginia, the glares of disdain that came my way were an unfamiliar and eye-opening experience.

As the years passed, I wanted nothing more than to retreat to the forest, raise my girls, and smell the flowers. I published picture books, some with interfaith themes, as my own small way of saying, "Hey, we're not so different. In fact, we're very much the *same*."

My personal experiences with Islamophobia eventually went from eye-opening to gut-wrenching when my husband endured a nasty Islamophobic tenure ordeal, which resulted in the loss of his job and our first home. We moved from the United States to the United Arab Emirates. I was existentially exhausted and felt powerless. But as a parent, I had to get up and out, every day. Many of our neighbors were refugees from

Syria, Iraq, and Palestine. Being among these amazing people was humbling. When I asked them how they were doing, they'd often respond with *"Alhamdulillah fi kulli hal."* This common phrase translates to "Things are a little hard right now, but in all circumstances praise belongs to God."

This perspective reminded me that back in the United States, I still had a physical home and country to return to. (Thanks, Mom, Dad, and Frances for opening your abodes.)

I got to thinking and writing. The result is *No True Believers.*

Yes, things are a little hard right now. There are desperate factions in our nation that are using the tactics of fear and propaganda to drive our country mad. To divide, dismantle, and disenfranchise. And while I don't know what the future holds, I do know that with humility, self-belief, and radical love, new beginnings are possible.

*Alhamdulillah fi kulli hal.*

# ACKNOWLEDGMENTS

THANK YOU, GOD, for this incredible blessing called life. *Alhamdulillah fi kulli hal.*

Eternal thanks to my parents, Debra and Lt. Col. Stephen York. Next to God, you're my saving grace. Also, Dad—thank you for your service in the U.S. Marine Corps (twenty-five years!) and for allowing me to pick your brain about your civilian life afterward as an intelligence analyst for counter-extremism and cyber-infrastructure with both the FBI and DHS.

To clan Vanessa—eternal kisses. To Frances and Sarah Lumbard—I couldn't ask for better in-laws. To everyone else in Virginia, Tennessee, and beyond—warm hugs!

To my agent Kevin O'Connor and independent editor Rachel Abrams: your early encouragements were invaluable.

A cosmic bow to fellow Deadhead and epic homey Daniel Ehrenhaft. You're the best mentor. Truly. A round of bubbling date-juice to the rest of Soho Lab—Bronwen Hruska and Jon Fine. (Yay! We finally got here!)

To Emily Easton and the fine book lovers at team Crown: my highest esteem. Seriously, I'm speechless and delighted. And I think you're brave. A massive thanks, forevermore.

To my boxing coach, Keeyon Tate—our workouts got me through some tough days, but as you reminded me à la Floyd Mayweather, "All work is easy work." Good mantra.

Lastly, my beta readers! M. Lynx Qualey of Arablit.org, Safia Benbrahim of @BookishDubai, and Amir Web, DC's best-dressed historian, much love. To Iman Bakkioui-Lahroussi, a brilliant Amazigh scholar—hijabi hats off to you! To Tylor Brand, historian of the Middle East at Trinity College, *shukran jazeelan!* To Ustadh Ammouri, my eldest's oud teacher from Aleppo, forever honored. To Shannon Dilks, a homeschooling momma and Christian, big hugs. And to Zahra Awadallah, Sufi, writer, and blerd, you're the beta reader I most needed. My sincerest love and forever support. May the universe reveal an EDS's cure.

And to Joseph Lumbard—my partner and bestie—thank you for loving my quirks, from books to cats. Yes, I'm addicted. But then again, so are you!


P.S. Thanks to both Edward Norton for making great movies and Chuck Palahniuk for his iconic book *Fight Club*.

# ABOUT THE AUTHOR

RABIAH YORK LUMBARD is an award-winning author of the picture-book retelling of *The Conference of the Birds*. After embracing Islam at the age of eighteen, she earned a BA in religious studies from George Washington University and is completing her MFA in creative writing from Spalding University. *No True Believers* is Rabiah's deeply personal debut novel, which draws on her experience as an American Muslim at home and abroad. She lives in Doha, Qatar, with her husband and their three daughters.

rabiahyorklumbard.com